**He was a Henry and he could handle any-
thing…couldn't he?**

"I told you to get out of here, you bastard! Why the
hell won't you listen to me?!" Emmett flailed out, caught
the plastic water pitcher on the bedside, and hurled it with
amazing accuracy.

Samantha had to duck or it would've hit her head.
"You ought to be ashamed of yourself, Emmett Henry! I
never had the opportunity to meet Beth Henry, but I
know that your mother raised you to keep a respectful
tongue in your head, and so did your father. Jackson Henry must be rolling in his grave right now, ready to kick
your butt. Talking to your brother that way, and he's been
here at this hospital, by your side, for over a month. I've
half a mind to drag you out of that bed and make you
clean up this mess."

The anger died almost as soon as it flared up, and
Emmett's face blanched the instant he realized it was her.
She took one step forward when he reached up, yanked
the IVs out of his arm, and slipped out of bed. He started
crawling on the floor, feeling his way, attempting to pick
up, setting things on the bed as he did, stopping every
few seconds to hold his head. A soft moan slipped out,
pain his constant companion.

Wyatt Henry has always been his brother's keeper. It's been his job. That, and learning how to be a horse farmer and a man above measure like his father, Jackson Henry—the Henry Way. Emmett made his arrival when Wyatt was two years old, and his kid brother has lit up his world ever since. He's been the light in the darkness—when his mother died when he was only six, when his father died in a tragic accident on the farm. So what does he do when that light could be snuffed out?

When Emmett jumps in to help a damsel in distress in a barroom fight, he suffers a severe head injury that leaves him blind. It nearly destroys him, taking Wyatt with him. Wyatt has to try and help his brother pick up the pieces. He won't give up on him, no matter how depressed and angry Emmett is. While he is dealing with Emmett's challenges, Wyatt will face a life-threatening illness of his own. Through it all, his wife Samantha will be at his side as they work together to take Jackson Henry's advice and make mountains into molehills.

KUDOS for *Making Mountains into Molehills*

In *Making Mountains into Molehills* by Heidi Sprouse, Wyatt Henry is dealing with his brother Emmett's blindness due to a head injury, when Wyatt gets an unexpected and unwelcome surprise about his own health. Both strong willed and stubborn, neither brother wants to ask for, or accept, help, so they are their own worst enemy. Can they adjust to their new circumstances, or are they doomed to be unhappy for the rest of their lives? As well written and intense as the other two books in the series, this one will catch your interest with the very first page and hold it all the way through. ~ *Taylor Jones, The Review Team of Taylor Jones & Regan Murphy*

Making Mountains into Molehills by Heidi Sprouse is the story of a family of strong willed, stubborn, and honorable men and women who overcome obstacles and problems with courage and love. Emmett Henry has been blinded in a bar fight where he was defending a young woman and the man abusing her hit Emmett over the head with a chair. Emmett's brother Wyatt is determined to help him through this difficult time, but then Wyatt is stricken with a life-threatening illness, and now Emmett has to help him. The Henrys are a strong family, but are they strong enough for this? Filled with wonderful characters and real-life situations and problems, *Making Mountains into Molehills* will both warm your heart and break it, while keeping you glued to the edge of your seat. A worthy addition to the series. ~ *Regan Murphy, The Review Team of Taylor Jones & Regan Murphy*

OTHER BOOKS BY

HEIDI SPROUSE

and

BLACK OPAL BOOKS

A Man of Few Words

Hindsight's 20/20

ACKNOWLEDGMENTS

Thank you to the team at Black Opal Books for believing in me, helping me to make an incredible story come to life. Faith, Jack, Arwen, and Lauri, you do beautiful work and make sure my best shines. To Dan Barrett, my fellow author at Black Opal Books, thanks for putting me on this path!

MAKING MOUNTAINS INTO MOLEHILLS

HEIDI SPROUSE

A Black Opal Books Publication

GENRE: FAMILY SAGA/ROMANCE

This is a work of fiction. Names, places, characters and incidents are either the product of the author's imagination or are used fictitiously, and any resemblance to any actual persons, living or dead, businesses, organizations, events or locales is entirely coincidental. All trademarks, service marks, registered trademarks, and registered service marks are the property of their respective owners and are used herein for identification purposes only. The publisher does not have any control over or assume any responsibility for author or third-party websites or their contents.

DEDICATION

To the amazing men in my life
who have taught me what
it is to be a rock in times of trouble.
My father, Stephen Smith Pedersen.
My husband, James Sprouse III,
and my son, Patrick James Sprouse.
My heart belongs to all of you.

PROLOGUE

E m, behind you!" Wyatt Henry barked sharply, fear biting off his words, as the *animal* who had bashed Minnow Allen's face into the table only moments before slammed a chair on top of his brother's head.

Mindy was her given name, but she'd always been a little slip of a thing and the nickname stuck. She was much too small to catch Emmett, but reached out for him anyway as he dropped like a sack of rocks to the floor, her china blue eyes wide with terror. Wyatt saw red.

Surrounded by the fog of tobacco smoke and the clamor of voices as the barroom crowd screamed and shouted in alarm, Wyatt closed the gap in seconds. *Too late, you're too late!* He went after the sorry excuse for a human being like a pile driver. Filled with a berserk fury, the blood thundered in his ears and his heart pounded in his chest as he slammed into the giant of a man and took him down. Hard. How *dare* anyone hurt his kid brother?

It didn't matter if they were thirty-three and thirty-one respectively. It was a gut reaction to stand guard over Emmett, to protect him, to answer any threat. One more good whack of the guy's head against the floor with a sickening thud, and the monster was out cold.

Gasping for air with the adrenalin pumping through his body, Wyatt turned with a jerk and knelt next to his brother. Minnow—the *preacher's* daughter for God's sake—was hunkered down beside Emmett. What the hell was the kid doing here in the first place?

She held Em's bandanna to his head and blood was everywhere. On her hands. On the floor. Soaking Emmett's hair and running down his face. He was unconscious. He looked dead. *Please God. You've taken so much. Don't take my baby brother. Please.*

Wyatt's chest became tight and it was hard to breathe what with the fist of fear squeezing around his heart. He knelt beside his baby brother, because that's what he would always be, and held on to his arm as if that would pin down Emmett's soul. The rage and the sorrow were crashing inside of Wyatt, threatening to tear him apart. Minnow was sobbing, the tears raining down while her nose continued to bleed and he had to clamp down on his resentment of her. She was underage, shouldn't have been here. Of all the nights to be rebellious and get herself into trouble.

Wyatt squeezed his eyes shut but couldn't erase that moment when the tattooed, bald man sitting with Minnow wrapped her blonde hair around his hand like a rope and slammed her face into the unforgiving oak. That was when everything went crazy, Emmett knocking over their table to get to them as fast as possible to avert disaster, to make the stranger pay. His brother gave the jerk a jab in the gut, attending to Mindy and giving her his bandanna. Before anyone could even breathe, the chair came down on Emmet's head. Wyatt didn't even have time to cross the room.

Wyatt shook his head. He would've done the same. It could be him in the floor right now in the middle of the chaos as the wail of a siren approached. Emmett had just been faster. He always had been a leap before you look kind of kid, the kind that ran before he walked. This time, Emmett ran too fast, straight into disaster.

CHAPTER 1

His elbows were driving into his knees, and Wyatt welcomed the pain, any kind of distraction from the thoughts and images crashing in his head. He was still covered in blood—*his brother's blood*—and didn't even care as his fingers threaded through his hair. His eyes began to sting and tears splashed on his boots and the floor between his feet.

Pounding footsteps, running down the hallway, came his way, putting on speed. He looked up and almost lost it at the sight of his angel, his wife. Samantha wore an old flannel shirt, his dad's—and that hurt too, a quick jab to the gut, bringing on an intense longing for his father. She was exactly what he needed, especially right now with her blonde hair pulled up on top of her head and poking out every which way, a smudge of flour on her face, holes in her jeans, and mismatched shoes. Nothing ever looked better.

Wyatt stood up and gathered her in, buried his face in her hair, smelled her shampoo, soap, deodorant, and a sweat born of fear. He inhaled deeply, filling his lungs, and began to tremble. At any instant, he would come apart at the seams and unravel in her arms.

Sammie reached up to press her hand to his cheek, stroke it, and stare into his eyes. Her gaze took in his clothes, the blood staining everything, his hands, and her blue eyes shimmered. "What happened?"

A second of hesitation and Wyatt dropped back into the chair, hand gripping the back of his neck. He had a monster of a headache and it had nothing to do with the beer and everything to do with his baby brother, in emergency surgery. Fast. Everything had happened too fast. *Stop the world. I want to get off!*

"We were at Joe's Bar and Grill, just having a beer and some pretzels to unwind when all hell broke loose. Mindy Allen was there—yes, I know she's too young— with some excuse for a man and he bashed her face into the table, used her hair like a rope to do it. Em was on him in an instant to break it up—and—and—*that bastard*—hit him in the head with a chair, damn it! I went crazy, tackled him. I was too late." Wyatt leaned forward and his voice was a jagged whisper. "I can't lose Em. Not him too, Sam. He's the only family I have."

He buried his head in her stomach as she stroked his

hair and murmured words of comfort. Wyatt wanted nothing more than to scoop her up, walk out into the bitter snow of early January, and carry her home to bed. To lose himself in her arms. Her body. Sleep. To find out this was all a nightmare. But in his life, the nightmares were real. He closed his eyes, carried back to day the darkness snuffed out the light of his youth…

ℰ∽ℰ∽ℯ

Daddy packed them up in the truck early in the morning. The sun had just woken up and peeked its face over the edge of the world. Wyatt opened his eyes in the truck, Emmett tucked up against him in a blanket, and their rooster was crowing. He squinted as the light stabbed at him. "Daddy? Where we going?"

His father stroked his head and kissed his cheek, the rough stubble of a faint beard scraping Wyatt's skin. Daddy was shaking and pale as a ghost, his dark hair a mess. His eyes, usually warm as chocolate like they wore a smile, looked unspeakably sad. "Going to Grandmama's and Grandpop's, baby. She's cooking a big breakfast, said she was missing you boys."

Something wasn't right, made Wyatt's stomach hurt, but he was so sleepy and couldn't keep his eyes open the rest of the ride. He didn't know how long the two of them napped on Grandmama's couch. Daddy was gone. The uneasy feeling stayed with him while he tried to clean his plate and saw the looks pass between his grandparents. They seemed scared and that terrified him. Uncle Wyatt and Uncle Emmett, their namesakes, took him and his brother out to the barn. The stomachache got worse. His uncles were quiet, not full of the mischief Mama would laugh at and warn them about. Mama always said, "Look out now! Here comes trouble," anytime his uncles were out and about.

Night came and Daddy still hadn't come to see them. When Wyatt stood at the window and saw him come inside from yet another errand, his father's back was stooped, his head hanging low. Henrys held their head high.

That scared him most of all, watching that stranger walking to the door, dragging his feet. Daddy was usually full of it, couldn't keep him down. Mama said he'd always give them a run for their money, whatever that meant. Maybe like a bank robber?

Wyatt had already made Emmett brush his teeth, wash his face, and put on his pajamas. Just like Mama would. Wyatt's eyes started to burn. He missed Mama. No one had said anything about Mama, and they hadn't seen her all day long. His stomach twisted really hard, and he held on to his middle, wondering if he was going to get sick, when there was a soft knock on the door and his father walked in.

"What's wrong, Daddy?"

Emmett sat on the big double bed in the guest room

they shared whenever they spent the night at Grandmama and Grandpop's. Wyatt stood in the corner watching his father close the door and stand still, like a statue.

"Something's wrong with Mama," Wyatt whispered and the fear rose up inside of him, making him feel like he was going to smother.

He couldn't move, didn't want to come any closer, didn't want Daddy to tell him anything, make it real. Not a dream.

His father got down on his knees. "Boys, come here." Daddy's voice broke, like he'd been crying. Daddy never cried and that was the scariest thing of all. Emmett jumped off the bed and ran to their father, throwing his arms around him. Daddy met Wyatt's eyes. "Wy. Come here. Now."

He came, even though all he wanted to do was run. Daddy sat cross-legged and pulled them in close, said the words that Wyatt wanted to un-hear, erase from his mind.

"Wy—Em—I've got to tell you something bad. Something hard. I know. It won't make sense to you. It doesn't make sense to me. Boys—Mama was sick, and we didn't know it. The angels in heaven came to get her last night to make her better. I guess—" He choked down a sob, but the tears were coming on fast, raining down on their heads, mingling with theirs. "—I guess God needed her to stay to be another angel, to watch down on us from up there."

Terror squeezed Wyatt's heart, making it pound so

hard it hurt. "But Daddy, we need her down here!" He screamed as loud as he could. "I need her now, Daddy! Go get her!" Emmett didn't say anything, only started wailing.

Daddy held on so tight that Wyatt couldn't breathe. "I can't bring her back, Wy. I want to, but I can't get to heaven. We can only go when God says so."

"No, Daddy! No! No! No! Bring Mama back! You bring our mama back!"

Wyatt started to punch at the wall of his father's chest, his arms, and kept on hitting him until he couldn't lift his hands anymore. He wanted to howl at the top of his lungs, to run all the way home, to knock everyone down. Daddy didn't say a word and looking at his face, filled with such a terrible pain, his coffee eyes crying, Wyatt collapsed in his arms. He sobbed his heart out. Daddy tucked him in tight against his chest, Emmett too.

After the longest time of crying together, Daddy rocking them in his arms, their father lay down on the bed and held them close. Wyatt couldn't stop crying. They had to let him go to Mama, to wake her up, like Sleeping Beauty and Snow White. No one else knew how to break the spell. Only Wyatt could do it, like the prince. She called him her prince sometimes. He could do it—but it didn't work. When he kissed her in the coffin, she felt cold, like wax, and Mama, his beautiful mama, never woke up.

≈≈≈

"Mr. Henry? Excuse me, Mr. Henry?"

Wyatt's eyes snapped open as Sam started. She had dozed off in his lap as the sun crested the horizon. She slid over to the next seat so that Wyatt could meet the surgeon's gaze head on. The doctor had just come from surgery, a very long surgery that had eaten up the night. He pulled up a chair and sat down. Met Wyatt's eyes. Set his shoulders. Took a deep breath.

Something about the man reminded Wyatt of Jackson Henry, his father. A mountain of a man. Something about the kindness in the doctor's espresso eyes, the threads of silver in brown hair, his firm jaw, and sturdy handshake. The surgeon held on longer than necessary, and Wyatt felt like he was giving him a shot of strength, hope. Anything. "Doc, is my brother going to be all right?"

The surgeon…Martin, David Martin, that was his name…looked down for an instant, making Wyatt's heart plunge and his mouth go dry. Samantha took his hand and held on tight and that was a comfort. Whatever came at them, she would be there by his side to face it, and give him something to hold on to. But he feared what they had between them combined wouldn't be enough. *Lord, give me strength.*

Dr. Martin set his shoulders and met Wyatt's gaze. "I really don't know yet. The damage was considerable. He had skull fractures, splinters of bone in his brain, bleeding, and swelling. I've done everything I can. Now we have to wait for the swelling to go down, to find out what kind of recovery he'll have. He's heavily drugged, in a medicated coma. The next twenty-four hours are crucial. Get him through that, and we can be hopeful. You can go sit with him now. He's in critical care."

A squeeze of Wyatt's shoulder and the doctor stood. He helped the young couple to their feet and showed the way to the end of a long corridor. In the last room on the left, a stranger lay buried in covers, wires, and bandages. Wyatt bit back a sob. Emmett wouldn't want to hear him crying.

He pulled up a chair and took his brother's hand. "I'm here, Em. Sammie and I are here. You're going to be all right. Do what you have to do and come back to us."

He bowed his head and pressed it to his brother's limp fingers. The sobs he'd been fighting since Emmett fell in the bar, since the blood started pouring out of his brother's head like a fountain, since he saw him laid out in a hospital bed, got the best of him. Wyatt let them come. Sammie set another chair beside him and sat quietly, stroking his hair, rubbing his back. She wrapped an arm around his waist. His lifeline.

❧❧❧

"Wyatt." Samantha was standing beside him. She'd gone home to take care of the horses. She looked exhausted with dark smudges like bruises under her eyes, her gaze dull, her skin gone white. Wyatt didn't want to know what he looked like. "Wyatt, it's been twenty-four hours. Why don't you come home, get some rest, change your clothes, and come back? Em's made it through the first stretch. They'll call if he's in danger."

She touched his arm and he pulled away, growling at her. "I'll stay!" Wyatt glanced up, saw the hurt in her eyes and his voice dipped down low as he nearly caved in on himself. "I couldn't sit with Mama at the end, but I caught Dad's last breath, and I was there the day Emmet came into this world. Damn it! I will be here if he's going out. Do you understand?"

Samantha pulled up a chair and stayed by his side.

℃⁄℃⁄℃

The first twenty-four hours ran into two days, three, seven, all of them blurring together. Wyatt lost all sense of time as he sat by his baby brother's bedside and talked to him—or *at* him—until his throat was raw and there were no more words to say. Sammie was by his side more often than not while he held his vigil. Occasionally, Wyatt would find himself dragged under by fatigue, Sam's touch the only thing that helped him to come back up and hang on. At night, he tumbled on to the cot placed at the bedside by helpful staff members for cat naps, but he never fell into a deep sleep while he waited for Emmett to open his eyes, or cross over, whichever came first.

☙❧

"The swelling's gone down considerably. We've weaned Emmett off of the medication that has kept him in a coma. You may see a response in the coming hours or someday soon. It's a guessing game." Dr. Martin squeezed Wyatt's shoulder, shaking him awake with his words, and checked the monitors attached to his patient. A quick notation on his brother's chart and the surgeon was gone.

Wyatt leaned forward and pressed his hand to his eyes, letting a curse slip under his breath. He didn't want maybes or somedays. Emmett Henry needed to wake up and get out of that hospital bed. *NOW!*

"*Dammit!*"

Unable to sit another instant, he shot up and began to pace. One glance at his reflection in the window and he came to a halt. Who was that stranger? Appalled, yet fascinated at the same time like a victim in a horror movie, Wyatt went into the small bathroom and stared at the mirror. What he saw made his jaw drop.

The five o'clock shadow didn't do anything for him. Rugged on some, it just made him look like a wreck, as well as the bags under his eyes and the lines of worry in his face. His hair was unkempt and needed a trim. Wyatt reached up and gave a strand a tug. Was that a white hair?

He spun away and strode out into the room, glaring at the figure that appeared to be getting swallowed up by the bed. "Wake up, damn you! Wake up now!"

His shout rang across the room and echoed off the walls, yet there was no response from his brother. The only sounds—Emmett's even breathing and the blipping of the machines that proved he was still alive—slowly driving his older brother out of his mind.

"To hell with this!" Wyatt's boots clomped down the hallway of the hospital as he sought some kind of release from the torture of watching his brother sleep. This limbo was near impossible to live with, not knowing if Emmett would ever come back.

Wyatt navigated the maze of each floor of the hospital and found himself in the cafeteria, staring at food that turned his stomach. He sat by a window and gazed out sightlessly while he drank a cup of coffee that gave him the shakes. His return trip was no better. The pitying stares from the nurses' station only stirred him up more until he was seething, ready to explode.

The instant he hit the door, Wyatt closed the gap to the bed with great strides and kicked the chair out of the way. "Emmett Henry, you wake up now, damn you! Jackson Henry didn't raise a quitter!"

He grabbed his brother's arm and shook him, hard enough to jar Em's whole body. Defeated, Wyatt dropped onto the bed and held onto his brother's limp fingers. There was the slightest flicker of movement, nearly stopping his heart.

Emmett squeezed his hand.

CHAPTER 2

Samantha stood in the kitchen, humming to herself as she tackled a mountain of dishes. What with preparing supper and putting together the makings for a pie, there must not have been a clean dish left in the house. She sighed heavily. There would be more after dinner. She had to do them right now. There were too many to fit in the sink!

She pulled her hands out of the steaming suds and stared at them. Red, rough, cracked from working inside and out, from breaking things and fixing them. They'd been through the mill. Her fingers strayed to her hair, pulled up in a top knot, skimming over flyaway bits going this way and that. A quick glance down revealed bare feet. No nail polish. Blown out jeans. Her father-in-law's flannel shirt, one of her favorites, because it belonged to that great man and smelled like Wyatt, he wore it so often. No, she wasn't winning any beauty contests. Samantha closed her eyes and thanked God that she'd married her best friend, someone who took her the way she was.

The scent of apples and cinnamon, filling the cheerful, homey room, made her stomach grumble. Her tongue longed for hot apple pie with ice cream. Wyatt's favorite. Maybe Emmett would stay too. She'd made chicken and biscuits, enough to feed an army. Her stomach protested again and her tongue skimmed over her lips. Sammie couldn't wait. The phone rang and she dried her hands on a towel, telling her appetite to pipe down. "Hello?"

"Sammie, get to the hospital as quick as you can. Emmett's been hurt bad in a bar fight at Joe's. For God's sake, hurry." Her heart started to skitter at the sound of the receiver slamming down with a bang that made her jump. Wyatt sounded terrified, and her husband never sounded scared of anything. He was a Henry, and Henrys were rock solid.

The moment she got the call, Samantha left the pile of dishes in the sink. She barely had the presence of mind to take the pie out, shut off the oven, and turn off the bubbling pots on the stove. She snatched her keys, didn't even grab a coat, or get her purse. If they pulled her over, so what?

She drove like a mad woman, running across the parking lot, slipping and sliding, shivering from the cold of winter as her feet carried her inside on legs that felt like they were made out of gelatin. A glance down and she almost began laughing hysterically. Her shoes didn't match and they were soaked, leaving footprints down the hall.

The instant Samantha saw Wyatt, her heart nearly broke. She went to him and tried to pick up the pieces that were left of her husband yet was afraid she was out of super glue this go around.

Her husband was a Mount Rushmore of a man. All of the Henrys were, but how much could he take? Losing his mother had torn him apart—and his father had nearly broken him. Losing his baby brother? That would take him down.

Sitting by Wyatt's side with surgical slippers kindly supplied by a nurse, she kept vigil for hours for Emmett. He was wrapped up in bandages and tubes in a bed that appeared to be much too large as it devoured him while machines made all kinds of noise. Samantha held on to her brother-in-law and her husband, tried to be the tie that would bind them both, keep them safe—and thought she would snap in two.

That was a week ago. The longest week of her life. Sammie stood in her kitchen, digging her fists into the small of her aching back. Still wearing her father-in-law's flannel shirt, the threadbare jeans making another appearance yet again because she kept grabbing them off the floor, the sound of Wyatt's voice gone raw during that phone call still echoing in her mind. She never wanted to hear him sound that way again. Hopeless. In all the years they'd been together, Wyatt Henry had only sounded that way once before, pulling the rug out from under her feet…

 espesp

The foal just didn't want to come. Stubborn thing. Samantha had been in the barn for hours, doing her best to keep Maggie comfortable, quietly encouraging the mare. She kneeled in the straw and massaged the horse's heaving stomach, blowing her bangs out of her eyes, swiping a sleeve across her forehead to get rid of the sweat. Lord, but it was hot. It had to be close to one hundred degrees. They needed a barn fan, full blast. Where was Wy? He was supposed to be back from his dad's over an hour ago.

The barn phone rang out, blaring compared to the horse's heavy breathing and the relative quiet of the large cavernous space that was empty otherwise; the rest of the herd was in the pasture, many taking advantage of shade trees.

Samantha gave the mare a pat. "I'll be right back, Mags. See if you can get that little critter moving along." She stood and stretched out the kinks in her back and neck. The phone kept ringing. "Persistent, aren't you? All right, all right. Just give me a minute."

Crossing the entire length of the barn and grumbling every step of the way, she snatched the receiver off the wall. "Wyatt, that had better be you telling me you're on your way. Maggie's in labor, and she needs your magic touch."

There was a gasp on the other end, a shuddering breath, the sound of someone quietly falling to pieces. Samantha gripped the phone with both hands, shaken to the core because somehow she knew it was her husband. "Wyatt?" she whispered.

"Sam. You've got to come to Dad's. There's been an accident. Just come."

His voice broke, and all she could hear was soft sobbing. She dropped the phone and flew across the path that ran between the two houses. It had to be a quarter of a mile at least, but Wyatt had the truck. Was it Emmett? Dad? Horrible imaginings filled her mind.

Her heart was tripping so fast, sure to explode, making her stumble to a halt and drop to her knees. "Please, God. Keep them safe."

She got back on her feet and ran even harder until she burst out of the woods. Wyatt and Emmett sat on the porch while an ambulance quietly pulled away.

Why was it so quiet?

Her eyes scanned the house, the barn, and out to the field, caught sight of the massive tractor tipped on its side, and her stomach gave a lurch. She almost got sick but choked it down and made it to Wyatt's side.

"We couldn't get it off of Dad in time, Sam. We tried, God, how we tried—but all we could do was hold on— and watch him die!"

Wyatt couldn't even get to his feet, just pulled her into his arms as he crumbled while Emmett silently cried beside him, his shoulders shaking, and somehow that was worse than wailing at the top of his lungs. Samantha's tears mingled with theirs. If she could cry long enough and hard enough, her tears would drown the world. Jackson Henry, their foundation, was gone.

℘℘℘

She shook herself and gripped the sink, close to losing it, but how could she complain? Wyatt was so punch drunk tired, he could barely see straight or walk. Whenever she came to the hospital, she made him lie down on the cot beside the bed, stroking his hair, singing softly, promising to wake him if there was any change until his body finally gave up the fight. She would take Emmett's hand next, bow her head, and press it to his limp fingers. She'd hum, sing, talk, and pray. What else was there to do?

Right now, alone in her kitchen, with no one else to hold up and no prying eyes, Samantha gave into weakness, allowing the tears to roll down her cheeks. She wanted someone to take care of *her*. For one week, she'd been getting up at the crack to take care of two herds of horses, spending her days at the hospital to be with Wyatt and Em, only to come back to put the horses back in the barn at night. Sleeping alone in a bed that was much too big without her husband meant long, wakeful hours, staring up at the ceiling. Praying some more.

Samantha couldn't help picturing her husband's thick, wavy hair like an oak stain scattered across her pillow with his slate eyes, so like a blue sky on the edge of gray on a cloudy day, filled with light as he gazed at her and held her in arms strong enough to carry the world. She ached for him with a longing that brought on a pain that was physical. Samantha was just running on empty.

She sank down into a chair at the kitchen table and bowed her head, her shoulders beginning to shake as the sobs finally broke the dam. A soft knock sounded at her door and a moment later, a diminutive, round, white-haired woman was at her side. Emily Hastings was their next door neighbor. A gentle soul, she'd been widowed several years ago but managed to carry on, bringing cheer to others with her sunny personality. Many thought of her as a grandmother for the entire road.

"Samantha, there, there, dear. Don't carry on so. I've tried to catch you but you've been in and out so much. This was the first time I saw the truck parked long enough to pin you down. Now tell me. Are things that bad with Emmett?" Her neighbor's pale blue eyes were filled with compassion and that only made Sam cry harder. She turned and allowed herself to be wrapped in a floral house dress, the scent of home baked cookies, and a hug.

"Oh, Mrs. Hastings, we just don't know. He's had a terrible head injury and he still hasn't woken up." Emily began to gently rock her, murmuring words of comfort, exactly who Samantha needed what with her mother on the other side of the country vacationing. Her elderly neighbor was a close substitute.

The sweet lady patted her back gently and tucked a loose strand of hair away from Samantha's face. Emily sat down at the table and took her hand with fingers bent by arthritis and equally cracked from daily chores. "Then we must pray together. Henrys are made of solid stuff. I've no doubt that the good Lord will help young Emmett to pull through. Beth and Jackson were taken too soon. That's not going to happen this time."

The two women bowed their heads and closed their eyes as Emily whispered the same plea that had been in Sam's heart since that day the awful phone call came. She gradually became aware that her kitchen was filling up with her neighbors. Mrs. Hastings had set a fresh apple pie on the table and more dishes were set beside it. Wives bringing in casseroles, sacks of potatoes, jars of vegetables and preserves canned by their own hands during the summer. Husbands nodded to her and gave her shy smiles as was their way. Before Samantha went back to the hospital that morning, she was assured that the

Henry horses would be cared for as long as necessary because that was what it meant to be good neighbors.

When she came home that night, her kitchen was sparkling, her dishes were clean, her floors swept, and her fridge stocked with food. Trailing through the rooms of their farm house, she discovered that her laundry was washed and neatly folded on the counter in the laundry room and everything was in order. Samantha sat down at the table and cried again—in gratitude. She slept well for the first time in a week.

The next morning, Samantha held back a sigh as she took up her post at her brother-in-law's bedside once more. She took in the changes wrought in her husband and wanted to cry again. He looked so beaten down, on the edge of defeat. There'd been a brief glimmer of hope the night before when Emmett squeezed his hand, then nothing and the waiting game was wearing on Wyatt.

She picked up his hand and studied the cuts on his knuckles, finally scabbed over, the redness and swelling from the barroom brawl only a memory; that first night, Wyatt had the hands of a prize fighter. Gently, her lips grazed each cut. "Do you remember Tommy McGee?"

A low rumble of laughter rose up as he slid down in his chair and rested his head on her shoulder. "How could I forget that one? Little punk. Never bothered you again, did he?"

Sam closed her eyes and the scene unfolded like it was yesterday. The first day of school in third grade, over twenty years ago, rolled out in her mind like a film on a projector…

∽∾∽

"Hey, Wyatt. Wanna come over to my place and pick apples? The trees are just bursting with them, and the boughs are nearly touching the ground, we've got so many. Mama doesn't know what we're going to do with them all. You could bring some home, make a pie." Samantha stuck her hand out, and he took it.

She held tight to Wyatt's hand as they walked, her eight-year-old heart full. She knew that this boy was going to be her best friend for life. Funny. They'd fought over the teeter totter that morning and she knocked him flat on his butt. Who would have thought the Henry boy would be sweet on her by the end of the day?

"My daddy does make a really good pie. Grandmama taught him how."

He turned her way, his dark hair blowing in the breeze, and gave her a crooked grin. A gap from a missing, top tooth, knocked out in a tussle with a horse on his father's farm, made him even cuter. The sun caught Wyatt's gaze, a touch of blue on gray, and Sammie's mouth went dry, her heart starting to race really fast like a hummingbird flitting around. Maybe Wyatt Henry would be the boy she would marry!

"Hello, Sammie! Earth to Sammie O'Dell. Do you hear me? Your mouth is hanging open so wide you are going to catch a fly!" He rubbed shoulders with her, then froze. His head tilted and his smile faded away, his eyes opening wide. *"Say, Sammie. Your hair sure is pretty, like sunshine, like Mama's—and you've got eyes like hers too. Daddy called them cornflower blue. They're really nice."*

His words were almost a whisper, and he leaned in closer to her. Samantha swallowed hard. He was going to kiss her!

"Oh, look at the two lovebirds, Sammie and Wyatt sitting in a tree, k-i-s-s-i-n-g!"

A boy from their class, Tommy McGee, came running up behind them and barreled between them with a sneer, pushing Samantha down on the way. Tommy was a skinny, little runt of a kid, the kind who would take anything away from someone else if he couldn't have it for himself.

Samantha was so steamed it would be no surprise if smoke was coming off the top of her head, her hands curling into fists, even as angry tears burned behind her eyes. Wyatt stopped long enough to help her to her feet, and then he let out a roar, taking the other boy from behind in a rush, knocking him to the ground. He shoved Tommy's mouth into the dirt, making him sputter. Her hero's fists started flailing, pounding his victim left and right.

"You teach him a lesson, Wy! No one messes with a Henry!"

Wyatt's kid brother, Emmett, had tagged along on the way home, trailing behind with a group of first grad-ers. At the sign of a fight, the group of boys gathered around, everyone putting in their two cents.

Sammie watched, holding her breath, wondering if she should run for help when Tommy started to wail. "I'm sorry! I'm sorry! Enough, I say! I'm sorry!"

☙❧❧

"You always were the bold defender, just like in that bar with Em." She laid her cheek on Wyatt's hand.

He closed his eyes and his breath came out in a hiss between clenched teeth. "Didn't come out on top this time."

They both fell silent, listening to the monitors, watching the still figure lying before them. Hoping. Pray-ing. Samantha wondered if Emmett, the Emmett they knew, would ever truly come back to them. She bowed her head and stared hard at her brother-in-law's hand, willing him to wake up, do something, when there was a twitch. "Wy! His fingers, did you just see them?"

Wyatt came up fast and grabbed his kid brother's hand. "Em? Emmett! Can you hear me? Sam and I are here, Em. Wake up, won't you? Come on, little brother. Come back to us." His voice cracked and Sammie wondered for the umpteenth time how her husband was still on his feet.

Emmett's head started to move from side to side and a crease appeared between his eyes as he let out a terrible moan. His fingers came up slowly, fumbling at the bandage on his head. Wyatt caught his hand and held on tight. "No, Em. You've been hurt. You've got to leave your head alone."

Another moan and Emmett shifted, tossing his head from side to side, beginning to thrash and Wyatt pinned him down. "Should I go get help?" Sammie asked nervously, afraid her brother-in-law might do damage to himself.

"No, no. I've got him," Wyatt called out over his shoulder. Turning, he softened his tone and spoke in a soothing voice. "Em, it's all right. Calm down. You're going to be all right. Open your eyes. Say something to me. Let me know you hear me."

Emmett's body went still and slowly, he opened his eyes, wide and unfocused. "Wy?" He whispered. "Wy? Sam?" His voice rose in pitch as he turned his head this way and that. Fear stamped his features.

Samantha went to the other side of the bed and took his free hand. "I'm right here, Em, and so is your brother. You've been out for a week, sweetie. Easy."

Emmett squeezed his eyes shut and opened them again, turned his head both ways and let out a groan that was inhuman. Wyatt's hand held on even tighter. "What's wrong? Do you need something for the pain?"

Em shook his head, and his words shot out, piercing them all, right through the heart. "Wy—I—I can't see!"

Samantha felt like the floor just dropped out from under her feet into a gaping chasm. Judging by the look on her husband's face, he'd already fallen through the hole.

❧❧❧

Dr. Martin came right away, returning with a team of doctors. They ran tests and scans, questioned Emmett, who was remarkably clear all things considered, poked and prodded. They had no answers. It could last a day. It could last forever. As the initial hours of blindness ran into a week, her brother-in-law was *not* handling it well, hope dwindling with each passing day, replaced by an all-consuming fury and still, ever faithful, Wyatt stood guard, and Samantha as well. *Wherever you go, I will go. Lead and I will follow.*

No one said phase two of Emmett's recovery would be easy. Samantha cringed as he shouted at them once again, a daily occurrence, angry at the world, swinging his pillow, knocking things off of his bed stand. Wyatt tried to calm him, but his brother only shook him off. "Leave me alone, Wy. Just leave me alone. Can't you see? I'm just a mess. I'm such a godawful mess!"

Then the unexpected. Em suddenly shoved his way out of bed and crashed against the wall, ripping the IVs out of his arm and sending the rack holding medication and fluids clattering to the floor. Samantha tried to stop him, but he just pushed her out of the way. He rammed Wyatt next, his strength taking them both by surprise.

Emmett staggered through the hallways, plowed into the nurse's station, and his scream tore through the wing as he grabbed his temples. He sank to his knees, and an instant later, his eyes rolled back in his head. Em sprawled on the floor and began shaking uncontrollably.

"He's seizing!" a nurse shouted. "Someone get Dr. Martin!"

Another doctor arrived and, together, they did their best to protect their patient from harm, administering medication. Five minutes later, his body became still. Two steps forward, three steps back as the drugs took him under and back to bed, unconscious for another day. When he came to, Emmett was sluggish for all too brief a time, anger and violence coming back in force, turning him into a stranger.

✧✦✧

Samantha stared at the heart marked on the calendar and scraped at her face with both hands, fighting the stinging at the back of her eyes. She'd already cried enough tears to last a lifetime in the past six weeks. Valentine's Day and none of them even noticed. She wanted to sit down and bawl—a little bit for herself on a forgotten sweetheart's day. More for her Wyatt, tormented by his brother's injury. Most of all for Emmett who might not ever be the same again.

She wanted to have a good cry, but Sam didn't. She washed up in the bathroom, changed into a pretty shirt that brought out the blue of her eyes, and brushed her hair, leaving it down for a change. Wyatt was going to get her company, like it or not. He'd sent her home soon after Emmett came to from his seizure because her brother-in-law had been downright nasty, throwing things, cursing, shouting. Angry—man, was he angry. In all of her years of knowing the Henry men, she'd never seen someone so mad. Wyatt made her go home, but *he* wouldn't leave Emmett's side. Time to give him some relief.

✦❧✦

"Get your hairy ass out of my room and stay the hell out!"

Samantha could hear Emmett's shouting all the way down the hall as she stepped out of the elevator. A crash...dinner, perhaps?...followed next. She hurried to his room, her hand on the door as Wyatt slipped out.

At the sight of her, his face softened and he pulled her into his arms. "Aww, Sam. I told you to stay put, but thanks for coming anyway. Hold on a second." He fished in his pocket and pulled out a small box. "Happy Valentine's Day. Sorry it almost got away from me." He bent down and kissed her, making her dizzy.

Those three words made her heart light and a tremulous smile appeared for the first time in days. Sammie lifted the lid to find a delicate ring with a ruby in the shape of a heart. She slipped it on her finger with a hand that trembled. "Wy, how did you manage? I didn't bring you anything."

He grinned even though he looked exhausted, dead on his feet. "You brought you, and that's enough. They had it in the gift shop. I've got a rose in there, but it's on the window. If Em got a hold of it, it would be history."

Samantha glanced at the door and back at her husband's worn face, and some anger of her own flared up like flames fanned to life from the red embers hidden beneath the ashes. She looped her arms around Wyatt's neck and planted a kiss on his lips. "Why don't you go to the cafeteria, and I'll meet you in a few minutes? We'll have coffee and dessert. I need a minute with your brother."

She gestured to the closed door. Wyatt's eyebrows raised, and he shook his head, but he didn't argue. His lips brushed her cheek and he walked slowly down the hallway, giving her a chance to slip inside Emmett's room.

Her brother-in-law was lying back, hands pressed to his head, and his room was in shambles. His dinner tray was on the floor, food splattered on the wall. Papers were all over the place and vases of flowers from friends and neighbors were shattered, strewn across the floor as well. At the click of the door, he came up fast.

"I told you to get out of here, you bastard! Why the hell won't you listen to me?!"

He flailed out, caught the plastic water pitcher on the bedside, and hurled it with amazing accuracy. Samantha had to duck or it would've hit her head.

"You ought to be ashamed of yourself, Emmett Henry! I never had the opportunity to meet Beth Henry, but I know that your mother raised you to keep a respectful tongue in your head, and so did your father. Jackson Henry must be rolling in his grave right now, ready to kick your butt. Talking to your brother that way, and he's been here at this hospital, by your side, for over a month. I've half a mind to drag you out of that bed and make you clean up this mess."

The anger died almost as soon as it flared up, and Emmett's face blanched the instant he realized it was her. She took one step forward when he reached up, yanked the IVs out of his arm, and slipped out of bed. He started crawling on the floor, feeling his way, attempting to pick up, setting things on the bed as he did, stopping every few seconds to hold his head. A soft moan slipped out, pain his constant companion.

Samantha knelt on the floor beside him and took his arm, throttling down her voice to a gentle murmur. "Em, stop. I didn't mean it about the mess. You're going to hurt yourself. You've just got to stop being so mad at the world. It's not helping you get better."

He turned to her and felt for her, drawing her into a clumsy hug. "I'm sorry, Sam, sorry I talked to you that way. I don't mean to behave so badly. It's just I feel so bad, I can't take it. I'm not sure it's going to get any better than this."

Sam choked back tears and stroked his cheek. "I know, Em. It's not me you have to say sorry to. It's Wy."

His face collapsed, and he broke for the first time since the accident. Before then, he'd lashed out at everyone who came near him. Samantha held on, smoothing his hair, calming him. She helped him back to bed and pulled up the covers. "Why don't you lie back and rest for a bit, okay? I'm going to find Wyatt, and you can make that apology."

"Okay—and Sam, thanks for understanding. Happy Valentine's Day." Somehow, he managed a grin that broke her heart.

Before she left, she quietly straightened up the room. Samantha stopped at the nurses' station, told them about Emmett's IV, then headed to the cafeteria to have a quiet moment with Wyatt. They shared a piece of chocolate pie and sipped at coffee, fortification for their return, but there was no need. When they stepped in, it was as if the fuse finally burned out, a subdued Emmett waiting for them.

"Wyatt, come here. Please," he called out when the door opened.

Wy did as asked and sat down on the side of the bed. He took Em's hand and was jerked into a bone-crushing embrace.

"I'm sorry, so sorry, for all of it, how I've been. You've been a rock through all of this, and I've just been downright rotten. I'm going to work on my attitude, I promise, but I need you to do something for me."

Samantha had to turn to the window, unable to look at the pain written on Emmett's face or the emptiness of his golden eyes that called to mind honey gleaming in a jar in the sun. Since the fight, the light in his gaze had been hidden by the cloud of his anger. In this instant, only hurting, intense and deep, was revealed.

Wyatt's voice cracked. "Anything, Em. You know I'll do anything for you. Just say the word."

Emmett kissed his brother's cheek and gruffly told him, "Go home, Wy. You and Sammie have been here long enough. Give me some room and time to heal. Take a breather. Drop in and check on me, but go back home."

Wyatt shook his head and pulled back. "No, Em! No, I'm not going home until you do."

Emmett hooked him at the nape of his neck and gave a good squeeze. "Please, Wy. I need a break. *You* need a break. I'm out of danger, but I'm so drugged up, and I'm a mess. You don't need to be here for this. I've got to learn how to deal. Besides, the horses need you." His face twisted, and he had to pause a moment. "Go take care of my babies. Tell them I miss them. Go on now. I love you, brother, more than ever. You too, Sam. Go have your Valentine's Day the way you should."

Wyatt didn't like it, but he did as he was asked, kissing his brother and dashing tears away as Samantha waited. As they walked out, she held his hand all the way to the truck, and when he wept, she kept him anchored through the storm.

CHAPTER 3

Wyatt stood in the barn for the first time in six weeks, wrapped in the familiar smells and sounds. What should have been a comfort only grated on him. Everything rubbed him the wrong way. His hands balled into fists, and he bowed his head, gritting his teeth so hard his jaw popped. He wanted to hit something. To run until there was no place to run. To turn back the clock, make this whole nightmare go away.

Unable to do any of those things, he saddled up one of his favorite horses, Blackie, and headed onto their lane and down the road. Wyatt let the horse have his head and urged him to go as fast as the stallion wanted to go. There was too much snow in the pasture for a gallop. This was the horse's first chance to run in months, and he put on a wild burst of speed that actually made Wyatt's heart jump.

He welcomed the feeling, anything to take his mind off of the pain that had been with him ever since Emmett was hurt. Wyatt needed to take the edge off of his frustration and anger before he went back, give his wife the attention she deserved. It was Valentine's for God's sake, and all he'd managed was a cheap ring and a rose. Sam had been through hell too, yet he hadn't been there for her, not since he'd been at the hospital day in and day out.

"Damn!" he cursed, had been cursing far too much since a bizarre twist of fate blinded his brother. Mama— and Dad—would wash his mouth out with soap. *Who are you kidding? Em would be standing in line if he had half the chance, and Grandmama would finish the job with laundry soap.*

The thought of the time she gave him powdered detergent, so bad it made him puke, actually made Wyatt start to laugh. Emmett had stood by and watched the whole thing. First he had worn a devil's grin, but when he saw his big brother get sick, the tyke stepped up and put a handful of soap in his mouth. The two boys took turns tossing their guts in the toilet. They must have been about five and seven. A year after Mama died.

Wyatt slowed Blackie to a trot and finally a walk, turning back toward home. He leaned forward and rested his face against the horse's sturdy neck, relishing his warmth. "Thanks, boy. You're good medicine. You and the herd are just what I needed."

Back in the barn, he took his time rubbing the stallion down, brushing his coat, and giving him plenty of water. As Wyatt led Blackie into his stall, he thought of something else he needed more, the want so bad it made his gut clench and his head go light. The barn hadn't been the only place he'd missed for six weeks. He hadn't slept in his bed either.

The thought made his heart give a hiccup and his breath catch, his steps quickening on the way to the house. After all, it *was* Valentine's Day. He had to do his wife justice on this of all days, give her the love she gave to him unconditionally since the day Samantha promised to be his.

Wyatt stepped inside, slid off his boots, and hung his coat on the peg by the door. The kitchen was warm and bright. Something smelled good and made his stomach growl, but food wasn't on the top of his list of priorities right now. "Sam?"

There was no response, but the bathtub was running. A few steps farther, and he found rose petals on the floor, followed a trail all the way upstairs to their bedroom. A glance in the open doorway, and he saw candles scattered about, the covers turned back, inviting him in. The desire for his wife, powerful from the start, blazed up and burned even brighter, pulling him to the bathroom next to their room.

Wyatt mentally counted to three and slowly opened the door. Samantha was bent over the tub, pouring bubble bath, with nothing on to take away from her God-given glory. Her golden hair was pulled up off of her face, but a few, damp tendrils clung to her neck. She was rosy from the heat, her curves beckoning him, just calling for his hands to rest in all of the right places. His wife had hips and a soft swelling for a belly, full breasts, something for him to hold on to. A testament to her good cooking and she lit a fire inside of him every time he laid eyes on her.

"God, but you are the most beautiful thing I've ever seen." The words tumbled out.

Samantha turned the water off and slowly turned to face him. She crooked a finger, beckoning him.

"You said that on our wedding day. I'm glad to see that time hasn't changed your mind, although you might be delusional with exhaustion right now." He took one step closer and she was in his arms, her warm, soft body pressed up against his flannel and denim. If he didn't shed his clothes soon, Wyatt feared spontaneous combustion.

"I'd have to be dead to be numb to your charms. Touch me, Sam. Please, touch me. It's been so long." He yearned for her with all of his being. Many of the nights in the hospital, tossing and turning on the uncomfortable cot by his brother's side, snippets of dreams took him home to the arms of his wife when he gave himself up to her able hands.

Samantha gave into his need, running her fingers through his hair, down his neck, to the top button of his shirt. She was painfully slow undoing every one and skimming her hand over the flat plane of his chest. He couldn't help but groan. Samantha paused then pulled his white T-shirt over his head in one fluid motion and pressed her mouth to the spot over his madly beating heart.

"*Sam!*"

He couldn't say anything more as her hands moved down and undid his jeans, dropping them, shimmying the boxers to the floor next. She looked up at him, her blue eyes shining brightly in the glow of the candles scattered around the bathroom, and he could swear his wife was laughing on the inside. The woman was enjoying this!

Unable to wait a second longer, Wyatt swept her into his arms and stepped into the tub, sinking down into the suds. Cradling her in his lap, he sealed her mouth with his until both of them had to stop for air. His hands took their turn worshiping her gifts and, with a sudden move, he pulled her on top of him.

The water sloshed over the sides and Wyatt sank down. He didn't care if they ever came up. For a brief instant in time, there was no Emmett, no fear, no worry. Only two people sharing their hearts and bodies on Valentine's Day.

ひoひ

"Wow. Maybe we should take prolonged breaks more often." Samantha's laughter was a soft sigh as she lay tucked in under Wyatt's arm, her head resting against his chest. His heart was limping along. After a turn in the tub, another round on the bathroom floor when he recovered, and a final marathon in their bed, his body couldn't do much more. If the place was on fire, he wasn't sure they'd make it out of the house.

Wyatt kissed the top of her head. His hand slowly floated up and it was all he could do to play with a strand of her hair. "I'd rather not. I was in serious withdrawal. Being away from you at night nearly killed me."

She lifted her head and gazed at him, tears close to the surface. "Me too. Happy Valentine's Day."

Wyatt set his lips on hers and felt a stirring below. "Happy Valentine's Day to you. What do you say to one more time?" She buried her face in the pillow and started to laugh—but not for long.

ⲉⲟⲉⲟ

"How did you sleep?" Samantha was at the stove, fixing his breakfast. Coffee already waited for him at the table.

Wyatt stepped behind her and wrapped his arms around her waist. His hands reached inside her robe and felt her body, naked. Beautiful. His eyebrows sprang up. "Well—when I wasn't thinking about this amazing body of yours. What are you trying to do to me? I hope you'll keep that on reserve until I get the horses out."

She turned and kissed him until his insides practically turned to mush. "There's plenty more where last night came from. I'm just so glad to have you home, Wy."

Samantha stepped in and rested her cheek against his chest. He stroked her hair and cupped the back of her head, returning the kiss. "Me too, honey, me too."

They sat down and ate breakfast together, like the married couple they were. Wyatt gave her a gentle swat on her nice, round bottom and got one in return before heading outside. Working with the horses restored his inner balance, made him realize how much he missed being on the farm, needed it. His thoughts strayed to Emmett as he headed back inside. One more turn with his wife in the bedroom, maybe a nap—he was so tired, always so tired, and his head was starting to throb—then Wyatt would go back. Regardless of what Em said, he'd be back every day until his baby brother came home. Henrys stood by their own.

ↄ⁄ↄↄ⁄ↄ

A quiet Emmett was worse. Wyatt had been sitting by his brother's side for the past hour. Aside from a few niceties, the ticking of the clock was the only distraction while Em gazed at the ceiling with his blank stare. Emmett's emotions were usually close to the surface, transparent in his expression and his eyes. Beneath that calm exterior, Wyatt suspected a fierce storm raged and his fingers dug into his knees, itching to throw something, punch the mattress, anything to stir his brother up.

"Doc says I can go home tomorrow. The seizures are under control. If I can take the migraines, there's no reason to keep me any longer." Emmett's voice was flat. There was no anticipation for his homecoming. Not now. Not like this.

"You'll come to our place then." Wyatt rose to his feet and crossed his arms, anticipating a fight. Emmett didn't say a word. He just kept still and closed his eyes. That was the worst of all.

⁋⸙⁋

God love her, Samantha didn't blink or skip a beat. Without a second's hesitation, she went to the spare room to get it ready for Emmett upon word of his upcoming release. The bedding was efficiently changed and the windows opened a crack to let the fresh air in to the room that the brothers had shared when they would sleep over at Grandmama and Grandpop's. Little did they know that one day, Wyatt would inherit it and Emmett their father's home, much too soon.

Wyatt laid a hand on his wife's shoulder, making her go still. He spun her around and hugged her so tight, her breath came out in a rush. "Thanks, Sam."

He went to Emmett's next. Walking into the empty house was eerie without Em. It felt like Dad should be waiting for him in the house that kept all the memories of their growing-up years. The place had an abandoned air to it, like a ghost house.

A shiver went down Wyatt's spine, but he shook it off, taking the stairs two at a time to his brother's bedroom. He opened the closet door and the scent of his father's cologne reached out to him and wrapped itself around him. Wyatt closed his eyes and could swear that warmth brushed his cheek. *Dad. Help me to help him. Please. I'm out of my depth here. I know horses. Humans are trickier.*

A sense of calm washed over him as he pushed the air out of his lungs. Wyatt opened his eyes to find nothing except clothing, a jumble of his father's favorite shirts and jackets, intermingled with his brother's things. Slightly unsettled and off balance, he quickly gathered some essentials and headed home. He barely slept at all that night, thinking about Emmett's homecoming, and took care of the horses before the sun woke up.

Samantha was waiting for him when he stepped into the kitchen, her hair mussed and sleep in her eyes, wearing a cotton nightgown with pink rosebuds on it that brushed the dip behind her knee. She looked so pretty and heart-achingly sweet that he just wanted to pick her up and carry her to bed. Wyatt took her in his arms and buried his face in the sunshine of her hair instead. Somehow, she always made things better, no matter how big the problem, no matter how hard the earth shook.

"You got up too early for me. I didn't even get a chance to put on the coffee. It's just about perked now. Sit and I'll pour you a cup," she murmured with her head pressed against the wall of his chest, practically smothered in the flannel of his father's shirt, the same one Samantha had worn to the hospital on that first dreadful day—and for a string of days after.

They both grabbed the red-and-black-checkered shirt often, a source of comfort, a way to bring back a hint of his father's presence in the day to day. Wyatt didn't want to ever let go of the great man who had been forced to raise two boys on his own. That thought had him bucking up for whatever lay ahead with Emmett. Wyatt took a deep breath and kissed the top of her head. "All right, but don't bother with a big breakfast right now. My stomach's doing flip flops. Besides, Em might like something when we get home. That hospital stuff doesn't even qualify as food."

He accepted his cup and inhaled the steam drifting into his face, closing his eyes in pleasure. Funny how the simple things in life could still satisfy, even when your world was turned on its end. Samantha stood behind him and looped her arms over his neck, resting her chin on his head. "I wonder how he'll do at home. Your brother's got a stubborn streak a mile wide."

Wyatt chuckled and took her hand, pressing a kiss to the rough surface, dry and cracked from all of the work she did indoors and out. "It's a family trait. Runs deep in the both of us, I suspect."

That set Samantha off to laughing, and the sound made a bubble of happiness rise up inside of him. He set down his coffee and pulled her into his lap, his lips finding their way to hers. Regardless of what was wrong in his life, his wife was the one constant, the one thing that was always right.

❧❧❧

Strange. Leading his brother to the truck, protecting his head as he climbed in, guiding him up the steps of their grandparents' home, a place they both knew like the back of their hand. Emmett had always been independent. From a young age, he insisted on doing things on his own. He might throw a tantrum when trouble came his way, but Em always figured it out in the long run. This time, Wyatt wasn't so sure.

Watching Emmett with his hands out, walking cautiously like an old man, Wyatt realized they'd have to get a cane for him. Wyatt had resisted so far, hoping against hope there'd be no need, that this was temporary. But nothing had changed.

He'd take Em to every doctor in the country. No matter how many doors slammed in his face, one had to open and give them reason for optimism. Until then, listening to his brother curse as he rammed his knee against the door frame, they had to be practical. Wyatt would have to look into ways to make navigation easier.

The door closed with a click, and Emmett stood still, head down, breathing hard as the pulse at the base of his neck fluttered wildly. He wasn't letting on, but his kid brother was scared, scared to death to be in a familiar place that was now full of unknowns.

"Let me take your coat, Em." Wyatt helped him shrug out of it and hung it on the hook. Emmett fumbled awkwardly with his boots, but managed to get them off. His breath came out in a rush, and he stood rooted to the spot once more, motionless.

"You want to sit in the living room, have some coffee? Sam wants to cook you a big breakfast, something that's actually edible. I could put on the game…" Wyatt's words trailed off as he realized the mistake he'd made, wanted to bite his tongue. "We could listen."

"I'm really tired. I think I'll just lie down. Thanks anyway, Wy." Emmett turned and reached out, found his brother's arm, gave it a squeeze. He walked slowly toward the stairway, nudging along with his foot, hands extended. The relief was plain to see the instant his fingers brushed the banister. He gripped the railing, his knuckles white from holding on so tight, and Emmett took the steps slowly to the top.

"Welcome home, Em."

Samantha was waiting for him, strong emotions at war on her face, but she kept her tone gentle. She laid a palm on his cheek for an instant then took his hand. He let her lead him to his room. Wyatt trailed behind. He stood in the doorway as Emmett stretched out on the bed on a late sunny morning and stared with unseeing eyes at the wall. It pained Wy to know it didn't matter if his brother's eyes were open or shut.

"If you need anything…"

The words died as Em's eyes slid closed, one tear running down his face. "I won't," he said gruffly, dismissing them both.

Wyatt spun around and clomped down the stairs, stomping harder than he should have. He went out to the field, not even bothering with a heavy shirt or coat on a day when the air still had some bite to it. Out into the middle of the pasture. Kicking at the last of the snow. Sending clumps flying everywhere. Shouting at the top of his lungs until his voice went hoarse.

Samantha practically tackled him, snagging him around the waist, and squeezing hard. Shivering, Wyatt bowed his head and stared at the cloud his breath made. "What is Em supposed to do, Sam?"

"Take it one day at a time, and so will we."

He turned and welcomed the light in her eyes, her trembling smile. He took her hand and let his wife guide him home.

CHAPTER 4

March came in like a lamb. The same could not be said about Emmett. Samantha sat at the kitchen table and gripped her coffee cup, eyes closed, as she listened intently for the next burst of fireworks upstairs. A few days after his arrival, her brother-in-law had found his independent streak and insisted on doing *everything* for himself. Some things *did not* go well, but he would learn the hard way or not at all.

The front door opened and closed, and a whirlwind in the form of her mother blew its way into the kitchen, grabbing Samantha in a bear hug and kissing her on the cheek.

"We came straight from the airport. Your father is out in the barn right now, trying to talk some sense into Wyatt to let us stay on and help out for a while, just until things get settled. Two herds of horses! Lord, but that's a lot for one man."

Angela O'Dell was a no-nonsense sort of a woman. She had to be as a farmer's wife for thirty-five years. At five feet, two inches, she was a couple of inches shorter than her daughter and a bit more generous in curves, but her blue eyes were just as bright, her sunny hair bleached lighter by their winter months in Florida. They'd become snowbirds a few years before, heading to a warmer climate as soon as the harvest was in, returning in time for planting. Taking hold of her mother's hands, Samantha lost a little bit of the sharp edges of her anxiety. Besides Wyatt, she'd had no one to help her carry the burden of Emmett's blindness.

Nearly sagging with relief, Samantha gestured to the table and set out another cup. "I appreciate that, Mom, really I do, but I don't think that's a good idea right now. Em is *not* up to company." She poured coffee and creamer for her mother, adding sugar last. With a shake of her head, Samantha sat down and sipped at her cup in an attempt at letting her guard down.

A crash, bang, and violent streak of cursing brought it right back up. Both women jumped out of their chairs and sprinted up the stairs. The bathroom door opened, and Emmett stepped out, a hand raised in the air. "Sorry, sorry. The bathroom is still standing."

"What's got a bee in your bonnet, young man?" Angela set her hands on her hips and grinned, trying to find humor in the situation although unable to hide her dismay. Seeing Wyatt's brother blind was still a shock for Samantha and Wyatt when they saw him every day since he was injured. Samantha could only imagine how hard it was for her mother.

Emmett's face flushed with embarrassment, even as his lip twitched. "I didn't know you were back, Mrs. O'Dell. Welcome home." He waved a hand in the direction of the bathroom. "I'm sorry, Sam. I did it again. I knocked the shower head down, and then I tripped over the side of the tub getting out, sent the vanity flying. I don't think I broke anything. I tried to put it all to rights." He let out an explosive breath of frustration, his cheeks crimson at this point. "Just can't get my balance stepping out. My head starts to spin, and I get dizzy. That's when everything goes haywire."

"Well, now, I suspect what with having your head bashed in, that's to be expected. You're looking remarkably well, all things considered. Don't be so hard on yourself, Emmett. You need to give yourself time." Samantha's mother stepped forward and gave him a hug before taking his arm. "Do you need a hand getting back to your room to get dressed?"

He went an even brighter shade of red if that was possible, and his eyes glanced down because it was habit. Emmett was only wearing a towel. "No, no, Mrs O'Dell. I'll manage." Gathering the remaining shreds of his dignity, he held on to his towel with one hand and skimmed the wall with the other, taking refuge in his room. The door closed a little harder than was necessary.

The two women glanced at each other, and Samantha had to cover her mouth to hold back her laughter. She hugged her mother and held on for an instant. "Oh, Mom, I think that was just what Em needed to hear. You're the first outsider who has seen him since this happened—he insisted on no visitors at the hospital, and no one has dared since he came home with us. I think it's good to have someone like you shaking him up a bit."

Chuckling softly, they straightened the bathroom before returning downstairs to finish their coffee without further incident. The two had caught up on doings for the past few months when Emmett appeared at the door. Samantha's head snapped up as he stepped into the kitchen, feeling his way with his hands extended and his stocking feet.

Em had experienced many a stubbed toe, banged knee, and bruise since his arrival. "Is there enough coffee for me?"

Angela hopped up and pulled out a chair, giving him a point of reference. "I'll get that for you in a jiff. Sammie, you stay put."

Her mother gave him a kiss on his cheek when he sat down. She set a steaming cup of coffee in front of him, the sugar, and the creamer. A big smile bloomed on Emmett's face as the older woman set a spoon in one hand and took his other, showing him where everything was.

Samantha couldn't help but smile with him. It was the first time Em had come down from his bedroom since his arrival.

David O'Dell walked in with Wyatt at that moment and patted Emmett's back before sitting down at the table. His wife squeezed her husband's shoulder and set a cup in front of him and her son-in-law.

"You're looking fine, young man. You'll be back to yourself in no time." Broad of shoulder and compact, Samantha's father reminded her of a linebacker, ready to charge at any problem that came their way. The warmth of his coffee eyes, his steady gaze, and his dark hair threaded with gray gave her a badly needed shot of confidence that they would get through this together. It rubbed off on Em as well.

"Thank you, sir. I'm trying." Emmett pulled out a slip of a grin and drank his coffee to the last drop. He didn't leave the table as they all relaxed for a while and talked. Samantha's father told some stories from her childhood that had them all laughing. Even Em was fit to split his sides wide open, wiping tears from his eyes. His honey gaze began to gleam brighter than it had since that awful night in the bar.

Samantha found herself drawn in. It was such a good sight to see. Maybe, just maybe her brother-in-law would be all right. She had all the more reason to believe it when her parents went home a few weeks later and Emmett came down to breakfast. When they were finished eating, she started clearing the table, and Wyatt stood up to go to the barn.

Emmett stood as well. "Wy, hold up." He stepped toward the sound of his brother's footsteps. Her husband obliged and turned his way. Emmett cleared his throat, as if gathering courage. "I think it's time for me to go home." Meeting a wall of silence, he raised his jaw and crossed his arms. "If you don't take me, I'll find my way there."

They stood chin to chin, Wyatt's eyes flashing, more gray than blue with the storms brewing within. "You're crazy, you know that?" A moment's pause and he grabbed hold of his little brother in a bear hug. "Okay. I know I can't stop you when you set your mind to something, and if there's one thing that's stronger since you were hurt, it's your stubborn streak. It runs at least a mile deep."

Emmett laughed, sounding a bit choked. "What can I say? I'm a Henry, and I learned from the best. You and Dad taught me well."

❧❧❧

Wyatt stood in the barn, murmuring softly to one of forty horses after a hard ride. Whenever he was frustrated or needed time to think, her husband would seek therapy in the animals he loved and knew so well. Samantha could stand there and watch him for hours. His broad back. His strong shoulders. The muscles rippling in his arms with each movement, great strength restrained by his gentle ways. She pictured those hands on her body and her temperature started to rise, her breathing became a bit labored, and the blood thrummed in her veins. She closed her eyes and swallowed hard. All in good time.

She waited quietly, doing her best to be patient as Wyatt worked with his horse, trying to ease the tension that had been his constant companion since Emmett's world was turned upside down, tying him up in knots even more so since his brother went home.

He finished grooming and led the stallion into his stall, resting his forehead against the wooden door. No peace today.

Samantha slowly approached him, walking softly, and wrapped her arms around his waist. Pressing up against him, she felt his body go loose. He turned her way and she saw the clouds gathering in his slate eyes. That hint of blue was hard to find today. "I wish your hands were taking care of me head to toe right now."

She kept her tone light and tried to tease, but her heart ached to see the darkness in his gaze. Wyatt stepped forward and buried his head in her shoulder, inhaling deeply. "I don't feel like I can take care of anyone right now. My baby brother's life is falling apart and I can't even pick up the pieces."

"Hey, enough of that." Samantha stepped back and took his face in her hands, forced him to meet her steady gaze when he wanted to look away. His hurting hurt her, made her raw inside, but she would do her best to be his bandage. "You have been by Emmett's side every step of the way. He could not ask for better. When it comes to the title big brother, you have lived up to it in every way."

"I still don't like it, Sam, letting him go home. I feel like he should be here where I can keep an eye on him." His voice cracked and his eyes were bright, tears close to the surface.

Samantha couldn't hold hers back, swiping at her cheeks even as she held on to his arm and offered him a source of comfort. "You'll check on him every day, and you're only a phone call away. There's a health aide coming in every morning. You've got to let him do this for himself, figure this out."

Wyatt let out a shaky breath and held her close. "I know, I know. I've never been good at that. When he was learning how to walk, I always wanted to hold his hand. Em wouldn't let me, even pushed *me* down sometimes. I can't do this for him either, and it's tearing me up inside."

Samantha reached up and gave him a kiss, hoping to heal. "Maybe I can patch you up. Let me try." He closed his eyes and gave a slight nod, setting his shoulders, taking up his burden again. The Henry way.

ജാ

She didn't feel like getting out of bed. Her head was throbbing and her whole body felt like it was heavy, aching all over. Samantha let out a groan as the coffee began to perk and the smell had her running to the downstairs bathroom. She hit her knees just in time and let the heaves have her until there was nothing left. On shaky feet, she managed to wash up but had to steer clear of the kitchen, unable to face the coffee scent again.

Wyatt was waiting for her when she stepped out, his hand taking her chin and tilting her face his way. "All right, that's it. Bed." He didn't even wait for her response, just scooped her up in his arms and took the stairs.

"But I need to get your breakfast, and the laundry is piling up. I've got to work on my garden and—"

He pressed a finger to her lips as he set her on the bed and pulled up the covers.

"Sam, I know you think this place will fall apart without you, but I can muddle through for a day or two. I won't like it, but I'll manage. You need to take care of yourself. I knew you weren't right last night, picking at the best chicken and biscuits you ever made." She stuck out her tongue at the thought, making Wyatt chuckle. "See what I mean? You fell asleep before I even turned out the light." He pressed the back of his hand to her forehead and winced. "You've got a fever too. Stay put. I'll bring you some tea, toast, and aspirin, then I want you to sleep. Doctor's orders."

She didn't want to do what he said, honestly, but Samantha's body had other plans. A few bites of toast, enough tea to swallow the pills, and she was out as soon as her head hit the pillow. She woke up periodically to go to the bathroom what felt like a hundred times, even though she didn't have anything to drink. Wyatt checked in on her throughout the day, bringing her something to eat and drink, keeping her hydrated, making her take more medicine. Samantha even slept through dinner, a first, straight through to the next morning.

At five in the morning, her inner clock pulled her out of bed. She was still dragging, but managed to get breakfast started. She set the coffee pot on the stove and sat down at the table, resting her head on her arms when the strong scent filled the kitchen again. Usually a smell that filled her with anticipation of that first invigorating sip of hot coffee, today it made her stomach turn for a repeat performance. Another trip to the bathroom, and she was annoyed. This had to stop.

Intent on making sure Wyatt's cup and plate was filled when he came down to the kitchen, she opened the window and stood by it, inhaling deep gulps of fresh air, holding her breath as she poured coffee into his mug. Another fortifying breath at the window, and Samantha set bacon on eggs on the table. A glance at his breakfast, and she pressed one hand to her stomach and the other to her mouth. Breakfast was not in the cards for her that morning.

Wyatt walked in whistling and crossed the room quickly to give her a kiss on the cheek as she rested her hands on the window sill and continued to breathe deep. "Hey, beautiful. How are you doing today?"

Samantha found a smile even though she felt awful and kissed him back. "Better than yesterday. Get eating before it's cold."

He eyed her closely, his eyebrows drawing together as a crease formed in the middle of his brow. "Hmm. I think you're lying to me, but I know how stubborn you are so I won't pick at you. Promise you'll take it easy today?"

She swatted at his bottom as he turned away. "If I'm stubborn, it's a trait I've acquired by association. I don't have anything big planned today. I've got to run to the store, take care of a few errands. Then I might even put my feet up on the couch and eat bon-bons."

"Sounds good to me. Maybe I'll join you." Wyatt grinned and polished off his breakfast. He gathered all of the dishes and washed them up quickly in the sink, grabbing his cup on the way to the door. Samantha followed him, even though the last thing she wanted was to be close to that coffee scent. "I'm off to the barn, and then I'll go over to see Em. I think I'll walk the path today. It looks like a fine day, good for getting some extra fresh air. I think it's putting the roses in your face." He snatched a kiss and headed out.

The taste of coffee on his lips, just a hint, was enough to head her sprinting back to the bathroom. As soon as she was done retching, Samantha rinsed her mouth and dumped the pot of coffee down the drain. She also added one more place on her list of stops for the day. She was heading to the doctor's.

℘℘

"Well, Sammie, have I got news for you." Doc Smith gave her hand a squeeze when he returned from his lab in the room next to his office. The old farm house had been converted years ago and included a pediatrician's office as well as a laboratory that could provide fast results for minor issues, such as strep throat or an X-ray analysis.

Samantha took in his big smile and the butterflies in the pit of her stomach went to war with the nausea that had been her companion the past several days. Suddenly breathless, she whispered, "It's not the flu?"

The white-haired man, a benevolent figure that had been a part of her life since childhood, caught her with his twinkling, green eyes. "Definitely not. Wy's going to need a supply of cigars in nine months. You, my dear, have a bun in the oven. Finally, sweetheart. I'm so happy for you."

Ten years of trying. Ten years of hoping. Ten years of waiting and fearing that the dream was dying. Samantha's heart beat so hard she thought it might explode, and she burst into tears. A river of happy tears, enough to drown out three months of sadness. "I've got to tell Wyatt right away!"

She jumped off of the examining table, kissed the doctor who was more like a grandfather, and shot out the door, intent on one goal. Getting home and giving her husband a little good news for a change. God did work in wondrous ways, bringing miracles when they needed them most.

CHAPTER 5

Wyatt stepped out of the barn and flipped up the collar of his father's flannel shirt. The late April day had a bit of a bite to it even though the sun was shining brightly overhead. He decided to take the path between his house and Emmett's, go check up on his brother.

In the shade of the mighty oaks and tall pines, some patches of snow remained. Ghosts of his past followed on his heels all the way back to his childhood home…

❧❧❧

"Take that, Wy!"

Eight-year-old Emmett whacked him dead center on the back of the head with a snowball as they stomped their way to Grandmama's and Grandpop's. It was an official declaration of war.

"I'm gonna cream you, Em!"

Wyatt whipped around, scooped up a good handful of snow, and packed it into the form of a sizeable snowball. One good launch and he nailed Emmett in the gut.

Dramatic as always and inspired by Sunday movie marathons of old Westerns, his kid brother grabbed at his midsection, staggered, and toppled backward. A pitiful groan rose up as he sank into several inches of fresh powder, kicking up a cloud of white upon impact.

Wheezing with laughter, Wyatt offered him a hand up. A hard tug and Em had him on the ground. Some good-natured wrestling ensued without a victor until they were both huffing and puffing, staring up at the clouds. Snow sprinkled down on them, dusting their hair and faces. Emmett poked his tongue out to catch a few flakes and glanced at his sidekick with a big grin. "Wanna do it again?"

ഗഗ

Wyatt shook off the memory. That was his brother, always ready to get back up again. Until now. Wy's eyes began to burn, and his heart thumped painfully. Life had knocked his brother down pretty hard this time, knocked him flat. What if Emmett couldn't be the comeback kid this go around?

All the way through the woods, Wyatt couldn't squash his misgivings. Breaking out in the opening by the house, staring off into the distance at empty fields didn't help. He couldn't even bring himself to walk into those barns without any horses to fill them. Lord, but that had been one of the hardest days of his life as the neighbors helped him to bring Em's herd next door. There'd been nothing for it. The trek back and forth between the two Henry Homesteads had been too much and Emmett couldn't take care of his beloved animals, no matter how much it killed him.

Staring at the front door of his brother's house—*my father's house*—Wyatt took a deep breath and squared his shoulders. Time to face the lion in his den, again because there was nothing else for it. Emmett had insisted on going home and dammit all, that meant getting a daily visit, like it or not.

A quick rap on the door to announce his entrance and he stepped inside, slipping out of his boots into his sock feet. "Well, hello there." A chipper voice greeted him and an equally cheerful little slip of a woman stepped out of the kitchen.

Ginny McRay was a veritable ray of sunshine. The home health aide came in for a few hours each morning to do light housekeeping, prepare Emmett's meals, and assist him in any way necessary. With her fiery hair, green eyes that snapped, and small stature, she made Wyatt think of the fairy folk. He couldn't help grinning at her. "How's the patient?"

The girl smiled back at him, even as she winced. "He's sulking in the living room. We had an altercation over the shower. Would you like a cup of coffee?"

"No thanks. I've had my quota for the morning." She gave a wave and returned to the kitchen where the sound of pots and pans clanging together in the sink drifted out. Cute little thing. Spirited. Too bad his brother was too ornery to notice.

Wyatt wandered back to the living room to find Emmett in what had become his favorite spot—one of two recliners facing the fireplace which was still burning to take off the chill of early spring. His brother was glowering, his arms crossed and jaw set.

Struggling not to laugh at Em's expression, Wyatt gave him a slap on the back and dropped into the other chair. "Hey, want a beer?"

"I don't know if Hitler will let you get one. She found my empty can on the counter from last night and flew off the handle at me, chewed me out about my seizures and migraines." Emmett leaned forward and set his elbows on his knees, hands pressed to his forehead. "*She has got to back off!* That insufferable woman tried to help me take a shower today. Next thing, she'll want to put me in diapers. That happens, put me in the ground."

Wyatt had the sinking feeling that was exactly what his baby brother wanted. "Hang in there a minute." He walked out to the kitchen and returned with two cold cans, ignoring the tapping foot and angry expression of the woman in the kitchen, setting one can in his brother's hand. "Here. You're a big boy. You can face the consequences of drinking a beer."

Emmett dusted off a crooked grin as he popped the top and the foam spilled over the side. A few long swallows and he sat back, letting out a contented sigh. "Thanks, Wy. I've got to have something to look forward to. There's not much else right now."

"I hear you, brother. I hear you." Wyatt stayed with Em until the home health aide was gone, and they drank the beer down to the last drop.

⋐⋑

"What's the word today?"

True to form, Wyatt came back the next day just after lunch. He stopped in around the same time each day. Knowing the health aide would leave soon, he'd fill a few hours of the afternoon so that Emmett wouldn't be alone for too long. Wyatt didn't like it, would much rather have him at home with Samantha to keep Em company. To know exactly where Emmett was at all times. To be a safety net, ready to catch him if he fell, but as in all other things in his brother's life, it was Emmett's way or no other way.

Stubborn. Why'd he have to inherit that Henry trait

in such a heavy dose? Wyatt inwardly cursed and struggled to contain his feelings of frustration, the helplessness. He focused on the girl before him and forced himself to put on some pretense of being calm, inviting her to be open.

Ginny's eyes were clouded with worry and her smile ran away from her face. She propped a shoulder against the wall and shook her head. "Not so good. He's up in bed with a migraine right now. I was waiting outside the bathroom when he took his shower, and I heard him moaning. I caught Em just before he lost his balance and fell. I helped him to lie down. That was a few hours ago. I've checked in a few times. He's down for the day."

Wyatt nodded and squeezed her shoulder. "You can head out now. I'll stay with him as long as he needs me, okay?"

She nodded and thanked him. He quietly took the stairs, taking care to tread softly the closer he came to Emmett's room. His brother's hearing had become extremely sensitive since the injury, especially when one of his killer headaches set in.

Wyatt pushed the door open to find Em with his head buried in a pillow, his face white as the wall, his hands twisted in the covers until his knuckles stood out. Wyatt sat down on the side of the bed and laid a hand on his back. "Pain bad?"

"Yeah." Emmett's face twisted then smoothed with an effort.

"You get sick?" Wyatt paused, held his breath.

"Twice. Nothing's left. Practically turned my stomach inside out." Emmett winced again and bit off a curse. Wyatt started massaging his shoulders and the back of his neck. Eventually, the crease between his brother's eyes went away, and his body went slack.

"Sleep it off. I'll be downstairs if you need me." Wyatt slipped out, walking aimlessly through the empty rooms of the house, picking up pictures here and there. Each photograph was a sharp reminder of people who were no longer there, of Em the way he used to be, stabbing at him. Finally, Wyatt dropped down in one of the recliners and stared into the fireplace, seeking some comfort from the flames. There was none to be had. Like a toothache that wouldn't go away, nothing could take away this hurt except the source. As long as his brother was suffering, that wasn't happening.

A few hours later, Emmett shuffled into the room. It hurt to watch him, his steps uncertain, hands extended, peaked from his bout with headaches that had plagued him with alarming intensity since his injury. Em sat down in the other recliner and began to rub at his temples, his eyes closed.

Wyatt couldn't keep quiet. "I'm taking you to another doctor in a couple of days. We'll hear what he has to say."

Emmett's face twisted in a grimace. "We already know what the doctors have to say. You just don't like what you hear." He stood up and reached out, stopping when Wyatt's arm blocked his way to give it an awkward pat. "I'm going back to bed. I'm worn out. You don't have to stay." A dismissal if ever there was one. Em wouldn't say it, but Wyatt got the message. *You can go to hell.*

Wyatt trudged back home, muttering to himself, fighting the urge to punch a tree or rip the branches off. The walk wasn't enough to settle him or burn off his anger. He took to the barn and started mucking stalls with more gusto than was the norm, pitching out the manure, hauling it by the wheelbarrow-full to the compost pile, trip after trip until his muscles were screaming. The stalls were practically clean enough to eat off of by the time he was done, and he went into a mad flurry, sending the hay flying into every one, a cloud of dust and particles floating in the air around him.

Winded, unable to catch his breath, he stopped, his hands gripping the handle of the pitchfork. The feeling of being out of control, on a roller coaster gone haywire, swept over him. He'd been on this treacherous ride since that blasted night in the bar. Wyatt wouldn't ever set foot in the place again.

The door opened and shut behind him, bringing a cool gust of air that washed over him and the scent of growing things. The world was being reborn. Why not Emmett? Footsteps approached, and his wife was there for him *again*, his one constant in life.

Thinking back to his father losing Mama at such a young age, Wyatt had to give Jackson Henry credit. How the man survived having his heart ripped out Wy would never know. He turned and gathered Samantha in, tucking her under his collarbone, inhaling the scent of her hair, a combination of sunshine and her shampoo. He drew his strength from her.

"I take it Em's not so hot today?" Her hands moved up to rub his back in soothing circles, inching their way to his hair, threading in. Forcing him to meet her steady gaze.

He swallowed hard, fought the burning in his eyes. "Another migraine's kicking his butt and he's ticked off at me. I told him about going to another doctor, and I could read my kid brother's mind. Emmett wanted to tell *me* where to go." Wyatt pressed his forehead to hers and closed his eyes. "I just want to fix him, Sam."

She laid her palm on his cheek, her voice trembling. "I know. I know how hard this is on you, but you can't do anything more than you're doing right now. The best we can do is pray and have faith. Together, and by the grace of God, Emmett is going to get through this."

He buried his head in the crook of her neck and held on. Wyatt didn't know how long he stood there in the silence, wrapped up in the scent of fresh hay, springtime, and his wife. With the steady beat of her heart against his chest and the flutter of her pulse at the base of her neck, Samantha reminded him of why he was thankful to be alive. She was his. He took her hand and they walked outside, out to the pasture, greeted from time to time by one of the herd and the cracks in his heart became a bit smaller. It would keep him going for another day to take up the fight again.

∽∾∽

Wyatt sat at the kitchen table, reading the morning paper. He was on his second cup of coffee after taking care of the horses at the crack of dawn. Samantha sat across from him, her feet in his lap, swapping sections and stealing sips from his mug. Every now and then, he reached out and stroked her hair or she would bless him with a kiss. A simple ritual, he made a point of sitting down with his wife to enjoy a few minutes of peace each day before they each carried on with their chores. She started to giggle at the comics, a sound he could never get enough of, and Wyatt couldn't help smiling at the wonder that was his wife.

"We're like an old married couple, you know that?" She told him, poking him in the stomach with her bare toe.

Wyatt tickled the sole of her foot, making her squirm and pulled Samantha into his lap, the better to nuzzle her neck and make the blush rise up in her cheeks, feel her become pliant in his arms. "Well, we are married, but there is nothing old about you."

The phone rang and he snatched a kiss on the way to pick up. "Hello?"

"Wyatt, it's Ginny." She was breathless and sounded frantic, making his pulse start to jump. "I just got here, and Emmett's gone. I'm going to go look for him, but I thought you should know."

Her anxiety gave his heart a little lurch. "No, stay put in case he comes home. I'll go out in the truck. Sam's here if he shows up or you need anything, okay?" He hung up and headed for the door, slipping on his boots, Samantha trailing close behind. "Em's not there. Wait for him in case he finds his way here, okay?"

She nodded, fear in her eyes. "He couldn't have gone far."

Wyatt's mouth twisted in a grim smile. "Don't underestimate my kid brother. He's a Henry." A quick kiss and a hug would have to fortify him on his way out the door. Wyatt cranked up the old Chevy and rumbled down the driveway, scanning to the left and the right, peering out at neighboring fields, trying to rein in his runaway heart. Emmett had been exploring his boundaries, walking in the front yard, up and down the driveway, anything to get out of his head, but nothing beyond his property.

The thought of him lost or hurt made Wyatt's mouth go dry and his heart started to skip. He rolled to the end of the driveway, ready to peel out, and there was Em, clinging to the mailbox. He was pale and breathless, his pant leg torn at the knee and blood seeping through. He looked a tad terrified, mirroring the way Wyatt felt.

"What the hell do you think you're doing?" Wyatt called out through his open window.

Emmett followed the sound of his voice and grinned, a hint of his former, daredevil self shining in his golden eyes. His hands skimmed over the hood of the truck, helping him to navigate to the passenger door. He fumbled for the handle and climbed in, letting out a gust of air as he did. "I escaped my jailor for a while."

"How'd that work out for you?" Wyatt fished a bandanna out of his pocket and pressed it to the hole in Emmett's jeans.

Em nodded in appreciation and held on, wincing at the pressure. "Fell a few times, got back up again. I'll live."

A low rumble of a chuckle rose up from Wyatt's belly, and he turned the truck around. They pulled up to a stop by the walkway leading to the house, and Emmett turned to face him. Uncanny really, as if he was staring right at him, or *through* him.

"I'll let you take me to the doctor on one condition. No more babysitters."

Wyatt took his hand and gave it a hearty shake. "Deal." He reeled his brother in for a hug and pounded his back. "If you go for a stroll again, tell us, all right? So we can send out the dogs and search party after a few days, you know? You scared Sam to death, and poor

Ginny—the girl was practically in tears. You want to come in for fresh apple pie?"

Emmett started to laugh. "I guess I could be persuaded." They got out of the truck and walked into the Henry House side by side. It felt good, right, the way things were meant to be.

ↄↄↄↄ

Wyatt couldn't sleep. Tossing and turning, he stared up at the ceiling, watching the light begin to change, dawn creeping up on him. Emmett was right, damn him. Three doctors' visits in the past week, and Wyatt didn't like what he heard.

The last one had been the worst. A five minute exam, a quick scan of Em's records, and he told him bluntly, "If your sight isn't back now, it won't be coming back." The physician handed him a fold-up cane, shook hands, and showed the brothers to the door.

Wyatt rested an arm on his eyes. That was definitely not the news he wanted to hear, and he was not ready to accept it. As for Em, the diagnosis threw him for a loop into a pit of depression. That was a week ago, and he hadn't climbed out yet.

Wyatt rolled over, seeking comfort in the warmth and touch of his wife to find the bed empty. He must have dozed off when she slipped out. The sound of retching had him throwing back the covers. This was the second morning in a row and fear clutched at his belly, made *him* feel sick to his stomach. Dawn's light was tiptoeing in when he went downstairs and found her standing at the window, clinging to the windowsill, breathing in the fresh air that made the curtains flutter. His breakfast was on the table. Even when she felt sick, his wife took care of him.

He put on a smile and whistled as he crossed the room, dropping a kiss on her cheek. "Hey, beautiful. How are you doing today?"

"Better than yesterday. Get eating before it's cold." She smiled, but Wyatt didn't like the look of her, could tell she was lying to him. *Stubborn. Could be worse than a Henry.* He asked her to take it easy and went on with his day, but she was in the back of his mind throughout the hours that stretched for an eternity, his afternoon at his brother's absolute torture as Emmett sat in that damned recliner and stared blankly at the wall, saying nothing.

Wyatt was glad he chose to walk again. By the time he hit his porch, his shoulders didn't feel quite so tight, and the dull ache at the base of his skull, brought on by dealing with Em, eased up some. He stepped inside to be welcomed by the cheerful music of the coffee pot perking and the scent of fresh-baked apple pie, making his stomach grumble. His wife's thoughtfulness lit a warm glow in his heart that made him feel like smiling for the first time that day—until he heard the retching again.

A sinking feeling jabbed at him deep down in his gut. Samantha was as healthy as the proverbial horse, was hardly ever sick a day in her life. Dad used to say the same about Mama.

Wyatt tapped on the bathroom door and pushed it open to find Samantha at the sink, splashing cold water on her face. She turned to him, throwing him off balance with a huge grin lighting her up, her sky blue eyes sparkling bright enough to blind him.

"You okay?" he asked.

She lunged at him and wrapped her arms around his neck. "Better than okay, Daddy."

His heart swelled big enough he was sure it would burst. How could so much love be contained? Wyatt scooped her up in his arms and carried his wife to their bed. He laid her down and lifted her shirt, running his hands over her belly, noticing the slight swelling for the first time. He kissed her belly button and began to sing softly.

Sam began to laugh, a joyous sound, and reached down to play with his hair. "What are you doing?"

"Practicing."

He looked up at her and the tears rose up, tears he welcomed. Let the river come and cleanse away the pain. Wyatt took her in his arms and held on tight, hoping this bubble of happiness would never burst.

CHAPTER 6

Samantha leaned against the fence and gloried in watching her husband at work. While most would call it breaking horses—training them how to take the bit and get used to a person in the saddle, the touch of a human—it was more like gentling the fine animals for Wyatt. He had a way with horses, of getting acquainted, what she'd come to know as the Henry way. Jackson Henry had it and passed it on to his oldest. Emmett was a master—before. Thinking about a world that existed in which Emmett lived without horses was like watching a man with an amputation of his arms and legs.

Her heart aching, she pushed that thought to the back of her mind and concentrated on the soothing sound of Wyatt's voice. She closed her eyes and a cool breeze danced across her skin, pulling at her hair, easing the slight sense of nausea that was with her all the time. Doc reassured her it should be gone in three months. Samantha sincerely hoped so.

"Hey, beautiful."

Her eyes snapped open. Wyatt was standing in front of her, drawing her gaze like a magnet. Tall. Sturdy. Solid. His mouth turned up in a grin.

Samantha's heart started to flutter, like a school girl's, and she climbed up a rung on the fence to loop her arms around his neck. "Hey, handsome." She pressed her lips to his and their foreheads touched. For a moment, the rest of the world went away. "I'm going to Em's to check in on him."

Wyatt stiffened under her touch. "Good luck with that," he told her gruffly. "My brother's been a real bear since he sent Ginny packing. Don't be surprised if the same happens to you." His face softened, and he gave her a kiss to send her on her way. "Let me know if you need any help."

She chose to walk. Like Wyatt, Samantha found the path between the two Henry houses to be therapeutic. April was marching on to a close and the air was warming some. She'd be able to shed Jackson Henry's shirt soon.

Memories tugged at her of two boys shoveling a path, a good quarter of a mile long, in the middle of winter, the snow flying left and right while they grumbled, snowball fights, snow angels, and snow wrestling often getting in the way. Her father-in-law was a smart man. He knew how to keep his sons out of trouble.

The farther she walked into the past, the more her heart lifted along the journey, the fresh air and movement invigorating, only to feel her spirits sink as she stepped out of the woods. The present rammed her, head on.

The place had an abandoned feel to it. No horses in the field. No cheerful whistling as Emmett worked outdoors, always busy with some project or other. No tall, familiar figure sitting on the porch step, the glider, or leaning against the railing. Just an emptiness that hurt on a physical and emotional level.

Samantha tapped at the door. There was no response. She stood outside, indecision tugging at her, anxiety making an unsteady stomach begin to pitch some more. She breathed hard through her nose, took the knob in her hand, and stepped inside. "Em? Hey, Em. It's me, Sam."

Still no answer. She wandered into the kitchen. A box of cereal stood on the kitchen counter, opened. No sign of a bowl or a spoon. Walking through the remaining rooms was like following the path of a hurricane. Hurricane Emmett.

A pillow and blanket were bunched up on the couch. Furniture was knocked over in the dining room, a desk pushed over in the study. Books and magazines were tossed on the floor. Picture frames and knickknacks were scattered about, knocked off shelves, the mantle, the walls. Her heart kicked into overdrive. She swallowed hard. Closed her eyes. Prayed for guidance. For Em.

Reluctant to find any more wreckage, her feet pulled her up the stairs. Samantha heard retching, and her heart pounded harder. She ran the rest of the way and burst into his bedroom. The bed covers were twisted, pillows and clothes piled on the floor, empty bottles of alcohol all around. "Em?" she called out again, her voice rising in pitch.

"Go away," a raspy voice answered, followed by the sound of someone getting very sick. It sounded like he was being turned inside out or torn apart.

Samantha pressed a hand to her stomach and had to cover her mouth to avoid joining him. She'd already had her bout with throwing up when she woke up and was not keen on a repeat performance.

Taking a firm hold of her resolve, she opened the window to let in some fresh air, taking away the combined stench of alcohol and vomit before pushing open the bathroom door.

Emmett was hunkered down on the cold tile, head in his hands, moaning softly. Disgusted, because he'd brought this on himself, Samantha drew herself up and crossed her arms, a sharp edge to her tone. "I don't have the least bit of sympathy for you, Emmett Jackson Henry. I've been throwing up every day for weeks, sometimes several times a day, definitely *not* by choice."

He came up to his feet fast, swaying, skin going from

white to gray, and took a few faltering steps toward her. "Are you sick too?" His hand reached out imploringly, his golden eyes staring straight ahead, boring into her.

Samantha could see the fear, the pit of darkness growing bigger, about to swallow him up. For an instant, a four-year-old boy stood in front of her, bereft of his mother. She'd seen Wyatt brought low too in rare glimpses of the past. Beth Henry's death had hit hard, affecting both of her sons forever, leaving a wound that would never completely heal.

Seeking to be a bandage, she grabbed his fingers and held on tight as Emmett started to tremble. "No, oh no! I'm pregnant."

He made a small sound, caught between anguish and joy, before his arms closed around her in a fierce hug. "I'm so happy for you, Sam. So happy. *Someone* in this family deserves happiness." His face cracked, nearly splitting down the middle, and the sobs took over.

Watching a Henry cry was near unbearable. Samantha led him to the bed, straightened it out, and pulled up the covers. She sat on the edge until the shudders stopped, and he drifted into a fitful sleep. If only this was a fairy tale and all would be right in the world when the prince woke up.

Unable to sit still, she went through the house, tidying up, restoring order, getting rid of the alcohol. Samantha was sitting in the recliner, flipping through a book, singing softly to herself when Emmett came down the stairs. He looked like death warmed over. His hair was disheveled, the stubble on his face headed for a beard, the shadows under his eyes dark as bruises. She couldn't help but wince at the sight of his clothes hanging loosely on a frame gone leaner with the strain of his injury and illness.

He paused at the bottom of the stairs, focused in on the sounds from her direction, and crossed the room. When his hand brushed against the chair, Emmett knelt down and bowed his head. "Help me learn my house. All of it. I'm terrified of the place I've always known. Help me to make sense of it."

Samantha rested her palm on the crown of his head. "Anything. You know your brother and I would go to the ends of the earth and back again for you, Em."

The next day, like Lazarus, Emmett Henry came back from the dead.

❧❧❧

It took a team effort to put Humpty-Dumpty back together again. Wyatt came to pitch in as they helped his brother to come up with an incredibly anal system of organization. From the food in Emmett's cupboards to his medicine cabinet, cleaning supplies, and clothes—*everything* was arranged in an orderly fashion, catalogued in that meticulous brain of his. There was no clutter and no mess, the house neat as a pin to provide Emmett with a world that he could navigate.

Day by day. Hour by hour. Step by step. He mapped out each inch of his home, down on his hands and knees at times. Ramming his feet and his shins into anything that got in his way. Falling down. Getting back up. Unstoppable until the Henry House was his again. Samantha had never been prouder to be a Henry watching Emmett's comeback. One look at Wyatt's face told her he felt the same.

☙☙☙

"Hey, Em!" Solo day. She was supposed to leave him alone, but Samantha couldn't help it. She had to check in on her brother-in-law's progress, make sure he was all right. A crash in the kitchen, and she was scrambling through the house. "Emmett?!"

He was at the sink, cursing so bad it turned her ears red. The lid from a pot was on the other side of the room on the floor, and tomato soup was splattered all over the stove. Thankfully, Emmett had the good sense to turn off the burner before tending to his scalded hand.

Samantha bumped hips with him. "Let me see that hand." He turned the water off and presented the offended appendage to her. As Emmett turned, he revealed a nasty black eye. She gasped and pressed her palm to his cheek. "Okay, never mind the hand. It's not that bad, even though it must smart. What happened to the eye?"

Emmett's face twisted in a sheepish grin. "I had a

war with the cabinet. The cabinet won. That's what happens when you forget to close the door."

She tsk-tsked, led him to the kitchen table, and slid out a chair. "Sit a moment." A bit of rustling in the freezer and Samantha flipped ice cubes into a towel. She handed the bundle to Emmett and made sure he pressed it to his eye. "Well, it's not pretty, but I guess you'll live."

"Thanks, Doc. You're not even supposed to be here."

They both burst out laughing, Sam so hard she had to wipe her eyes. She sat down next to Emmett and his hand found its way to hers.

"Want some slightly burned soup?" he asked.

It was hard to say no. Harder still for Samantha to stay put while he pulled out bowls, spoons, and poured the soup, sending up another blistering streak of curses when some ran over his finger as he tried to judge even servings. They ate without further mishap. Emmett cleaned up—on his own—and walked her to the door. He even waved, making her choke up on her walk home. She'd come to accept such extremes in emotions, from mountain high to rock bottom low when it came to her brother-in-law's bumpy road to recovery. That didn't mean she was used to it.

By the time Sam made it home, her eyes were dry. She went about taking care of her chores, finishing with dinner preparations. She stood at the sink with a mountain of dishes and let out a sigh. There always seemed to be piles of monumental proportions. Add the fact that late

May was uncharacteristically hot, and her mood didn't improve. She braced one palm against the counter, the other digging into the small of her back. Her peanut might not be big, but that added weight and shift in gravity took a toll by the end of the day. Samantha wasn't a slacker either, not with a Henry for a husband.

She started to hum along with "When a Man Loves a Woman" on the radio, swaying in a shaft of sunlight, and it had a hypnotic effect. Slowly, the knots in her body began to unravel. Her breath came out in a rush, and she closed her eyes.

The door opened with a creak and swung shut, heavy footsteps coming her way, without as much spring as usual. Wyatt was dragging a bit too. The closer he came to the kitchen, the more he slowed down, coming to a stop in the doorway. He let out a low whistle. "Wooee. There is nothing more beautiful than a woman, barefoot and pregnant, in the kitchen."

"Do you know how many feminists are screaming in agony right now?"

He was at her side in a heartbeat, spinning her around and making her head light with a kiss. Her whole body started to tingle and she forgot all about being tired. Another kiss like that and Sam might forget her name— or lose her mind.

His lips, almost as talented as his hands, grazed her jaw line and burned a trail down to her collarbone. Samantha struggled to form a coherent thought. "Em—I checked in on Em. He's doing all right. Got a black eye from the cabinet, but—"

Wyatt quieted her as his mouth sealed hers. "No more about my brother right now. Emmett's going to be all right. Tonight, it's just you and me."

He started humming, something incredibly sweet and sexy, swaying her around the room in a dance. Somehow, her feet carried her up the stairs, to the bathroom, and into the tub once her husband filled it to nearly overflowing with warm water and bubble bath. He lovingly washed her head to toe, shampooing her hair, and making her ready to overheat. Carried her into the bedroom, into their bed, over the edge.

ℰↃℰↃ

"Wy, I'm scared." She squeezed her eyes shut and her whole body went stiff. The ground was a long way down. A squint through a crack in one eyelid and she could see him shaking his head.

He put his foot in the stirrup, swung up behind her as easy as breathing, and wrapped an arm around her. "I've got ya, Sammie. For Pete's sake, you're nine years old! Haven't you ever been on a horse before?"

"No. My daddy raises crops. The only animals we have are a dog and a cat." She'd accepted a dare to go riding. After all, Samantha had watched the Henry boys do it every day after school. How hard could it be? She'd

never expected to be terrified. Wyatt started to laugh and that had her boiling mad. "Don't you make fun of me, Wyatt Henry, or I will never talk to you again."

He cut off right away, like someone had covered his mouth. There was a pause, and his soft voice was nearly a whisper in her ear that made shivers run up and down her back. "Just relax. Ricky Ricardo's a really good horse. He won't ever let you down, just wait and see."

Wyatt's heel tapped the horse's side gently and they started to amble forward, taking it slow, letting her get used to the motion and the feel of the great animal beneath her. Samantha's grip on the saddle horn eased. It really was kind of nice. She wasn't about to do it all by herself, but with a Henry behind her, there was nothing to fear. "Go faster."

He gave another tap of his heel and Ricky Ricardo surged ahead, breathing harder as his hooves pounded over the field. Excitement bubbled up inside of Samantha and she called out, "Faster, Wy! Make him go faster!"

"Hold on tight! Ya, Ricky! Show her what you've got, boy! You could've been a race horse!"

One more tap and they were in an all-out gallop, the trees and grass a blur as they bounced up and down in the saddle. Wyatt's legs tightened around hers and she did the same around the horse, holding steady to ensure they weren't going anywhere. Samantha started laughing and flung her arms up in the air. Free! She'd never felt so free before in her life, like she was flying.

❧❦❧

Samantha woke up, tucked in against Wyatt's side, as the moonlight streamed in through the window and turned him to silver. Her breath caught, taking in the beautiful sight of him, and she set her hand on his chest. He still had that power over her, to make her feel free every moment by his side.

His hand settled on hers and his mouth curled up in a smile. "Go back to sleep, beautiful. Morning will be here before you know it."

"I don't mind, not as long as you're in it." She snuggled closer and slid into more sweet dreams with Wyatt.

❧❦❧

"Emmett, it's me!" Samantha called out, closing the door behind her.

There was no customary greeting. A glance in the kitchen revealed a tidy room, but no occupant. The rest of the downstairs revealed the same. Heart picking up the pace, she took the stairs two at a time to search upstairs. Still no sign of her brother-in-law.

She jogged down the stairs. "Now stay calm, Samantha. Stay calm!" The words were a litany, spoken out loud.

She stepped out on the back porch, expecting to find him in the chaise lounge that looked out over the fields.

Emmett would often stretch out and close his eyes, said the cool breeze was refreshing, that he enjoyed the sound of the wind in the trees and birdsong. When the migraines took hold, which was much too often, it was one of the few places that could give him any peace. Thank God there had been no more seizures.

The porch was empty and now her mouth went dry. He hadn't pulled a stunt like walking to their house again, not since that day that Emmett decided to go it alone. A quick scan of the barns and the fields solved the mystery. A lone figure walked the fence line of the horse pasture, one arm raised, touching the sturdy wood from time to time, using it as a guide. Her breath came out in a rush, like she'd been punched in the gut. Samantha didn't realize she'd been holding it.

It didn't take long to catch up. He wasn't walking fast, taking his time as he moved relentlessly forward away from the house. She wondered how far he planned to go. After all, the property went on for acres. "Emmett Jackson Henry, just what do you think you're doing?" Samantha huffed and puffed as she reached his side.

He didn't stop, just kept walking, and his face went tight. "What's it look like? I'm taking a walk. Don't worry. I stick by the fence. I learned the hard way that's the only way I can find my way back." A few more steps and he stopped. "Don't tell Wyatt. Please, Sam. You know he'll freak out. I just have to do something, or I'll go out of my mind."

The sun lit his gaze, setting the gold on fire, and for an instant, it was as if he could see again. Samantha took his hand and gave a tug, making him pick up the pace again. "All right, I won't say a word. Promise you'll be careful."

He smiled, the Henry smile that had made her fall in love with his brother, and pulled her in to kiss her cheek. "Careful is my middle name these days."

She reached up to skim her fingers lightly over the bruised bump on his forehead, a run in with the door when he was doing laundry a few days before. Nearly knocked himself out cold. "Daredevil is more like it."

That set them both to laughing, and he looped an arm around her waist. They kept walking and didn't stop until Emmett was ready to turn back, proving he *could* manage to find his way. Her brother-in-law's world may have grown smaller, but he had found some freedom of his own.

CHAPTER 7

No more, Wy. No more doctors."

Emmett's head was pressed to the window as the truck rolled to a stop in the driveway, keeping his disappointment hidden from view. He couldn't hide the weariness in his tone.

Wyatt slammed his hand against the steering wheel. "I'm not giving up. Do you hear me? As long as I hear of another doctor, if anything will give us hope, I'm going to take you if I have to carry you, drag you, or knock you unconscious. I wasn't fast enough in that bar. At least, let me do this!" Damn his voice for choking up at the end.

This visit had been harder than the rest. They'd spent the entire morning at the clinic while his little brother had test after test, scans, X-rays, was poked and prodded like a specimen under a microscope. Emmett was asked to do different tasks to demonstrate his motor skills, agility, and balance, one that brought a headache on so fast and intense, he threw up and had to lie down.

All that, and the specialist came around his desk to press a hand to Emmett's shoulder. "I'm sorry, Mr. Henry. I wish there was more that I could do." His compassion was worse than the offhand dismissal of so many others. The man had been so thorough and obviously knew his stuff, only to crush their hopes yet again.

Thinking about more wasted moments, the frustration and anger rose up inside of Wyatt, strong enough to strangle him. He let out a gust of air and pressed his head to the steering wheel, wishing he could tear his own eyes from his head, give them to his brother.

Emmett turned and hooked an arm around his neck. "All right. All right. I'll keep going. God, I love you, Wyatt, but you're so stubborn. Will you stop blaming yourself for that night in the bar? *You* didn't do this to me. Minnow didn't do it. I didn't do it. That—I can't even come up with a suitable word for that man—did it. Got it?"

Wyatt wiped his arm across his eyes. "Yeah. Let's forget it about it for now. I know something that will make you feel better."

He climbed out of the truck, Em whipping out his cane as he did the same. He was getting pretty good at using it, although only outside his own house. At home,

Emmett figured out how to get around without it, giving himself a tad more normal.

Wyatt didn't say a word, just let his heavy footsteps lead the way and stepped into the barn. He'd come to accept his brother *needed* to do things on his own, hated to be coddled. Bonnie and Clyde, a couple if ever there was one, were waiting in the first two stalls. In a low voice, he greeted the mare and brought her out, setting the reins in his brother's hand. "Talk to Bonnie-girl. She's missed you."

Emmett stood still as a statue the instant Bonnie nuzzled his hair. A heartbreakingly sweet moment later, his arms came up around the sturdy column of her neck, hiding his face, but not before revealing his pain.

Pierced to the heart, Wyatt cleared his throat and brought Clyde out next. He saddled him up and finished with Bonnie. Emmett was positively glowering, his arms crossed. "I'm not doing it, Wyatt. I'm not going to be led around like a kid at the circus or somebody helpless."

"You do what you want then, Em, but it will be awfully cruel to make Bonnie wait here while I take Clyde. You know how much they love to go together." He poked his foot in the stirrup. One smooth, fluid movement and Wyatt was over. He turned toward the exit and let Clyde have his head.

The stallion whinnied and Bonnie answered. Wyatt looked back over his shoulder and almost fell off the horse. Emmett was whispering in the mare's ear, as if preparing her. One hand took the saddle horn, the other her mane, and he managed to get his foot in the saddle after a few misses. A deep breath, Wyatt mentally counted to ten, and his brother was up and over.

Bonnie didn't hesitate. She went straight for Clyde, a true sidekick. The stallion trotted out to the field and his mare was right behind him. Emmett was white. His jaw clenched, knuckles standing out, he was clutching the saddle horn tight—this from a man who took to riding like a fish to water.

"Em, relax. Bonnie-bell isn't going to let you get hurt. You've practically been in a saddle since the day you were born." *You could do it with your eyes closed.* The irony of it took Wyatt back to their childhood.

❧❧❧

"Let go, Dada! Let go!"

Emmett couldn't have been much more than two. Their father had him perched on Ricky Ricardo's saddle. Mama was at the fence, standing on the rung, wearing a big smile. If she was afraid, it didn't show.

Wyatt's arms tightened around Em's waist, scared enough for all of them. He was crazy about his baby brother. A glance down and the ground seemed so far away. What if Emmett fell? If anything happened to the baby of the family, he'd never forgive himself.

"Come on, Dada! Giddyup!" The toddler was unbelievable, bouncing up and down in the saddle. His hands took hold of the reins. "Go, Ricky! Go!"

Jackson Henry tipped his head back, and laughter rolled out, a deep musical sound that Wyatt could never get enough of. "All right. Wy, you hold on and take the reins if your brother gets out of hand."

A step back and Emmett was in charge.

One tug and Ricky lifted his head. "Go, Ricky! Go, boy!" Em called and tapped his flanks. That got the stallion moving, brought him up to a trot. Wyatt seriously thought he would faint or topple overboard. Emmett was only two years old, for Pete's sake!

"Careful now, Em!" Wyatt reached around his brother, intent on taking the reins. Emmett gave one more tap with his foot and they began to gallop.

"Wee! Look at me Dada! Look Mama!"

Now their mother looked terrified, and Wyatt felt like he was going to throw up. Emmett just laughed and spread his arms wide.

Their joy ride was over almost as soon as it began, Daddy coming up alongside of them on Mama's horse, Lucy. He reached over and grabbed the reins, bringing Ricky Ricardo to a slow walk. "That's enough flying for today, Em." One look at his youngest boy's obvious happiness and their father couldn't help but chuckle. "I guess we'd best give you a parachute and no matter what, I'm right here to catch you."

᧞᧞᧞

Jackson Henry's voiced echoed in Wyatt's mind. *'I'm right here.'*

Wish you were, Dad. He rested a hand over his heart and knew his father was with him every day. *What do I do, Dad?*

Watching Emmett now, rigid in the saddle, scared so bad it rattled him, Wyatt realized his mistake. He should have got on with Em, helped him through this first attempt at the saddle again. Wyatt reined in and waited until Bonnie was abreast with Clyde. His hand reached out and gave his brother's arm a squeeze. He could feel a shiver running through him. "I'm sorry, Em. I shouldn't have taken you by surprise like that. We'll go back."

Emmett pulled away, yanking his arm hard and picking up the reins. "You're the one who said it would be mean if Bonnie was left in the barn. It's worse not to give her a real ride. Let's go. Clyde will show her where to go."

Again, his brother proved what Henrys were made of.

They went around the pasture a few times, Wyatt keeping the speed under control, going easy and slowly, and his brother began to unwind. Emmett got used to the rhythm he knew so well and his hands loosened their grip. There might have even been a smile or two, until they came back to the barn, and it was time to groom.

Emmett slid down, holding on tight to the saddle. He pressed a kiss to Bonnie's cheek and simply stood there until Wyatt came and slipped her saddle off in order to start brushing. A hand came into his line of vision, and his brother took over, finishing the job, head to toe. When it was time to lead her back to her stall, Emmett stepped back, tight lipped, eyes glittering dangerously.

Wyatt turned around after he closed the gate, and his brother was gone. Heart in his throat, he hurried out to find him sitting on the porch steps, head in his hands.

"Don't do that to me again, Wy. I can't take it," Emmett mumbled as he heard approaching footsteps.

"You did fine, really. It's like riding a bicycle. You never forget." Wyatt put an arm around his brother's shoulders, felt like he held on to a slab of stone.

"It's too hard, like a mean tease, Wy, reminding me of what I can't do anymore, what's been stolen from me. You dangle it in front of me and snatch it away. Come to my place tomorrow, and I'll show you what I *can* do."

∽✺∽

Wyatt was dragging. Bone tired and aching, the heat of late June, and the workload of two herds was wearing him down. Not that he'd grumble, not with the price his brother had paid. He gave a perfunctory knock on the door and walked in, heading straight for the kitchen and an ice-cold beer. A pop of the top and it went down nice and smooth. He leaned on the counter and savored a swallow. "Yo, Em! Where are you?"

"In the living room." He followed the sound of his brother's voice to find him on the floor, lining up shoes on a mat by the back door. To make sense of the insensible meant organizing every inch of the place, top to bottom. A bit obsessive if anyone asked Wyatt, but he understood. This house was one thing his brother could control. Emmett heard approaching footsteps and stood up. "Where's Sam?"

"Hello!" A cheerful voice called out, accompanied by the sound of the front door being closed. Samantha walked in carrying two sacks of groceries.

"What are you doing carrying all of that?" Exasperated, Wyatt stepped in and took the bags from his wife, stealing a kiss as he did.

She smiled and followed him into the kitchen. As soon as he set them down, Samantha started unloading everything on to the counter.

Emmett had trailed after them and laid a hand on her shoulder. "Thanks for going to the store. I can take it from here. You two go relax while I get dinner ready. You're going to be my guinea pigs."

Surprised, Samantha backed away from the counter, Wyatt looping an arm around her shoulders. They stood and watched his brother methodically sort through all of the items on the counter, setting aside those he needed for dinner, putting the rest away. A glimpse inside each cabinet and the refrigerator proved that everything was neatly arranged by a system.

Once the groceries were put away, Emmett moved to the side, turning to the cabinet he needed in order to pull down bowls, pots, and pans. Bread crumbs, egg, salt, pepper, and onion, carefully chopped to fine bits, all made their way into hamburger to become meatballs. Once they were browning in a large sauce pan, he filled a big pot with water and set it on to boil.

A quick, thorough washing of his hands and the fixings for a salad were next. Emmett laid out an assortment of vegetables and took great care as he began to slice them into small pieces. Wyatt held his breath and Em stopped. He straightened his shoulders, his jaw firm. "Do you two mind with your hovering? There's a pitcher of sweet tea in the fridge if you want it, Sam. I just made it fresh today. Go sit and relax, put on TV or the radio, make out. Something other than just hanging around. I've got this."

"I'd say my brother is back."

The couple exchanged a grin. Wyatt did the honors and poured a tall glass of the refreshing beverage for his wife, adding one for himself since she couldn't share the pleasure of a beer. Once they were settled on the couch, he slipped off her shoes and put her feet in his lap. His hands went to work on her toes and the soft soles that were feeling the burden of that little bundle already.

Samantha worked hard to keep things running

smoothly at home, and Wyatt would never forget it. Watching her head tip back and her eyes close as she let out a small moan of pleasure, he rubbed a bit more. "How's that, darlin'?"

"Keep on doing what you're doing, and I will never move again." Her sweet smile was enough to keep him going, inching his way up her calves, working at the muscles that had hardened into stubborn knots. "Oh, Wy."

Her skin became flushed, her lips parting. The pulse beat frantically in the hollow of her neck on the edge of her collarbone and he couldn't resist temptation. Wyatt pressed his mouth to that flutter and felt a stirring of his own deep inside until a slight kick from her tiny occupant had him pulling back, laughing. "Well, I guess Junior told me."

Samantha rubbed at her belly, wearing that secret grin that only appeared as her eyes turned inward and she focused on the new life blooming inside of her. She shifted and set her feet on the floor. "All right, your turn, Mr. Henry."

She didn't have to ask him twice. Wyatt turned his back to his wife and she set her hands on his neck, her thumbs pressing in hard, making his head drop forward with a sigh. Her fingers moved on, down to his shoulders, applying pressure and making him gasp. On down his back, to the base of his spine that really ached by the end of the day and made him feel like an old man. "Sam, you are incredible."

She snorted and slid back. "Lean back and put your head in my lap." He obliged and her fingers danced over his temples, moving round and round until he could hardly stand himself. A groan escaped him that sounded like a dying man.

"Hey. Keep it PG out there, got it?" Emmett called from the kitchen. The lid of a pot clanged and they could hear the sound of dishware being placed on the table, followed by silverware. A few more minutes ticked by, Wyatt nearly slipping off to sleep and Samantha not far behind him, when his brother's voice rang out. "Chow's on!"

Wyatt stood slowly, feeling mellow and as if he had all the time in the world. He offered his hand to Samantha and helped her to her feet, grazing her fingers with a kiss. Hand in hand, they walked to the kitchen and froze. The food was laid out on the table in serving dishes, glasses filled with drinks, a bouquet of wild flowers acting as a centerpiece.

Everything was just so, perfect. Wyatt swallowed hard, unable to say a word or he'd lose it.

One glance at his wife and he saw the tears shimmering in her eyes.

"Well? Are you going to stand there all day? Sit down you two. Happy anniversary." Their special day was the next day. Emmett had remembered.

Wy was at a loss. He sat down slowly and bowed his head. Sam's fingers rested on the nape of his neck as his eyes burned.

"Thanks, Em," he said. "This was really nice of you. I—we—appreciate it."

Samantha echoed his words and they began to eat. Wyatt was in awe, watching his brother serve himself, eat his food, clear, and wash up without mishap.

He'd come so far since January. He even topped off the night with homemade chocolate cream pie. "It might not look pretty. I've no idea, but I made a test pie, and it tasted fine. Ate the whole thing."

His grin, like the kid who stole the last cookie from the cookie jar, made Samantha and Wyatt laugh until they nearly burst.

When they were all done, Emmett walked them to the door and gave them both a hug. Wyatt held on and pounded him on the back. "I'm so proud of you, little brother, so proud. You've crossed the Grand Canyon and made it to the other side. I wouldn't be surprised to find out you have a set of wings or a cape hiding under that shirt."

Emmett dipped his head, uncomfortable with the praise. Finally, he answered softly. "I had the best teachers. You and Dad showed me how to pick yourself up when you fall."

છ૭છ૭

"What do you want to do, Wy? You want to go to town, eat out?"

Wyatt was leaning back on the couch with his head in Samantha's lap as had become a habit of late when he'd come in from taking care of the herd in the morning, evening, or both. Whenever there was a need. Right now, feeling her touch him, there most definitely was a need.

"Go out? Out of the question."

Her hands finished massaging his temples and stroked his hair before they stilled. He peeked up at her through a slit of an opening in one eye.

"I want to go fishing, eat my wife's home cooking for a picnic dinner, and sleep with you under the stars. Is that enough of an anniversary for you?"

Samantha dropped a kiss on his forehead. "It's perfect. I don't even have to dress up."

She did anyway. Nothing fancy, just his favorite sundress, covered in pink rosebuds like the plants Grandmama had put in all over the place until their scent almost made him dizzy when he walked outside. Wyatt met his bride on the porch, his hair slick from the shower, in a new button-down shirt in blue that brought out a hint of the sky in his dusky gray eyes. He'd turned his sleeves up to the elbow and left a few buttons open.

Samantha stepped into his open arms and grazed his collarbone with her soft, warm lips. "God, how I love you, Sam. You're such a blessing to me."

Close his eyes and for an instant, a distant memory

of his mother hovered, wearing a sundress that was similar, with the sunshine in her hair and sky in her eyes. So like his wife and he thanked the Lord every day that this woman had been brought into his life. He was certain that he couldn't live without her.

Her laughter was music. "The feeling's mutual, Mr. Henry."

He ran his fingers through her hair, pulling out her ribbon, letting the golden strands fall. "You would not believe how you light up like the sun, light me up."

Samantha's mouth tipped up in a grin and she took his hand. Wyatt picked up the picnic basket and they walked far out across the fields, the tall meadow grass and wild flowers brushing at their legs, until they reached the pond. He spread out a blanket and stretched out. She handed over dish after delectable dish and they fed each other comfort food. Fried chicken. Potato salad. Fresh vegetables. They each had their fill and then Wyatt made love to his wife under the moon and stars. He cherished her, worshipped her body, and the baby within. With his breath. His hands. His body.

The frogs sang and the crickets hummed as the wind danced in the trees, making the branches sway overhead. As they stared up at the stars, Samantha nestled against his side, Wyatt held up her hand in the moonlight.

She buried her face in the crook of his arm. "They're so ugly."

He brought her fingers to his lips and kissed every

callous, every rough patch on her palm, every crack and line, making sure he didn't neglect a single one. His mouth traveled over her collarbone, to her jaw, and mouth next. "They're beautiful. Every mark on your hands shows your strength and how much you care for me."

Samantha rose up to take his face in her hands. "You are the best anniversary present a girl could ever ask for."

In one, swift move, Wyatt was up and had her flipped on her back. "No, that would be you, Mrs. Henry. What do you say we unwrap our presents one more time?"

Her laughter rose up in the night, and they opened themselves to each other.

CHAPTER 8

Gardening was one of Samantha's preferred chores, even in the oppressive heat of late July. She always plunged into the flowers first, her favorite, the task that required the least work and gave her the most pleasure. Wyatt's Grandmamma had planted plenty of perennials that came back year after year in all their glory. Tiger lilies, brown-eyed Susans, daisies, roses, and countless others that Samantha didn't even know the name for. She just had to nurture them and watch them grow. She could linger there all day, poking at the buds, pulling out the weeds, surrounding herself with blooming things. Like her. Samantha laid a hand on her belly and smiled to herself.

The vegetable garden was another thing. By the time she got done weeding on her hands and knees, plus watering, her back ached and her arms were sore. The end product would be worth the sweat, but right now it grated on her.

She paused to rest by the little picket fence that surrounded their peas, beans, squash, peppers, tomatoes, and what not, wiping her brow, when a jab down low in her belly snatched her breath away.

Fear made her grab hold of the swell of her stomach and cradle it. At four months, there wasn't much of a bump, but enough to prove *somebody* was in there. "Oh, sweet pea. You stay put, you hear me?"

Samantha closed her eyes and attempted to calm herself, breathing slowly through her nose. In and out. In and out. Another pain stabbed at her and tears sprang to her eyes. She hunched over and fought for breath, trying to protect her precious passenger, knowing in the end that this was a matter that was completely beyond her control. *Dear God, please protect me and this little one. Keep my baby safe.*

Strong arms wrapped around her, and she found herself drawn in against the wall of her husband's chest. "What is it? What's wrong?"

Somehow, and Samantha didn't question it after all of these years, Wyatt knew when she was in trouble. His radar came up, pulling him away from his animals, straight to her side. She leaned into him and took comfort in his strength, the smell of sunshine, hay, horses, and sweat.

Another pain and she clutched at his shirt. "Cramps. Really bad cramps." The next one doubled her over. "Oh, God."

Wyatt picked her up in one easy motion, cradling her as his long legs ate up the distance to the back porch. "Now take some advice from Dad. Don't go making molehills into mountains. I'm sure this is nothing." He spoke firmly, his slate blue eyes more blue than gray, proving his faith in his words. If her husband was afraid, he wouldn't show it, not to her, but his eyes would grow dark, the storm clouds rolling in.

He laid her down on the couch and slipped in behind her, giving her something solid to rest on. "You've been doing too much. Got to take it easy. Give yourself more breaks. Whatever needs doing will get done, and I can help."

His warm, gentle voice rolled over her, dropping low, as his hands, so good with the horses he loved, worked their magic. Round and round, they roamed over her stomach and he hummed softly in her ear.

Slowly, she relaxed and the tightening in her abdomen, a sensation similar to the pressure brought on during her menstrual cycle, let up. Samantha let out a long sigh and laid her hand on Wyatt's to give it a squeeze. "Okay. I'm okay now."

He dropped a kiss on her cheek and his relief washed over her in his voice. "Good. Now just rest a bit with me. Ease my mind, all right?" Another kiss and his hand trailed up to her hair to run through the heavy strands. Her eyes began to droop, anxiety let go, and she drifted off.

"You're sure? I don't mind bringing her in. Okay. I will. Thanks, Doc."

Samantha opened her eyes to see Wyatt standing in the doorway of the kitchen with the phone to his ear. He gave her a wink before hanging up.

A few steps was all it took for her husband to reach her before she could get up. "Just talked to Doc Smith. He said you were having Braxton Hicks contractions, said they're normal. If you feel them again, and they don't let up, we need to go in. I still wouldn't mind if you would anyway. Doc is always happy to see you. Said he'd make time for you any day of the week."

"Why? Were you scared? You didn't look it." She reached up to grab his collar and pulled him down for a kiss.

Wyatt pressed his forehead against hers. "I was terrified." His breath came out in a rush, as if he'd been holding it for hours, and his body went loose under her touch.

Samantha smiled and stroked his hair until his mouth curled up in a grin. "All right. Let's go to the doctor's office."

Truth be told, she could use some reassurance herself. Wyatt held her hand all the way to the truck, helped her up, and closed her door. When she ran her hand round and round over her belly, he cranked the truck up, reached across, and rested his palm on top of the mound of her stomach. If anyone could protect them, her husband could. Samantha could walk to the ends of the earth, but she wouldn't find better than a Henry.

A short drive into town, and Doc Smith ushered the young couple in the instant they walked through his door, apologizing to a few elderly ladies in his waiting room. When they saw a mother-to-be in their midst, everyone deferred to Samantha willingly. One woman even opened the door to the examining room, while another asked if she could touch her baby belly. "Glowing. You are positively glowing, young lady. Oh, how I miss those days!"

Misty eyed, the ladies resumed their seats, chatting away. As for Samantha's examination, it was performed promptly and without fanfare. She was given a clean bill of health, told to rest up when her body told her so, and they were sent off with cherry lollipops.

Not satisfied with candy, Wyatt pulled into the local ice cream stand and ordered large ice cream cones for the both of them. He settled Samantha on a bench under a tree, overlooking the pond, and nestled her against his side. She enjoyed the sweet delight, cooling off nicely, her hand resting on her stomach.

"Oh! Oh my goodness!" A healthy kick took her by surprise and made her gasp. She sat up straight, concentrating on her insides.

Wyatt's eyes widened in fear and his hand tightened over hers. "Do we need to go back to the doctor?"

"No, no! Feel this!" Samantha grabbed his hand and set it on her stomach. She held her breath, and there it was, another kick, then another.

A smile stretched across Wyatt's face. "Well, hello there, Junior! Someone's doing gymnastics in there. Guess he likes ice cream!"

The two of them sat there completely still, forgetting the vanilla ice cream dripping down their cones, transfixed by every movement. When the commotion finally settled down, Samantha looked up at Wyatt's silly grin. "How do you know it's a he?"

Her husband kissed her and stole a lick of her ice cream before it ran down her hand. "I don't. Just taking a guess. As long as the little tyke is healthy, I don't care what it is. You could have a horse!"

That had her giggling and taking a taste of Wyatt's cone to return the favor. "I'll be as big as a horse if I keep eating this way!"

A strong arm wrapped around her shoulders, pulling her snug against the steady thump of his heart. "Sam, I don't care what size you are as long as you and Junior are safe. You're my world." His lips stamped a kiss to the crown of her head, sealing his words.

"You're my universe. You have been since the day we met." Samantha closed her eyes and soaked up the warmth and solid presence of a Henry.

৩৩৩

The sun streamed across her pillow, poking her in the eyes, pulling her out of the deepest sleep she'd had in years. Samantha peered through the slit of one eyelid and groaned. She'd overslept. Reluctant to leave pleasant dreams behind, she inched her way up to a sitting position to find a pale, pink rose sitting on her pillow. A note was attached.

Dear Little Mama,
Stay in bed this morning. Husband's orders. I don't care what the doctor said. I say you're getting a day off.
Love,
Wyatt

A smile bloomed with his words and she picked up the blossom, bringing it to her nose to inhale its heavenly scent. A glance to the side of the bed made her eyes sting. A tray was waiting for her with fresh fruit, toast, juice, and tea. Steam was still rising from the cup. How he'd managed to slip in and out without her hearing his footsteps was beyond her.

She stretched for her tea cup and a head poked around the corner. "Just a minute. I'll bring it to you." Her question about his silent prowess was answered when Wyatt walked across the floor in his stocking feet.

"Wy! I'm fine! I'm pregnant, not an invalid." She accepted his offering even as her arms crossed, unable to contain her obstinate streak.

He kissed her and tapped her nose. "No arguments. I want you to take a breather today. Humor me, all right?" Wyatt knelt down by the side of the bed and kissed her stomach next. There was another jab that stole her breath and had him chuckling. "*If* someone will give you a break!"

A few more smooches and a little cuddling would have to tide her over. No rest for the weary horse farmer as Wyatt headed outside. When Samantha wandered down after snoozing, feeling sinfully lazy, her laundry was neatly folded, the dishes were done, and a fresh, strawberry rhubarb pie was on the counter. A pie! She could only shake her head at the wonder that was her husband.

The glider called to her from the back porch. Samantha sat down and propped her feet up, enjoying the view, waiting patiently for Wyatt. She didn't see any sign of him in the field, but knew he'd be in for lunch. The heat of the day and the glider's gentle swaying sent her off to sleep once more. She woke with a start. The angle of the sun had changed dramatically, proving Samantha took more than a catnap.

The afternoon's nearly done! The passage of that much time and the fact that Wyatt failed to join her for lunch or to at least check in on her made Samantha nervous. Trying to squash the sudden surge of anxiety that made her heart start to race and her stomach to churn, she slipped on her shoes and made her way to the barn. The only thing that set her at ease was finding her husband with Emmett's favorite mare. Bonnie was lying on her side, breathing hard—getting ready to deliver.

"There. That's it. Easy girl, easy." Wyatt was stretched out against her back in a bed of clean hay, stroking her neck and her side. Such a way the man had with these sweet animals and how they responded to him.

The mare snorted, her whole body tight, and then she went loose as Wy continued to murmur in her ear. Samantha rested a hand on her stomach and felt her little one roll from side to side. To think this would be happening to her soon. She closed her eyes and pictured her husband delivering their baby. No one could do a better job.

"Don't even think about it. We're not doing things that way when it's your turn. A doctor. In a hospital. Got it?" His hands took hers and gave a gentle squeeze; she hadn't even heard him approach.

Samantha opened her eyes and laughed. "How did you know what I was thinking?"

"We've known each other for over twenty years. I can read your mind and finish your sentences."

The mare appeared to have fallen into an exhausted sleep, the calm before the storm. Wyatt stretched, his bones cracking, making her catch her breath. In his plain white T-shirt and blue jeans, he was a marvel of a man.

"Could you bring me a cold drink please? Bonnie would have to pick one of the hottest days yet. I've been sitting with her since this morning."

Samantha clasped her hands behind his head and gave him a kiss. "Hope that will hold you."

By the time she came back with ice water, Wyatt was leaning on the stall, rubbing at the nape of his neck with his eyes closed, a line etched between his eyes. "You all right?" she asked, worry cropping up.

"Yeah. Heat's just getting to me. Giving me a headache, right here. Throbbing like the devil."

Samantha took over, massaging his shoulders, the rigid column of his neck, and the base of his skull.

His head dropped, and he sighed. "That's better. Thanks."

He drank the glass down in a few gulps and wiped the sweat from his forehead just as the mare woke up and gave what could only be described as a groan. She gained her feet and gallons of yellow fluid gushed from between her hind legs, followed by a white bubble.

The horse sank down on her side again, letting out another moan as her head rested on the hay. Completely sympathetic, Samantha ran her hands over the horse's belly in a soothing pattern, one she found herself doing to her own stomach more and more with each passing day.

Wyatt gave her a wink and hastily brushed her lips with his. "Show time."

Watching her husband kneel in the hay, lifting the horse's tail, continuing to talk in a low, soothing tone—what it did to Samantha. She felt a rising up inside, a tightening and a rush that made her long to place herself in his competent hands.

After what seemed like an eternity, but couldn't have been more than twenty minutes, one hoof appeared in the bubble. Samantha couldn't help sucking in a deep breath and gripping the railing. It didn't matter how many times she'd seen the miracle of a foal's birth. A moment later, a second hoof appeared. The tears filled her eyes and ran unchecked down her face when she saw the nose appear. The head soon followed. With a great grunt and a bunching of her muscles, Bonnie managed to release her baby.

Samantha clapped her hands together. "You did it, Mama! You did it!"

Wyatt did what he could to help, breaking the membrane around the foal and cutting the umbilical cord. With a great heave, the mare managed to take to her feet once more. Within minutes, the placenta came out in a rush and her baby managed to stand on wobbly legs. After a few, faltering steps and some nosing around in the wrong places, the foal began to suckle. Samantha couldn't stop smiling. *Soon! Our little one will be here soon too!*

Wy leaned against the stall and wiped the back of one forearm along his forehead. He was pale with exhaustion, but grinning fit to burst. "Well, that went pretty smoothly. Just wait until Clyde gets a look at his little boy. We'll have to let Em come up with a name."

He closed his eyes and sagged, all of the air going out of him. Samantha rubbed at his shoulders. "Let's go in, Wy. I'll get you cleaned up and you can lie down."

Reluctant to move, he stood still and his shoulders drooped. "Mmm. That feels too good. I've just got to take care of the placenta and get some clean hay in here. You go ahead in. I'll be right there."

She didn't go anywhere. Samantha was waiting for him, enthralled by the mother and baby, when Wyatt wrapped his arm around her shoulders. "Let's go, Little Mama. I don't know if you've noticed, but the sun's gone to bed."

The stars were twinkling overhead, the moon so big and bright it looked close enough to snag it with her fingers. Sam took Wy's hand and led him inside. She helped him to take off his boots and gave his hand a tug, guiding him upstairs. Into the bathroom. Peeled him out of his clothes and filled the tub with steaming water. Wyatt sank in almost up to his nose and dozed off almost immediately.

Shaking her head, Samantha got down on her knees and washed him, lovingly adding shampoo to his hair, rinsing it out, and running her hands through the thick stands. He stirred and smiled up at her even as he winced. "This feels really good, but my head is killing me."

"It's because you haven't eaten anything all day. That and the heat. You should listen to your own advice about taking a break when you need it." She offered him a hand and helped him to stand, toweling him off, and leading him to bed. Wyatt slipped on his boxers and sank onto the mattress.

Samantha set her fingers gently on his temples and began to give him a massage. Slowly, the tension eased from Wyatt's body and his mouth curved up in a grin. "Thank you for taking care of me. You're going to be a wonderful mother."

She kissed him on the forehead and stood up. "As a mother in training, I'm going to tell you what's good for you. I'm getting you something to eat." At the first sign of his urge to protest, her hand went up in the air. "Don't worry. I'll eat too. Then you're going to take two Tylenol and you are going to sleep—late. Those horses will be all right if you aren't out there at the crack of dawn."

She shushed any chance of arguments and went downstairs. Eying the choices, cereal seemed like the easiest option. Something light and easy on the stomach after waiting too long on a hot day. Samantha hummed to herself as she sliced bananas and strawberries to cover the corn flakes. She'd just put the milk away when hands rested on her arms and slowly turned her around. "You're supposed to be in bed!"

Wyatt looked dead on his feet, but his eyes glowed at the sight of her. "Why make you carry that upstairs? Let's sit on the porch. It's cooled down and there's a nice breeze. Then I'll go to sleep like a good boy, promise."

He picked up his bowl while Samantha took care of

her own. Ever the gentleman, Wy held the door open and they shared a perch on the glider. The crickets started singing their evening chorus as the bowl nearly tumbled out of Wyatt's hand, his head falling on to his chest.

Samantha put the dishes in the sink and came back for her husband. He gave her a crooked grin as she wrapped an arm around his waist and they made their way back upstairs. Wyatt dutifully accepted his painkillers and tumbled onto the bed. Sam turned out the light and slid in next to him. She moved against him, spoon style, and rested her hand on his hip. "Wyatt?"

"Hmm?" he murmured, almost gone already, but his hand patted hers.

"Wy, do you think tomorrow night you won't be such a good boy?" She held her breath, waiting for his response, sure he had faded away.

He took her by surprise, flipping over, his hand threading through her hair. "That's a promise."

His breath kissed her cheek and his lips were next, sending her into sweet dreams.

CHAPTER 9

The sun just peeked over the horizon, and Wyatt felt like he was walking into a wall of heat on a morning in mid-August, sucking the wind right out of him and making his shirt stick to his skin. A dull aching started up at the back of his skull, poking at him and grating on his nerves. Headaches had been following him around since the day the foal was born, anything from a nuisance to a pounding monster. One glance at Doc Holliday lightened his mood and made him chuckle every time he thought about his brother's sense of humor in choosing a name for the newest addition to the herd. *Leave it to Emmett to throw a good guy into the mix with Bonnie and Clyde.*

He pressed a hand to the back of his neck and applied pressure, wishing Samantha was giving him a massage—and then some—but she had enough on her plate. Besides, he didn't want to worry her and knew she'd fret about any trouble with his health. Wyatt breathed in and out slowly through his nose and pushed the pain away. There was work to do.

'*Just pace yourself. The horses aren't going anywhere and whatever doesn't get done will be there tomorrow.*' Jackson Henry's voice rang out in his mind just as clear as if his father was at his side.

A grin tugged at Wyatt's mouth even as longing for the man yanked on his heart. Dad always did have the best advice. If only he was here now to share the load. Even so, Wyatt's steps were a little lighter and he managed to find a whistle as he watered and fed the herd before letting them into the pasture. He worked steadily through the morning, lost in the rhythm of his day and didn't even realize lunch time had arrived until Samantha greeted him in the barn.

She came bearing gifts—sweet tea and a picnic basket, but her kiss was best of all. His wife led him out of the heat to the shaded porch while they enjoyed each other's company and her good food. Samantha's home cooking, the feel of her arms wrapped around him, and a cool breeze held the headache at bay.

Wyatt could have lazed with her on the glider for the rest of the afternoon.

"Stay right here with me, Wy." She cooed, stroking his hair and making his eyes droop. His whole body went loose at her touch. The woman cast a spell on him every time.

With a sigh of regret, he sat up and snagged her around the neck for a kiss. "Sorry, darlin', but I've got to fix a weak spot on the fence or some of the herd could get out. Clyde's been feeling his oats. I wouldn't put it past him to test his boundaries, try and go back home to Em's place. I'll take a raincheck. You save me a spot."

Dropping one more kiss on her sweet mouth, another on her baby belly that was swelling by the day, he was off to complete his self-appointed task.

After a good trek with a few heavy boards on his shoulder and a hammer in his pocket, Wyatt was just about done in. He leaned on the fence for a moment, just to catch his breath, then went to work on the broken board, using the claw end of the hammer to tug at the nails. They were a bear and fought him on the way out, a testament to the quality of his father's workmanship.

With a great yank, the board finally came loose and almost sent him flat on his butt. Wyatt set the new board in place and started hammering away, the vibration traveling from his hand all the way to his shoulder, when the pain slammed into the front of his head so hard, it made him lose his lunch. He doubled over, hands on his knees, and struggled to get his stomach to stop rolling. Time to call it quits. Wincing with every blow, Wyatt finished the job and managed to put the hammer away because it had been ingrained by his dad. *'You take care of your tools.'*

Samantha was at the kitchen sink when he stepped inside, swaying to a tune on the radio, wearing a sundress that was his all-time favorite, a pale blue that really brought out her eyes. Her hair was piled up high on her head, making him long to cross the room and pull it down. Wyatt would love to make love to her, the want and need for her warring with his insides, but the thunder in his head wouldn't let him.

He brushed her cheek with a kiss. "Going to lie down. Bad headache," were the only words that managed to tumble out of his mouth. The trip to the bedroom felt like a mile long and the stairs kept sliding in and out of focus. Wyatt closed his eyes as soon as he hit the bed. Bless her, but Sam brought him water and pain pills. She put a cold, wet cloth on his forehead and stayed until sleep came for him.

When his eyes opened, Samantha was lying next to him and the sun was touching down. Wyatt sat up with a jerk and the room began to tilt even though the headache was nearly gone.

Sam opened one eye and took his hand. "It's all right. I already took care of the horses. Lie back down with me. You need to rest."

Wyatt did as he was told even as his hand drifted up to caress her cheek. "You shouldn't have." His fingers trailed down her body to rest on her stomach and he felt her shiver at his touch. "What about the baby?"

Her face softened and she ran her fingers through his hair. "You worry too much and do too much. I walked outside and those horses were so hot, they were lined up to come in. All I had to do was open the door. I ran the hose to fill their water buckets and brought a coffee can of oats at a time for their feed. I was careful, promise." She rested her hand on her bulging belly and began to circle round and round.

Mesmerized, Wyatt's body became heavy and he gave up the fight. When he woke up a few hours later, judging by the clock, his stomach was growling. "I'm hungry. How about ice cream sundaes for dinner?"

Samantha's mouth curved up in a smile and she snuggled in against his chest. "Works for me."

They walked downstairs hand in hand, like two kids going on a date. Wyatt took out the containers of ice cream while Sam gathered all of the toppings. Whip cream, cherries, chocolate syrup, nuts. All the fixings for a whopping sundae. They both dressed up their own pint of vanilla and went to work.

She polished hers off first. "I win again. Remember when I beat you at that sundae eating contest on the last day of school in sixth grade?"

Wyatt pushed his empty container away and licked off his spoon, patting at his overly full stomach. He might pay for it later. "*I* won that contest. Ate all twelve scoops."

Samantha stood and gathered up the fixings. "Oh, I beg to differ. I might have only eaten ten scoops, but I kept mine down. You lost yours on the side of the road when we were walking home."

Wyatt snagged her around the waist and pulled her on to his lap. "God, I love you for keeping me honest. How 'bout we go back to bed and I'll repay the favor for taking such good care of me?"

"Deal." Her head rested against his chest and the blood rushed to his head with the pounding of his heart. Over twenty years together and the feelings only grew stronger between them.

Wyatt stood up, still holding Samantha in his arms and began the trek upstairs. She squealed and argued, telling him to put her down. He didn't give in until his feet hit the bedroom door. Thanks to his wife's extra set of hands, she pushed it open and he took the last, few steps, sinking with her onto the thick, soft comforter. It was like floating off on a cloud as he paid her the tribute that was her due and his headache? Gone for the first time in days. Sam was the cure.

໒ɔɛʒ

"Hey, Wy, give me a hand here!"

Asking for help. Something Emmett seldom did, especially when he was shaking with laughter. The two were in the middle of an experiment. Wyatt poured the

oil in the pan, Em used his judgement with the corn kernels, and now the popping was going like crazy, lifting
the lid right off the pot. Popcorn was everywhere, exploding over the stove. "Come on! Do something!"

Wyatt grabbed the bowl off the counter and started
catching as much of the overflow as possible before it
went on the floor or fell down in the burner. By the time
the dance of popping kernels had stopped, both brothers
were in hysterics, bent over with their arms wrapped
around their waists, they were laughing so hard.

When he could finally catch his breath, Emmett
straightened up and gestured to the stove. "How about
you finish cleaning up while I add the butter and salt?"

Like clockwork, they managed to finish their preparations. Wyatt grabbed two beers out of the fridge and
they settled in the living room, feet on the coffee table,
munching from the same bowl with the baseball game
blaring from the radio. Emmett tipped his head back to
finish his drink and nodded toward the source of the
sound. "You could've put on the television, you know."

Wyatt swiped another handful of popcorn. "Sometimes, I like to listen instead. There's more of a thrill to it
when you can use your imagination. That and the com-
mentators really get into it, trying to make you feel like
you're right there in the thick of it." He took one last
swallow of his beer and grimaced at the empty bottle.
"Hey, I'm going to grab another brewski. You want
one?"

Emmett nodded his approval and focused on the game, a crease forming between his eyes as he concentrated on the action. A smile tugged at Wyatt's mouth. He couldn't help it. It felt like old times again, like maybe Em could have a little piece of his old life back.

A whistle bubbled up, and Wyatt let it out, pulling two beers from the fridge and reaching for the bottle opener on the counter when a white-hot streak of pain ran through his forehead, pounding above his eyes and making his vision double. The whole room started to spin and his knees gave, the bottles crashing to the floor and shattering as he dropped. He landed on his hands and knees with a puddle of beer soaking into his pants. The smell of it made him feel sick, and he had to swallow hard. Wyatt pressed a hand to his forehead and waited for the room to stop going round and round, hoping the pain would let up.

"Wyatt? Are you all right?" Emmett stood in the doorway, his empty eyes scanning the room, his face tight. "Wy, say something for God's sake!"

"I'm right here. Just got a little lightheaded is all." He had to cut off a curse as his head continued to throb hard enough that his stomach flip-flopped. *Don't you dare.* His mind barked orders, trying to take control before nausea won. *Don't you dare.*

His brother moved toward the sound of his voice and Wyatt's head snapped up fast. This time he did curse as the pain bloomed and made his vision black out for an instant. "Watch it, Em! There's broken glass on the floor!"

Emmett moved cautiously, sweeping the kitchen tile with his foot until he nudged Wyatt. He got down on his knees beside him and took hold of his arm. "You all right?"

There was fear in his brother's eyes, in his voice. Wyatt didn't like to be the cause of it. He blew out hard through his nose and patted Em's arm. "Yeah, sure. Too much beer I guess."

"You only had one." Emmett stood and offered him a hand up, catching his brother when he swayed. "That's it. You need to sit down."

Wyatt allowed Em to lead him back to the couch only to pull up short. "Hold on. I've got to clean up."

Emmett gave him a gentle push until Wyatt was sitting down. "I'll manage. It's good practice. Just sit here and rest a minute."

With the jackhammer drilling hard inside his head and his stomach at war, Wyatt didn't have any fight in him. He leaned back and closed his eyes, concentrating on his breathing, trying to take charge of his stomach and clamp down on the stabbing in his head. Faintly, he could hear Emmett in the kitchen, the sweeping of the broom, the tinkle of broken glass, the opening and closing of cabinets.

The aching eased up and relief washed over him. Whatever it was had loosened its grip.

Emmett returned and rested a hand on his shoulder. "You're sure you're okay? I could call Doc."

"I'm good, really. I think I've just been overdoing it. Probably had some heat exhaustion from being in such a hurry to get things done this morning. Let's catch the rest of the game." Wyatt couldn't help laughing when his brother set a cold beer in his hand. "Now I'll be better than ever."

Emmett chuckled with him, but it sounded strained. His little brother was quiet the rest of the night. He continued a silent streak the next day on another round with a specialist about his eyes. It was downright out of character when Em submitted to all of the poking, prodding, tests, and questions without bristling.

When the doctor was finally done, he sat down on the edge of his desk and sighed heavily. Wyatt knew what that sigh meant and his heart plummeted—*again.* "I'm sorry, Emmett. I think your blindness is permanent."

Emmett was tight-lipped, the muscle bulging in his jaw he was clenching it so hard. He nodded once. "I figured as much, but Wyatt keeps dragging me to doctors who keep telling me what I already know. Besides, it's not me that I'm here for today. It's my brother."

Wyatt's body tensed, and he started to protest.

Em raised his hand to stop him. "You've brought me out time and again. You can stand to be the patient. Tell Doctor Edwards what happened yesterday. I'm not going to leave until you do, and you can't make me." His kid brother drew himself up to his full height, crossed his arms, planted his feet firmly on the floor, and set his shoulders. Talk about stubborn—bull-headed as only a Henry could be.

Wyatt might as well try and move a boulder. He could try to force Emmett to budge, but it would take one hell of a fight and Wyatt honestly didn't have it in him. He let out an explosive sigh and resisted the urge to curse. "I had a dizzy spell yesterday and a bad headache. It was no big deal."

The throbbing picked it up a notch, shifting from the base of his skull and hitting the ridge above his eyes, proving him a liar.

The doctor gestured to the examining table. "Why don't you have a seat, and I'll give you a quick once over? I won't be able to tell much without tests and X-rays, but we can see if anything is off." His brown eyes were steady, his expression calm, meant to offer reassurance.

Reluctantly, Wyatt hoisted himself onto the edge of the table and glared at Emmett, forgetting it wouldn't do any good. Em grinned and gave a nod. "If looks could kill, I'd probably be a pillar of flame right now, wouldn't I, Doc?

The specialist couldn't be much older than the brothers. He pushed his dark hair out of his face and let out a chuckle. "I won't lie to you, Emmett. Your brother doesn't look happy. Now, let me take your blood pressure."

Wyatt held out his arm and waited impatiently while Doctor Edwards slipped on the cuff. He was sure the aggravation didn't help any when the specialist let the air out with a hiss and shook his head. "It's too high. One-sixty over one hundred. You're headed toward the danger zone. I don't like it."

"Well, I don't like being blindsided like this about a doctor's visit. That might have something to do with it," Wyatt grumbled while the doctor pulled out a light and proceeded to examine his eyes. Wyatt squeezed them shut with a jerk. "That light hurts."

Doctor Edwards slipped the instrument into his pocket and rested his chin on his hand, a crease of worry forming between his eyebrows. "Your pupils are slightly dilated. Have you been having a lot of headaches?"

Wyatt shrugged. "Off and on. The heat's been getting to me. I forget to drink enough water, stay out in it too long."

"Tell him about Mama." Emmett's words tripped Wyatt up, taking him to a place he didn't want to go.

A moment of uncomfortable silence hung between them until Wyatt took the plunge. "Our mother died of a ruptured aneurysm when we were little. I'm sure this is completely unrelated."

The doctor studied him closely and Wyatt met his eyes with a defiant stare. He did *not* have the same thing as his mother. The thought rarely crossed his mind—and when it did, he squashed it.

"Well, it wouldn't hurt for you to be on the safe side and have some tests done. Call my nurse, and we'll set them up. As for you, Emmett." Doctor Edwards took his arm. "I'm sorry I couldn't give you better news."

Emmett thanked him, unfolded his cane, and led the way to the truck, proving how much he'd accomplished since that night in the bar. Wyatt followed him and couldn't resist slamming the door. He seethed for the entire drive, bristling all the way about Em's interference in his life. His brother didn't say a word.

The tires rolled to a stop in front of Emmett's house, and the engine cut off, tension crackling in the air. Suddenly, Em turned and gripped Wyatt's arm. "You're so busy taking care of me, Sam, and the horses that you forget to look after yourself. Promise me you'll get the tests. You're a pain in the butt, but I love you. Losing Mama was tough, and Dad nearly killed me. If something happens to you, I think it will finish the job."

Wyatt rested his hand on Emmett's and gave it a squeeze. "Now you know how I felt when you got hurt. I'll get checked out as soon as I can get around to it."

Emmett pulled his brother into a hug and pounded his back. "Make sure it happens soon."

That was two days before. Two busy days and now it was Sunday. The call for an appointment would have to wait until Monday. There was too much to do to be bothered over something as inconsequential as some headaches. Pushing it to the back of his mind like he was swatting away a bothersome fly, Wyatt dove into his day.

It started out good, waking up with Sam's arms wrapped around him and the baby nudging at him with her belly pressed up against his back. Someone else was revved up and ready to go. Wyatt rolled over and rested his hand on her stomach, marveling at the gymnastics going on in there.

Samantha opened one eye and her mouth tilted up in a sleepy smile. "I think someone is hungry." Wyatt's stomach growled in answer, making them both laugh. He leaned in to give his wife a kiss and hit the shower, singing over the pounding of the water on the tile.

His steps were quick and light on his way downstairs where he was stopped in his tracks by the sight of his wife, standing at the window with the sun touching her hair and making it glow like a brilliant halo.

She was rubbing her stomach as she gazed out over the fields and the pure beauty of the moment stopped his heart for an instant, he was sure of it. A second later, it was pounding harder, pushing him across the room, making him take her in his arms. "You just get more beautiful every day."

Samantha rose up on tiptoe to plant a kiss on his mouth. "I'm getting as big as a barn and I think you're delusional, but I'll take the compliment."

She fed him a hearty breakfast, gave him a cup of

coffee, and sent him out the door with a smile. "Watch the heat now. It's a cooker."

Cooker was an understatement. The heat was so oppressive, it felt like a hot, damp weight was pressing down on Wyatt's shoulders all morning long. Dark clouds were gathering on the horizon as he stepped out into the pasture. The wind picked up, becoming fierce as it whipped the trees to and fro. The weather was about to change and fast. A kaleidoscope headache, that unsettling flashing of lights that hit from time to time, almost tripped him up, but Wyatt ignored it. Had to get the horses in.

The animals didn't make it easy on him. Spooked by what they could sense, some raced away, others stampeded toward the open doors of the barn, while a few just stood and munched. Wyatt was engaged in an all-out tug of war with the last stallion when the skies opened up, dumping hail the size of golf balls that started pelting him in the head. Lightning split the sky and thunder boomed as he cursed at the tall, black horse.

"Come on, Hercules. Get your blasted hide in here!"

He had to use brute force, his shoulder shoved up against the horse's flank, before the stubborn animal finally went into his stall.

When Wyatt turned around, Samantha was waiting with a towel. "What are you doing out in this mess?! Get back in the house, Sammie!" he shouted over the howling of the wind, when a pain like he'd never known before ripped through his head and his legs gave, dropping him in a heap on the barn floor.

Samantha's scream rang in his ears, and his vision blurred.

The pain. He'd never felt such pain in his life. Crashing through his head. Rolling. Pounding with his heartbeat. If this was a migraine, he never wanted another one. Samantha let out another scream that went through his skull like a spike. Wyatt clasped his head in his hands. The agony was so bad that the barn could be engulfed in flames, burning him to a crisp, and he wouldn't be able to get on his feet.

He was vaguely aware of Samantha beside him, holding on to his arm, but the pain had teeth, dug in, made his hands curl into fists and his stomach twisted. He turned to his side and heaved. Again and again. Dry heaves continued, and his head was about to burst into a thousand pieces. "Make it stop. It's the worst headache I've ever had in my life. God, take me now."

"To hell with that!" Sam hissed in his ear, her nails digging into his arms.

Wyatt didn't even realize he'd spoken out loud.

"You lie still," she ordered. "I'm calling an ambulance."

A hasty kiss and she was gone, leaving him with an all-consuming pain that made him want to die. He couldn't have moved if his life depended on it.

CHAPTER 10

Heart in her throat, Samantha fought her way to her feet, cursing the bulk of her stomach and how clumsy her body felt as she hurried into the house and fumbled with the phone. It felt like the longest thirty seconds of her life as she waited for someone to pick up. She squeezed her eyes shut but couldn't erase the film in her mind that kept replaying that dreadful moment when Wyatt's face crumpled and hit the floor, so white one would think he was bleeding to death.

"Nine-one-one dispatch. How may I help you?" a no-nonsense, female voice answered.

"Please send an ambulance as quickly as possible to Forty-Four Henry Way. My husband, Wyatt, is out in the barn, and he's suffering from a severe headache and vomiting. Please, please tell them to hurry. I don't know what's wrong, but he's in terrible pain."

The dispatcher asked a few questions and disconnected to contact emergency services. At a loss, Samantha grabbed a pillow and a blanket, even though it had to be nearly one-hundred degrees. If Wyatt went into shock, she'd need to keep him warm. She ran outside, her hand pressed to her side as the baby jabbed at her. *Not now, Junior! Daddy needs help!*

Wyatt was where she left him, an arm pressed to his eyes, his hands curled into fists while the foot on one bent leg tapped the floor restlessly. She knelt beside him and felt the tension pulling his body taut. "I brought you a pillow." Samantha helped him to lift his head and Wyatt turned a nasty shade of gray. On the verge of panic, she covered him with the blanket and took his hand. He held on tight, his jaw clenched. Neither said a word, holding on to each other for all it was worth like they were on a sinking ship.

The sound of a siren approached, and Samantha sagged. "They're here, Wy. We're going to get you the help you need. Hold on!"

A slight nod was the only acknowledgement that he heard her. Minutes later, the sound of a door opening and shutting, accompanied by the flash of the lights, announced the arrival of two paramedics. They walked in with a stretcher and a large case of supplies.

A burly, blond man stepped forward and knelt beside them. "I'm Jake Thomas, and this is my partner, Steve Randall. Bring us up to speed."

The other emergency worker, a tall thin man with jet black hair, pulled out a blood pressure cuff while Jake waited expectantly with a pad and paper. Samantha let go of Wyatt as they went to work. "Wyatt was bringing in the horses while hail was coming down, hitting him all over. He stepped through the door and then fell to the floor. He said it's the worst headache ever."

Jake nodded and pulled a radio out of his pocket. He called into the hospital while Steve shot off vitals. "His pulse is dropping down to forty, and his blood pressure is going down as well. He's at eighty over fifty, right now. Sir, I need to check your eyes."

Gently but insistently, the dark-haired paramedic shifted Wyatt's arm and lifted his eyelids, peering closely with a small light.

The patient winced, and his eyes slammed shut. "It feels like a hot poker is stabbing me in the brain."

"All right," Steve said abruptly, his words clipped with urgency. "That's it. He's got one pupil dilated. Let's get him going. Whatever is going on, it's serious."

The two worked as a team to lift Wyatt off the ground, carry him to the ambulance, and get him settled inside. Jake offered Samantha his hand and helped her to climb in back. She sat on the edge of the stretcher and held her husband's hand. She would be there for him, no matter what.

His fingers tightened on hers while he continued to shield his eyes with his other arm. He didn't, or couldn't, say a word. A soft moan rose up, and he clamped his mouth shut. Samantha knew it was for her benefit. Wyatt wouldn't let on how much he was suffering, wanting to spare her.

Jake touched her gently on the arm. "Any conditions we should know about, Mrs. Henry?"

She shook her head. "He's always been healthy. Wyatt has hardly ever been sick in all the time I've known him and that's over twenty years."

Steve closed the door and seconds later, the ambulance pulled forward. Samantha closed her eyes and began to pray while the ambulance swayed and rocked its way to the hospital.

Every bump, every sharp turn went right through her as Wyatt's body tensed beneath her touch. She was so deep in prayer she didn't hear the paramedic's next question.

"Mrs. Henry?" A pause and he asked again, squeezing her hand to get her attention. "Mrs. Henry, is there anything of concern in his family health history, perhaps his mom or his dad?"

Samantha's head snapped up with a jerk as she pulled her gaze away from Wyatt's face, and fear wrapped itself in a fist around her heart, squeezing the breath out of her. "His mother—his mother died from an aneurysm when he was little."

Jake cursed under his breath and called up to Steve to step on it. The ambulance hurtled toward the hospital while Wyatt moaned softly, and Samantha gently stroked his hair, praying history would not be repeated.

∽∾∽

The hospital was chaos. Loud sirens, staff running to and fro. Patients crying, groaning, bleeding. Family members looking terrified. Samantha ran alongside the gurney as they raced toward an examining room, Wyatt's hand in hers, cursing the glaring lights overhead that must have been agony for him.

They reached a set of swinging doors, and Jake pressed her shoulder. "Mrs. Henry, you need to go in the waiting room now."

"Wait." Wyatt stopped their forward motion, his voice strained. He pulled Samantha in close and pressed his hand to the nape of her neck. In spite of the blinding lights overhead, he gazed at her, his eyes gone dark with pain, and whispered, "Love you, Sammie-girl."

He kissed his fingers and grazed her bulging belly with them before they wheeled him away from her.

"I love you too, Wyatt. You're going to be all right." *Please, God. Please. Let him be all right.* She couldn't move, staring at the closed doors, longing to run in after him and throw herself on the gurney, to shield him from whatever had gone haywire inside his body.

A nurse stepped up and took her hand. "Miss, let me show you to the waiting room. It's right this way." She spoke softly, her smile kind.

Samantha turned and stared at her, her mind crowded with terror, imaginings, and worry. "Would you show me where the phones are first, please?" She had to be strong for a few more minutes. Falling to pieces would be next.

The first call was relatively easy, and Sam kept it together. Her throat closed up during the second one, and she had to choke out the words. "Em, I'm at the hospital with Wyatt."

"What's wrong?" There was an awful silence on the other end and then the sound of desperation. "Samantha Henry, tell me what's going on *right now*!"

The tears started rolling down her face. She didn't even try to stop them. Let them fall. Try and drown out the pain. "Wyatt collapsed in the barn. They're running tests right now."

"I have to be there." No hesitation, not even a blink. Samantha had no doubt. Emmett would walk if he had to, crawling on his hands and knees every inch of the way if need be.

"Emily Hastings will be there any minute. I just called her. Em, pray for your brother, will you? Please pray like you never have before."

"I will." Her brother-in-law spoke so softly, she

could barely hear him and then the receiver clicked.

Somehow, she found her way to the waiting room and sat down in a chair by a window, her eyes drawn to a sky gone black while the downpour continued. Samantha didn't see any of it, only Wyatt's pain as his face caved in, taking down a man who was as strong as they come. She had no sense of the passage of time when an attractive, red-haired nurse sat beside her. Five minutes could have gone by or five days.

"Mrs. Henry? I'm Sally Masterson, one of the ER nurses. Your husband is in emergency surgery right now."

The nurse rattled off the tests that had provided conclusive proof that the current plan of action was the only choice. X-rays. A CT scan. An MRI. Samantha's hands curled into fists and she held her breath, dreading the prognosis.

The verdict: a ruptured aneurysm. Like his mother. The bulging blood vessel could've been there for years. Sam leaned forward and covered her face with her palms. Every headache. Every dizzy spell. Every time he'd felt off could've been a warning sign. Add all of the stress since Emmett's accident, her husband was a walking time bomb.

The nurse wrapped an arm around her shoulders. "Mrs. Henry, Dr. Andrews had to begin the procedure immediately because time is critical if we're going to save your husband's life. Otherwise, the doctor would be here right now with you. I want you to know that he is an extremely talented surgeon, and Mr. Henry is in good hands. Is there anything I can get for you, anyone I can call?"

Samantha straightened and nodded at the young woman at her side. "No. Wyatt's brother is on the way. Thank you."

Sally stood up and gave her hand one last squeeze. "I'll be sure to keep you updated on his condition."

A pat on the back and the diminutive figure in white retreated, leaving Samantha alone. A wave of despair rose up inside of her, nearly making her break down in the waiting room.

Samantha bent over and clutched her belly, fighting back sobs. Her stomach rose up and down as her little occupant became restless with her turmoil. She rested her hands on the swelling mound and began to massage it round and round. "It's all right, Junior," Samantha murmured softly. "Daddy *will* be all right."

He had to be. She closed her eyes and went back to praying while the waiting game continued.

Samantha heard Emmett's arrival before she saw him, the clicking of his cane coming down the hall, accompanied by the rather loud and distinctive voice of her elderly neighbor. "Slow down, Emmett, slow down. I can't keep up with a whippersnapper like you." She spoke lightly, trying to ease his burden as Emily so often did for those she cared for.

Samantha stood up and met them halfway. "Oh, Emmett!" she cried out and flung her arms around him, the tears back in force.

Emmett, being a Henry, became her rock, wrapping his arms around her and sheltering her with his body. He kissed the top of her head. "Hush now, Sammie. Hush. Getting so upset like this isn't going to help. Dad said you can make a mountain into a molehill with the right attitude. Any news yet?"

Samantha reached out, and Emily took her hand, forming a circle of love for Wyatt.

Samantha took a shaky breath and blurted out the dreadful words. "Wyatt has a ruptured aneurysm. He's in surgery right now."

For an instant, she felt a little give in Emmett, but he carried on his family tradition and shouldered her load as well as his own. He'd pick up Wyatt's too if need be. "*He will* be all right. My brother is indestructible."

Em squeezed her hand and she led him to a chair. They both sat while Emily patted them on the back. "You two sit. I'll go get you some tea." With that, the little white-haired lady was off on a mission because in her mind, tea was the solution for any problem, no matter how big or how small.

Emmett leaned forward and pressed a hand to his forehead. "This is my fault. I should have called you. I should have made him go to the emergency room."

"What are you talking about?" Samantha rested a

hand on his back and began to massage the muscles gone tight.

An explosive breath and the words poured out as if breaking a dam after being pent up for too long. "The other night, when Wy came over to catch the ball game with me? He went out to the kitchen and had a dizzy spell. I think he almost passed out, said his head hurt. When we went to my doctor's appointment, I made the doc give Wyatt the once over. He wanted my bullheaded brother to come in for tests." Emmett turned her way and gripped her arms tightly. "I should've made him go to the ER right then. I'm sorry, Sammie."

She pulled him in close and ran a hand through his hair soothingly. "Stop it right now. Don't you know? No one can make a Henry do anything. None of us could see this coming. The nurse said Wyatt could have had an aneurysm brewing for years. It was just a matter of time."

Time. So precious. They never had enough and right now, Samantha would do anything to make the sand in the hourglass stop falling down on her head, smothering her. She and Emmett held each other up, hoping against hope that the seconds would not run out for this particular Henry, not this time.

The minutes started running together, one hour into the next.

Emily Hastings dozed off in the chair next to Emmett while he continued to sit, ramrod straight, holding Samantha's hand. Her lifesaver. She was lost in her thoughts when he asked hoarsely, "What time is it? Feels like we've been sitting here an eternity."

The wait had gone on so long, they'd sent Emily home and promised to call her with any change or if they needed a ride home. She gave them both hugs and kisses then ordered them not to worry about a thing. Their good neighbors would take care of the horses for another round because that's what good neighbors did.

Samantha glanced up at the clock, something she'd been doing too often, trying to get the minute hand to stop turning. "Nine o'clock."

He stiffened further beside her and slammed his fist on his thigh. "What's that been? Eight hours? My God, what could they be doing in there?"

Just when Samantha felt like a powder keg about to blow, a tall figure in surgical scrubs slowly approached. He reached up and pulled his cap from his head, revealing sweat-dampened brown hair and a face strained by weariness. The surgeon scanned the room and his eyes locked with hers, eyes of a deep blue, drawing her into an undertow of compassion. She rose to her feet. Samantha would face this standing up.

Emmett came with her, tucking her in against his side, rock solid. She was grateful when his arm wrapped around her waist. He wouldn't let her fall. "Mrs. Henry? I'm Ben Andrews. I just finished up in surgery for your husband. It was really touch and go. Just when I thought we had him squared away, I'd find another bleeder or his vitals would drop. We've had to fight to stabilize him, but he's in recovery now."

Samantha reached out to the doctor and he took her hand. "What does it all mean, Dr. Andrews?"

He gestured toward the chairs, his eyelids heavy. "Do you mind if we sit? I don't have it in me to stand for much longer." At her nod, the surgeon sank down, kneading at the back of his neck.

Samantha eased herself back in her seat. Reluctantly, Emmett joined her. If he felt anything like she did, her brother-in-law probably wanted to run. Yell. Scream. Punch something. The stranglehold of his fingers around hers proved that she wasn't that far off the mark. "What's his prognosis?"

Dr. Andrews took a deep breath and met her gaze. She wanted to close her eyes and plug her ears, pretend this whole thing wasn't happening. Emmett stiffened beside her, his jaw tight, giving her the strength to hear what the surgeon had to say.

"Wyatt had a rather large aneurysm, and when it burst, it caused subarachnoid hemorrhage—bleeding into the space around the brain. That blood loss and pressure on the brain tissue is what made my job so complicated. We really don't know what the extent of the damage will be. On the positive side, you got him in my hands as soon as possible. I wish it had been before the rupture, but there's no going back." He paused and rested his elbows on his knees, the crease between his eyes carving its way in deeper. "On the negative side, we could see fatigue that will stay with him for months. Your husband may have weakness or paralysis on one side of his body and problems with speech, problems that may be permanent." The doctor eyed Emmett knowingly when the younger man cursed under his breath. This was hitting way too close to home. "Or he may have a full recovery. Right now, it's a waiting game."

Samantha was afraid to look up at her brother-in-law. When she finally glanced at his honey eyes, they were flaming, and his cheeks were streaked with red. Unable to restrain himself, Emmett let loose a blistering string of curses. "My brother and I have always had a lot in common. A brain injury was one thing I hoped we'd never share. I *have* to see him right now!"

"He's in recovery and then off to the critical care unit. Usually, I wouldn't allow visitors this soon, but I feel your presence is vital to Wyatt's recovery. If he's going to have a chance, he's going to need the people he loves most at his side. I'll take you to see him right now." Dr. Andrews understood a man's need to be with his brother, one that was as strong as a wife's need for her husband.

Samantha inhaled deeply, preparing herself. Em found her hand and threaded his fingers with hers. Whatever came next, they would face it together and be there for Wyatt—to pick up the pieces or let him go.

CHAPTER 11

He was swimming under water, his body heavy, everything moving in slow motion. There were sounds in the background, noises and voices, but they were far away and distorted. Wyatt couldn't grasp what they were or break the surface. Someone was holding his right hand, someone else had his right leg, as if they were keeping him anchored. He tried to lift his left arm, but it felt like a terrible weight was pressing down on him. A slight shift and his breath came out in a rush. His left leg was pinned too. Confused, Wyatt struggled to open his eyes. When he did, everything was a blur.

"Wyatt?! Stay with us, Wy. Don't slip away on us again. Emmett and I are right here." Samantha was the one holding his hand. He could smell her perfume, and her touch felt so good he wanted to cry. Try as he might,

Wyatt couldn't tell her. The words wouldn't come. His eyes sprang wide, this time with fear.

Emmett squeezed his leg. "Breathe, Wyatt. Just breathe. I know how you're feeling right now, like you're trapped in your own body. Let sleep lose its grip on you and shake off the meds. We know you're in there, brother. Come back."

Panic was rising up inside of Wyatt, threatening to smother him as his heart began to trip, and he started breathing hard. Samantha touched his cheek and it was all too much. Tears spilled down his face as he stared up at her.

She bent down and kissed him. In that moment, he could see her clearly and the memory came rushing back of his collapse in the barn. He moaned at the echo of pain in his head, a throbbing that was still at the edge of his consciousness, coming closer.

"Shh, Wy. Just lie easy. You were in surgery for a long time, and you've been out for two days. Try and relax." Sam's soothing voice brought him off the edge.

"My—Mmm—Not—Right." *Dammit! What's the matter with me?* Wyatt knew what he wanted to say, but the words came out wrong, and his head hurt worse trying to get them out.

Emmett stood up and moved around to the other side of the bed to take his left hand. "What's not right?"

Wyatt tried to hold on to his brother. The effort to close his fingers made him feel sick to his stomach, and a cold sweat broke out on his forehead. "Hand—my." He tried to move his leg and only felt worse. "Mmm—leg."

There was a strangled gasp from the other side of the bed. "I'll go get the doctor." Footsteps retreated rapidly, and the door clicked shut.

Wyatt was vaguely aware that his wife had left the room, but heard Emmett loud and clear, speaking at his ear. "You had a burst aneurysm, like Mama, but the doctor saved you, and whatever's wrong, we'll get through this. Understand me?"

His little brother's voice choked up, but Wyatt nodded and focused on his left hand. If he gave it complete concentration, he could wrap his fingers around his brother's hand and press with a ghost of his former grip.

Emmett squeezed back. "I felt that, brother. Just keep holding on."

Wyatt wouldn't let go. He couldn't. His life, his sanity, depended on it.

☙❧❧

Dr. Andrews stood at the side of the bed, his hand pressed to his patient's shoulder. He reminded Wyatt of Jackson Henry. "You had substantial bleeding and pressure on your brain. I'm not lying when I tell you it's a miracle you're still here, Wyatt. The weakness on your left side is a result of the damage. We'll get you started in rehabilitation as soon as possible. The sooner you're in therapy, the better your chances for a strong recovery. The most important thing you need to remember is to be patient with yourself and avoid getting upset. Otherwise, you'll be putting my hard work at risk with a setback. This is going to take time. Do you understand?"

Wyatt closed his eyes and clung to the memory of his father to give him strength. When he managed to open them again, Samantha and Emmett had stepped back to the side of the bed and were holding on to him, struggling not to cry, putting on a brave front. Wy would have to do the same. Slowly, like the petals of a flower closing up at night, his left hand came up and met the surgeon's halfway. "I'll—try."

Dr. Andrews held on and smiled encouragingly, bolstering Wyatt's courage. "That's all anyone can do. I want you to get some rest now. You're going to need it."

As soon as the doctor left, Samantha leaned in to kiss him, her hand on his cheek. So good, she felt so good, and he wanted to take her in his arms or make her slip into bed beside him. Make this all go away, make it a nightmare, and he'd wake up in the safe haven of her arms. The only thing Wyatt could do was hold her hand—and damn his eyes for crying.

"It's going to be all right. You're still here, and we'll help you through this." She rested her head on his chest. Gritting his teeth, he concentrated, focusing all his energy on getting his body to do what he asked of it. Wyatt's hand seemed to float into the air, as if it was disconnected from his body, and finally rested on her golden hair. That's when Samantha couldn't hold back her tears.

Emmett felt his way up the bed and gripped his brother's shoulder. "We're not going anywhere."

⌒⌒

Three days of lying in bed, and Wyatt was miserable. His emotions ran the gamut, from fury to the lowest of lows he'd ever felt. Emmett and Samantha's presence didn't help. They only made him feel more helpless as they watched him struggle to get to the bathroom and back into bed. Damn it all if he was going to use a bed pan. Might as well just shoot him.

Each journey across the room was terrifying. The weakness on the left side of his body was so bad, his leg gave out and pitched him to the floor several times, Emmett stepping into to haul him back up. Otherwise, Wyatt dragged the limb like deadweight, especially if he was tired—and he was tired *all* the time. His arm fought him, and he could barely lift it. Everything fought him, even his vision going double from time to time until he felt sick. The last thing he wanted was an audience. Wyatt finally understood why Emmett sent him home during his recovery.

On the fifth day since regaining consciousness, he fell for the third time coming back to bed. Emmett and Sam were at his side in a heartbeat, offering to help. Wyatt pulled away and the rage boiled up inside of him. "Will—you—stop? No—need to—watch!"

Emmett let go and stood back, hands on his hips, a scowl on his face. "*I* don't see anything wrong with you."

Samantha covered her mouth, doing her best to stay calm, but Wyatt could tell. She was about to lose it.

The flames of fury blazed higher, his head pounding the more his agitation grew. He grabbed hold of the bed and worked his way up, slipping and sliding, so mad he could spit.

With one monumental heave, Wyatt dropped on the bed, panting. "Tired—you—helping. People—helping my horses. Owe everybody." Saying that little made his brain feel muddled.

Nothing was simple anymore.

Emmett moved in and jabbed him in the middle of the chest with his finger. Spot on. "You don't owe any-body. You've done the same through the years, helping others out of a jam. It's what good neighbors do. You'll return the favor, but right now, it's your turn to be on the receiving end. Shut up and take it with grace."

"You—didn't." Wyatt rested his arm on his forehead and waited for the throbbing in his head to die down. Slowly, he sat up and snagged his brother's arm, then his wife's. "Need—you—do—me—favor."

"Anything." Samantha ran her fingers through his hair, making him tremble. "Just say the word."

"Go home." The hurt in Samantha's eyes cut deep,

and a wall of defiance rose up in Emmett as he drew himself up and crossed his arms, shaking his head.

Wyatt took his wife's hand with his right, biting his lip in concentration to take Em's with his left. "Please. Need time. No one watch. Please. You—you need—break—from—me too."

Sam couldn't help letting go of a choked sob as Emmett stepped in and wrapped them both in a bear hug. "I get it because I felt the same way. We'll go—for now, but you can't get rid of us forever, big brother. You got that?"

Wyatt could only nod because if he spoke, begging them to stay would be the first twisted words that tumbled out of his mouth.

სასა

Therapy? More like torture. Sitting in a small room, trying to do the impossible. Move. His leg didn't want to hold him or work the way it should. His hand argued all the time to the point that squeezing a rubber ball felt like moving a mountain. '*Stop making molehills into mountains. You're still here. Your mother wasn't so lucky,*' his father's voice barked at him, loud and clear.

Wyatt made it through one more set of exercises and had to accept a wheelchair ride back to his room because there was no other choice. He was too exhausted to walk on a journey that might as well be across an ocean, it seemed that far. The voice in his head, the one that worked perfectly, hissed at him, '*You're doing the best that you can.*'

That was a lie. He'd done less today than the day before. The therapist said it was natural, that he was pushing too hard and his body was arguing with him. Wyatt knew otherwise. He wasn't trying hard enough, running out of steam long before the finish line.

Sitting on the edge of the bed, staring at his limp hand on his knee, he felt like a pitiful excuse for a human being. Frustrated to no end with himself, he managed to make it to the chair by the window, sweating, cursing, half-dragging himself all the way. Wyatt leaned on the windowsill, his head resting against the blessedly cool glass while he waited for his heart to slow, his breathing to ease, and the ache in his head to go back down to a dull roar. A wave of depression rolled in, threatening to drown him. *Dad, what do I do? How do I knock this mountain down to size?*

His door swung open, the breeze lifting his hair away from his face. Quiet footsteps approached and a hand settled on the nape of his neck. "Hey. How are you doing today?" Samantha asked softly, music to his scarred mind.

He looked up and her smile was so beautiful, it hurt. Wyatt winced and squeezed his eyes shut. "Don't— deserve—you."

She moved in front of him and pressed a hand beneath his chin, forcing him to meet her gaze, and the fire in her eyes burned hot enough to singe the both of them. "I don't ever want to hear that kind of talk from you again. You're my husband, you're going to be the father of my child, and you're a Henry. Don't ever forget what that means."

Samantha took his hands and pressed them to her bulging belly. The baby chose that moment to give a hearty kick and Wyatt bowed his head. "What—if—I—gave—baby—*this?*" He broke off. His greatest fear, it was too hard to think about it, much less say it.

"You won't. Our baby will be as healthy as a horse." She sat on his lap, looping her arms around his neck.

Wyatt pressed his ear to her chest and listened to the steady, reassuring beat of her heart. "What—if—not? Never—forgive—me."

Samantha kissed his forehead, then his cheeks, and finally his mouth. He could taste her salty tears. Too many tears. "You heard what your surgeon said, Wy. We can have tests run every year and monitor the baby closely. Dr. Andrews promised to take the case on himself and keep an eye on the next Henry. We won't let anything happen—and if it does, we'll deal with it. Like now."

The sadness eased some and the weight on his heart lightened, a dose of her sunshine rubbing off on him. Wyatt kissed his wife and then her belly, a small smile turning his mouth up at the corners. "Still—don't deserve—you."

She caught the change in his mood and shook a finger at him. "What am I going to have to do to make you believe that's not true?"

His smile grew even bigger and one eyebrow raised up higher than the other, something he could still do with ease. "Lie—down—with—me. Teach—me—lesson."

Samantha tipped back her head and laughed hard enough to make her eyes water. It was the prettiest sound he'd heard in weeks. She stood and offered her hand. "Let me help you."

"You—carry—me?" At a rueful shake of her head, Wyatt stood up slowly and took one tortured step at a time. With his gaze centered on the patch of sky in her eyes, he felt like she was bearing him up. She lifted the covers and helped him slide in, lying down beside him.

He turned on his side to face her. No matter what happened to him, whether he was ever whole again or not, Wyatt would never tire of looking at his wife. He reached out with his good hand and trailed his fingers through her hair. "I want—home. I want you."

Samantha cupped his face in her hands and kissed him, making feelings stir that he thought had died on the day his brain nearly exploded. "Then show me the Henry I know. Fight like hell, and get out of here."

❧❧❧

"Come on, Wyatt. Five more and you're done for to-day."

Jonah, his therapist was like his high school football coach, pushing him until his body was ready to call it quits as he lifted a ten pound weight—*ten pounds!*—with his left leg. The sweat was pouring off of Wyatt's face, his shirt was drenched, and his whole body was quivering. To make matters worse, Emmett stood propped up against some nearby equipment through the entire, wretched session with a smile stretched across his face.

"What you grinning at?" Wyatt hissed through clenched teeth as he struggled through three more reps.

"One more, Wyatt! Let's go!" Jonah practically shouted in his ear, smiling in encouragement, his powerful muscles rippling as he gripped his patient's shoulder.

"Don't see *you* going anywhere," Wyatt grumbled.

His therapist only laughed and waited expectantly.

Wyatt closed his eyes and focused on straightening his leg, ready to scream or cry with the strain, but the weight came up one last time. A groan slipped out, and he slumped forward, his shoulders hunched while his over the top, much too enthusiastic physical therapist pounded him on the back.

Wyatt sucked in hard and looked up at his brother. "Asked—I—.you—question." His teeth clamped down on his bottom lip in frustration. The words were coming more easily, but they still got jumbled from time to time.

He tried again. "I—asked you—a question. What you grinning about?"

Emmett's hand explored the space in front of him, found his brother's arm, and gave it a good squeeze. "Listening to you, thinking about how far you've come, I know you're going to be all right. There's no doubt in my mind."

Jonah gave Em a slap on the back too. "That's the spirit. Let's take that attitude and use it while we give your arm some attention. Enough chit chat, boys. Time to get back to work, Henry."

Wyatt moaned and lay back on the bench, his right arm covering his eyes, but as soon as his therapist set the weight in his left hand, he was back at it again. This time, he made it through ten reps and the weight dropped from fingers that didn't want to do what he told them to. Emmett was there to pick it up, pushing him to do five more, just like his kid brother had since the beginning.

August had slipped into September and October wasn't too far off. If he had it his way, Wyatt would be back home by Columbus Day. Samantha wanted him to fight like hell. He'd do anything for his wife, even if it meant dragging himself through the fire.

"Five more, Wy. You can do it. Just five more." Emmett was hunkered down beside him.

Wyatt fought his way through the last set, grunting with the effort.

His brother was there to catch him when he fell back at the end, putting out the flames.

∾∾

The man in the moon was smiling in all his glory high overhead. The air was hot and heavy, sticking to Wyatt's skin. He wanted to cool down, but it was impossible with Samantha looking so darn amazing, turned to silver in the moonlight. They'd graduated that day, and their wedding was in one week. Not long now, not long at all, but temptation was a devil, urging him to take her in his arms and persuade her to forget about waiting for the night they said their vows.

Fighting the sizzle in his blood that was clouding his thoughts and stealing his good judgment, Wyatt reached out and took her hand, perched beside him on the log by their favorite swimming hole. She slid him a sideways glance, gave him a mischievous grin, and jumped to her feet. In one swift movement, Samantha slipped out of her sundress and walked into the water in only her bra and panties. One glance over her shoulder and Wyatt was hooked.

He shucked out of his T-shirt and shorts, his blood pumping so hard through his veins, his heart was fit to burst. One giant lunge and Wyatt had her in his arms. The mercury level, inside his body, spiked, and he was on the brink of vaporization. How was it humanly possible to wait seven more days?

Samantha looped her arms over his head and pressed her full body against his. Her mouth sealed his, and he forgot about breathing. God—God help him—take him. Take him now.

⋐⋑

Wyatt sat up fast with a gasp, the sound of Sam's laughter echoing in his ears, the combined sensation of cool water and the heat of her touch lingering. He let out a long breath and drew in another one, shaking it off. When he opened his eyes, Em was sitting in a chair drawn up by the bed, apparently dozing, feet propped on the comforter.

The sight was a bit of a disappointment after the dream. In a rusty, hoarse voice, Wyatt muttered, "Don't you have anything better to do than sit here?"

Emmett sat up and stretched until his bones popped, making him wince. He'd been there a while. "Not really and what's got a bee in your bonnet?"

Wyatt laughed in spite of himself and let the last traces of the dream fade away. He attempted to collect his thoughts. It was the last week of September and he was making progress. His speech was coming along day by day, but wrangling the words could still give him trouble as he tried to pin them down. He had to take his time and concentrate. "Nothing, nothing. Just had a dream about Sam. A good dream. Know what I mean?"

Emmett chuckled and gave him a grin. "Sure, brother, especially since I haven't had any female attention since this." His hand waved at his eyes. "So, since I'm sure you're feeling a little frustrated with all of that pent up energy, I think it's time for some exercise. Ready?"

His brother had been coming every day since his wife's pep talk. Samantha would drop off Emmett then visit with Wyatt after he'd been through his personal, daily hell. She didn't need to see him suffer and struggle. At least Em didn't have to *watch*. As for struggling and suffering, his brother had firsthand experience. They understood each other well.

Wyatt blew out hard through his nose and threw back the covers with his left hand, satisfied. Easier. It was getting easier. "Ready as ever."

Emmett felt by the bedside table and found the cane that had belonged to their father. Jackson had been hurt by a horse as a young man. Whenever Wyatt held on to the piece of art that had been carved by his grandfather, it gave his willpower a badly needed kick in the pants. He gripped the top and drew himself to his feet. Sucked the wind right out of him. Every time.

His brother held his arm a moment to steady him. Reassured that Wyatt was firmly planted, Emmett let go. "After you." As was his habit, he always let Wyatt go first, following the sound of his footsteps until they began to falter. Then Em caught up and hooked his right arm. They made the rounds, all three floors.

Wyatt lost his balance a few times, cursing when he had to be rescued. Standing still on the final stretch, gripping his cane with both hands and working up his nerve for the last twenty feet, he grumbled. "Sorry I'm a bear."

Emmett laughed and patted him gently on the back. "Not as bad as me."

They finally made it to the room, Wyatt's cane clattering to the floor as it fell from fingers gone numb and he dropped back on the bed. He studied his brother, propped up against the wall, and murmured bitterly. "We're some pair. You blind. Me gimpy." Judging by the expression on Emmett's face as he sat down with his arms crossed, his little brother didn't take too kindly to that description. "Sorry." Wyatt nudged Em's arm and watched him relax.

They sat in silence. Wyatt needed a moment to catch his breath, to fight the queasy feeling that hit every time he worked the left side of his body. Emmett sat straight and tall, his gaze turned toward a sunset that he couldn't see. Wyatt reached across, with his left hand to squeeze his brother's shoulder. "I knew you were strong, Em. Didn't know how strong 'til now."

Emmett leaned forward and Wyatt could swear he was staring right at him, straight at his heart. "Who do you think taught me how? You're tough as nails, Wy, and then some."

eↄeↄ

Columbus Day and it was nippy. The cold air poked under Wyatt's collar and made him grateful for his father's flannel shirt and blue jeans. The trees were exploding with color, leaves skittering by his feet, dancing in the air, making him want to get up and move with them.

It smelled like autumn, fresh and crisp. So much better than the inside of that hospital. Wyatt took a deep breath and filled his lungs. He could understand why Emmett detested the place and doctors so much. His own stint with round the clock care gave Wyatt a new appreciation for his brother's return every day to keep him company during rehabilitation. He sucked in one more gulp of air. Wyatt hadn't felt this alive in a long time.

His gaze was trained on the visitor's parking lot, waiting expectantly for one woman, his everything. Like clockwork, Samantha pulled in at four p.m. for her daily visit. She walked briskly across the parking lot, wearing a smile, her shield that rarely slipped no matter how his wife really felt. God love her, her arms were full of homemade pie—probably apple—and mums almost as brilliant of a yellow as the sun in her hair. She turned for a moment, distracted by geese flying overhead, and Wyatt's breath caught at the sight of her belly swelling, ripe and sweet as a Georgia peach. She started walking again, looked ahead. Saw him. Froze.

He stood up carefully, leaving his cane and suitcase on the bench. Wyatt would meet his homecoming on his own two feet without any help. With his eyes glued to Samantha's and his chin raised in defiance of his own limitations, he proved himself to be a true Henry. Step by step, across the parking lot, to her side. She set her presents down and his arms wrapped around her to pull her up against him. His body felt at ease, like it was his own, for the first time in months.

He pressed her head to his chest and rested his chin on her golden hair. "Mind bringing those back home?"

Her breath came out in a hiccup, caught between a sob and a laugh, and she kissed him. "Only if you're coming with them."

Wyatt took her face in his hands and fought to keep his voice steady, even as his smile nearly slid away, his emotions too powerful to be contained. "Take me home, Sammie."

CHAPTER 12

They held hands the entire ride to the farm, bringing back the innocence of childhood, the eagerness of their teen years, the anticipation of their wedding night. Today, with the fingers of his left hand wrapped firmly around hers, Samantha felt hope burning in her heart, glorious and bright as the setting sun touching down on the horizon. As long as he was by her side, they'd be all right.

They crested a hill and Henry land spread out before them in the distance, horses still in the field, the autumn foliage catching fire in the dying light before the night claimed the day. Wyatt whispered, his voice rough, "Pull over, Sam. Just let me look." At their home. Emmett's place. Their beloved animals. His life. One tear slid down his cheek, unbidden and unexpected. He scraped his arm across his face. "Wasn't sure—if I'd make it back."

Samantha rested her head on his shoulder and reveled in their perfect fit. "Me neither. I hoped and I prayed, but your mother kept popping up in my mind. I was so scared, Wy."

"Me too, but I'm going to be okay. Because of you and Em." He turned to her and she buried her face in his chest, so thankful to have the privilege again.

They sat a few more minutes, enjoying the quiet and stillness until she cranked the engine. A short trip down the road and the old truck rumbled to a stop near the back door. Wyatt stepped out, leaving his cane behind. Samantha took it, as a precaution, watching him sway slightly. She reached for his suitcase but he snagged it out of her hand, his eyes flashing. "Sorry. You go ahead, Mr. Independent."

A curt nod and he set his mind on his self-appointed task—walking one hundred feet from the truck, up the steps, and across the porch. Wyatt wouldn't take the cane, the railing his only concession. By the time he hit the door, sweat had popped up on his forehead and he'd gone white. He set the suitcase down and swiped his left hand across his forehead. Samantha could see it quivering.

She ducked under his left shoulder and gave him a devilish grin. "Come on now, Wy. Lean on me. The sooner I get you inside, the sooner I have you to myself."

That was enough to set him to wheezing with laughter. "How can I argue with that? I'm such a catch."

Together, they managed to cross the threshold. Wyatt lost his balance, falling to the floor in a heap, letting go of Samantha to spare her. She knelt down by his side and stroked his hair out of his eyes. "You okay?"

"Never been better." He brought her down by him and kissed her until *her* head was spinning.

They lay there, holding each other until the baby started fussing, judging by the increase of activity in her belly. "All right, Wy. I need to feed the beast. Insistent little bugger likes to stick to a schedule and right now is dinner time."

She stood up slowly and offered Wyatt her hand, planting her feet. He came up with a rush of air hissing through his teeth, dropped the suitcase, and finally had the good grace to accept the cane. "So embarrassed. I'm beat. Going to lie down while you make dinner. Sorry. Meant to be more energetic."

Samantha hovered by his side until he managed to sink on to the couch with a sigh. She dipped in and snatched a kiss. "Don't you go away."

He gave her a tired wink and a smile. "Wouldn't think about it."

She pulled the afghan up over him before heading to the kitchen, contemplating what to make. Something quick and easy, not only to appease the hungry one inside of her, but because Samantha was eager to be with her husband. That he'd surprised her and kept his release a complete secret had really thrown her for a loop. In a clatter of pots and pans, she briskly set about boiling water, heating a pot of sauce with meatballs, and chopping vegetables for a salad. "Almost done, Wyatt," she called out.

There was a mumbled response, enough to prompt her whirlwind of energy to continue, setting the table and pouring ice water just as the timer dinged. "There! That's got to be a record. All ready!" She hurried out to the living room and put on the brakes as soon as she caught sight of her husband.

His right hand was tossed over his head, the left dangling on the floor. His left leg was hanging over the side as well and his tousled hair was scattered over the couch pillow. He looked as if he'd been on a bender. Samantha crossed the room and kissed his forehead. "Time to eat, Sleeping Beauty."

His mouth turned up in a grin and he tugged her down beside him. "Good. I'm starving—for you."

They walked to the dining room holding hands, Wyatt leaning on his cane and Samantha. They took their time eating, soaking each other in until he started fading fast. He propped his forehead on his hand. "Sam. I can't make it—no way, no how am I taking the stairs."

"Then couch it is." She managed to hold back tears, barely, so happy to have him back home, even as his footsteps wavered. He resumed his spot in the living room and she kissed him gently on the lips. "Hang in there. Let me close up for the night and I'll be right back."

Samantha made quick work of locking the doors and turning out the lights. She went upstairs and slipped into a cotton nightgown, eyeing her reflection in the full-length mirror on her way out. A house, that's what she was, well on her way to being the size of a condominium. A strong puff of air blew her bangs out of her eyes in exasperation and she patted her belly. *You never were trying to win any fashion shows anyway—and Wy loves you just the way you are.*

Wyatt was dozing off when she returned. He jerked when she slid in next to him on the couch and tucked herself in against his side. "Sammie, don't have to sleep—here. Sleep—bed." His tongue was getting tangled, a sure sign of fatigue.

She pressed a finger to his lips. "I've slept here most nights since you've been in the hospital. Our bedroom has been too lonely without you."

"Mmm—lonely too." He murmured as his eyes drooped shut. Samantha rested a palm on his cheek and simply lay awake watching him. She was sleepless tonight, unwilling to miss a single minute with her husband. As the moonlight kissed his skin, casting him in silver, her hand slid down to feel the steady rise and fall of his chest, the throb of his heartbeat. She held her breath. Samantha was afraid he'd disappear.

As if he could read her mind, Wyatt came up out of sleep long enough to give her a smile. "I'm not going anywhere. Promise." Keeping a firm grip on his arm, she'd move heaven and earth to hold him to it.

ତେ୫ତ

"What do you want to do today?" Samantha slid her eyes to the pillow next to her, resisting the urge to pinch her arm and prove she wasn't dreaming. Wyatt's hair was a mess, his face lined with pillow marks, his eyes crusted with sleepy seeds. She'd never seen anything better. Her toe inched over and nudged his leg, making his mouth curve up in a grin. "Did you hear me, sleepy head? What are you in the mood to do?"

"Lie here all day." Grudgingly, Wyatt had accepted the fact that he still needed help with the herd, which meant a few more days of taking it easy. Sam was taking advantage of the chance to enjoy her husband. He rolled over on to his stomach and propped his chin on his hands. "Watch the Olympics."

His gaze fell on her protruding stomach which he'd affectionately dubbed Mount Henry.

A bulge rolled across her belly from one side to the other, making them both chuckle. His large, warm hand rested on her stomach and the movement stilled. In awe, he planted a kiss over her swollen belly button. "Amazing. Takes my breath away every time."

"How about a trip to the orchard? We can pick some apples and pumpkins. Go on a hayride." Samantha set her palm on his and her thumb went round and round. She had to touch him, feel him close to her. In the week since he'd been home, Wyatt had not been out of her sight.

"Only if I get cider and donuts for my efforts." Wyatt inched his way toward her mouth for her customary morning kiss. His left hand skimmed her hip bone, over her belly and onwards to her collarbone, finally threading into her hair. Samantha thought she'd disintegrate.

"That can be managed and I've got some more sweet stuff in mind when we come home." His lips sealed hers as soon as she managed to get the words out. Good thing because she wouldn't be making sense for a while, not when her husband had a way of turning her world upside down.

The day was fine for a trip to Richardson's Orchard, clear and crisp, great puffs of white hanging in a sky so blue Samantha had to blink each time she looked. Holding Wyatt's hand securely in hers, she still had the feeling this was a fairy tale and he'd be gone in a blink.

Her stubborn husband insisted on doing it all. Climbing ladders and sending her heart to her throat. Carrying a sack of apples. Going the distance and walking down a long stretch of trees. Wearing himself out.

When he stumbled for the fourth or fifth time, she set her hand on his arm. "Let me take the apples."

He pulled away from her and gave her dagger eyes. "*You're* carrying enough. I'll be fine. Just give me a minute."

Samantha shook her head and held out his cane. "Stop being an ox. Take this."

Wyatt's jaw set as he stared at it with loathing. He hated being reminded of his limitations and even more so when anyone saw them. Finally, his hand reached out and snagged it. "Going to make me look like an old man."

She grinned and took hold of the collar of Jackson Henry's flannel shirt. "Wyatt Henry, there is nothing old about you."

The bag of apples slid from his fingers and his arm wrapped around her waist. He dropped the cane and pressed his palm to her cheek. His mouth touched down and her husband blotted out the sky. The heat of the sun warmed her back even as the cool breeze of fall brushed against her skin. Samantha didn't feel any of it, not with the bonfire that her husband started deep down in the pit of her stomach.

"We're going to cause a scandal," he whispered hoarsely, setting his forehead on hers.

Samantha licked her lips and struggled to catch her breath, willing her heartbeat to slow. Her hands tightened on his shirt and she gazed up at him. How easy it would be to tumble into those gray-blue eyes. "How about that hay ride?"

Wyatt started to chuckle. "I can think of a lot more to do—in the hay." They set off, taking it slow to avoid any mishaps. The last thing Wyatt wanted was for anyone to see him fall. He set the apples in the truck and they made their way to the pick-up spot for wagon rides.

Ever the gentleman, he offered Samantha a hand and followed, struggling a bit as his leg dragged up the steps. Seeing him wince as Wyatt sat down, she took his hand. "You okay, Wy?"

He tucked her in under his arm. "Never better. I'm with you."

The wagon rolled off with a lurch, carrying them through the fields, up the hill, and overlooking the farm. They could see the point where Henry land merged and the sight of the horses grazing filled Samantha with pride. She rested her palm on her husband's chest and felt his heart pounding.

A glance up and she could see his eyes were wet. His close call made them all appreciate the blessings they had even more. The rest of the ride, not a word was said. Holding hands, breathing the same air, feeling each other's solid presence was enough.

When the wagon came to a stop with a jerk, Samantha didn't even realize they'd stopped. She was too lost in Wyatt's kiss. The driver cleared his throat and they pulled apart, the heat rising in their faces. "Hate to break this up, kids, but I've got my next load of passengers waiting on you, that is unless you want another go around?"

"No, no. Thanks so much, Clyde." Wyatt shook his hand and made his way to solid ground. He planted his cane firmly for support and entwined his fingers with Samantha's to help her down, dipping her and thoroughly kissing her for his encore. The waiting crowd broke into applause and gave them a few whistles. Wyatt turned a brighter shade of red, but hooked an arm around her waist. "You can't blame me, can you, not with a beauty like my wife?"

Samantha swatted at him and they moved out of the way to let the others board, Wyatt giving her a tug toward the field of pumpkins. She gave his hand a squeeze. "Whoa, Wy. Don't you think you've done enough for one day? I hear those donuts and cider calling." Her palm massaged her swollen belly to emphasize the point.

Her husband would hear none of it and kept moving forward, even though his limp was getting heavier as the day wore on. "Gonna do something, got to do it right. That means getting a pumpkin even though they'll think you stole one judging by the size of you."

She stamped her foot in aggravation and caught up with him. "Very funny, Wyatt Henry, just a barrel of laughs. I really don't think you need to be lugging around a pumpkin."

Wyatt pulled up short and rested both hands on his cane, bowing his head as he fought to remain calm. When his gaze finally met hers, his eyes were steady, but a storm was rolling in, blue darkening to gray. "Sam, I appreciate you thinking about me, but I've learned something important. Make the most of every minute. You only get one shot."

With that, he turned and started searching through the pumpkins. Samantha sighed and followed, settling on a round pumpkin that was a glorious shade of orange. "All right, how about this one? It's not too big, not too small. I'd say it's just right."

"Okay, Goldilocks." With his mouth tipped up in a grin and his good nature getting the best of him, Wyatt managed to hoist the pumpkin up in his right arm. He refused to let her carry it. Couldn't blame a girl for trying.

One step away from the truck and his leg gave. Rather than drop the prize pumpkin, he went down on his knees, dropped his cane, and caught himself with his left hand. It trembled, but held. "Wy?" Samantha reached down to take his arm as he remained on the ground, his head hanging low. "*Let me help you!*"

Before she could do anything more, Doc Smith stepped in. "Hand me that pumpkin, young man, and don't argue with your elder. Your daddy raised you better than that." The older gentleman was stern, but his eyes and smile were as warm as always. Wyatt obliged and accepted a hand under his arm to get him back on his feet. "Couldn't help but interfere. Saw the whole thing. Before this wife of yours tried to pick you up like a barbell, I figured it was best if I did something."

"Thanks, Doc," Wyatt murmured. "I would've managed on my own, but I appreciate it."

That got a belly laugh in return. "No, you don't, and I'm sure you would've got where you had to go if it meant crawling all the way home. You're like your father and your brother, as stubborn as they come. You two enjoy the rest of your day and Wyatt," Doc Smith stepped in close and squeezed the nape of his neck. "Stop pushing yourself so hard. You'll get there when you're meant to get there. I'm tired of losing Henrys before their time. Listen to what your body is trying to tell you, all right?" A cheerful whistling accompanied their good friend and neighbor as Doc walked on.

With the pumpkin resting in the bed of the truck, there was nothing left to do but get refreshments. Two, chilled cups of cider and sugar coated donuts smoothed things over, keeping the couple squared away for the ride home. Wyatt took two trips to set the pumpkin on the porch and the apples in the kitchen before he sank down into a chair at the kitchen table, the breath going out of him like a balloon without any hot air.

Samantha set a glass of ice water in front of him and started humming to herself, gathering all of her ingredients for apple pie. It didn't take long and two pies were bubbling away, browning in the oven, filling the kitchen with a scent that was heavenly and homey at the same time.

"Why'd you make two?" Wyatt asked, his chin resting on one hand while she took care of the dishes.

"One for Em, of course. It's his favorite too. You want to come with me when I take it over with some apples?" She glanced over her shoulder and saw his eyes slide shut. "Wy?"

He nearly tipped out of the chair before waking up with a jolt and gave her a crooked smile. "Think I'll go lie down for a while."

Samantha could see that he'd gone white. Wyatt tired easily since his ordeal. She wiped her hands on her towel and moved to his side. "You all right?" If only she had a nickel for every time that question came up. Her fingers stroked his cheek gently and he sighed, closing his eyes in pure pleasure.

"I'm fine. Just running on empty." He stood slowly and she could see that Wyatt had nothing left.

"You rest up. Remember what Doc just told you. Pay attention to what your body has to say." The trip to the orchard took too much out of him. Samantha bit her lip and her eyes burned. "I shouldn't have made you go today."

"You didn't make me do anything. I wanted to go and I had a good time." He pulled her in close and grazed her lips with his. His talented fingers caressed her belly and there was an answering kick that made them laugh. "Don't you overdo it either. Take your time walking to Em's." When Samantha opened her mouth to argue, Wyatt waved her off. "I know you'll walk so there's no sense denying it. Love you."

"I love you too. I won't be long." Samantha waited long enough to see that Wyatt was settled on the couch. She slipped on Jackson's red and black flannel that still smelled of her husband from their day at the orchard. Its warmth reminded her of Wy's arms wrapped around her. That put a smile on her face as she picked up a small bag of apples and carried the pie on an oven mitt. It was the perfect day for walking as the sun slid down lower in the sky and Samantha whistled all the way there. She had to share the song in her heart and its name was gratitude.

When she stepped out of the woods, Emmett was stretched out on the glider on the porch, wearing a matching flannel shirt, covered in a quilt, both passed down from his parents. He looked so peaceful, Samantha didn't want to bother him. As quietly as possible, she tiptoed forward, intent on placing her offerings on the porch.

"I hear you. Who goes there?" Emmett sat up with a cautious smile on his face, but his eyes were wary. She hated to see that uncertainty in a man who had always been so bold.

"It's your favorite sister-in-law. I brought you apples and apple pie." Samantha set her offerings down and gave Emmett a kiss on the cheek, getting a bone crusher of a hug in return. "Easy on Junior! You'll pop him out too early and he's underdone."

Emmett patted the spot next to him. Once she was

settled, he rested his arm on her shoulders. "May I?" He asked shyly, extending his palm toward her belly. She murmured her approval and he set his palm down ever so lightly. It was large and warm, like his brother's. The baby moved in response, giving a good tuck and roll before making Emmett's hand lift with a healthy jab. "I think you've got a boxer in there. Maybe the next Rocky Balboa."

Samantha rubbed at one spot that was sore from her little one's activities and let out a sigh. "It wouldn't surprise me. Girl or boy, this baby has definitely got a lot of get up and go."

She glanced at Emmett and saw his eyes staring out toward the horizon, catching the light of the sunset, gleaming like gold. If only someone had a camera for moments like this. "So, what have you been doing out here?"

He shrugged. "Listening to the wind making the leaves rustle as the trees creak and moan. Getting a taste of fall. Painting pictures in my head of what everything must look like."

Samantha chewed on her lip for a moment and looked at her surroundings with new eyes, as if it was the first time she'd ever seen the Henry land. "The maple, you know that granddaddy of a tree that your great grandparents planted when they married? That maple is so big that it takes up that whole side of your yard and the leaves have turned that deep purplish red color that means they'll fall soon. The birches have burst into shades of yellow. The oak trees are a medley of oranges and reds. The grasses in the field have grown high and turned to gold, waving in the breeze and the pines are standing guard, preparing for winter."

Emmett turned to face her and took her hand. "Thanks for that, Sammie." He took a moment to collect himself. "How about that apple pie? I'd love some. You want a piece with me?"

He stood and helped her to her feet, something that was getting harder every day. Samantha retrieved the pie and apples, setting them on the kitchen counter while Emmett pulled out plates, forks, napkins, and glasses. "You want coffee?"

She shook her head only to become annoyed with herself. He couldn't see her. "No thank you. Junior really starts going crazy in there if I drink coffee. I need a little something in the morning. It's mostly milk and sugar with a swallow of caffeine and that's all I can handle."

Emmett slid the plates her way and Samantha dished out two generous slices of pie. He took them from her and set them on the table. It was a marvel to watch him as he took out the milk, poured, and pulled out a chair for her, waiting expectantly. His house had become so ingrained on his brain, no one would even suspect he was blind.

They ate together, catching up on tidbits. As soon as her plate was empty, Emmett was whisking everything away like a waiter. "How's Wyatt doing?" He asked as the sink filled with soapy water and his hands scrubbed with a fury.

"Chomping at the bit to work with the horses. He overdid it at the apple orchard today. Wy's resting or he'd be here now too." Samantha grabbed a towel and began to dry, returning everything to its proper spot. Order was essential in this house to help Emmett navigate the world he lived in and keep him sane.

Once the kitchen was squared away, Emmett stood still with his hip propped against the counter. He flipped his hair away from his face and threaded his fingers through dark, wavy strands that were getting long. Samantha reached up to push his bangs back. "You really need a haircut. You want me to give you one?"

Emmett laughed bitterly. "I was just looking in the mirror the other day and I noticed that!" When Samantha only met his response with silence, his smile faded. "Sorry. I'd like that, Sammie."

He sat down at the table while she found the scissors, filled a glass with water, and wrapped a kitchen towel around his neck. Samantha combed his hair first, dipping the comb in the water. She began to work her way through, gently getting rid of any knots. As her hands snipped away busily, a humming rose up and Emmett's head drooped. He was sound asleep.

It squeezed her heart watching him, reminding her of his younger years. Samantha finished his haircut and swept up the trimmings, still humming. "Mama?" A small voice made her stop. It was the voice of a child, robbed of his mother much too young.

"It's just me, Em. You fell asleep during your haircut. How does it feel?"

He came up in a rush and ran his hands through his hair. Emmett grinned and caught her hand. "Thanks. Feels great—sorry about that. I was dreaming. Mama used to cut our hair, Dad's too." Emmett grew still, his thumb circling round and round. "Come to think of it, you remind me of her, Sam. Could be the reason Wy's always been crazy about you."

Samantha stepped in and kissed him on the top of the head. "I take that as a compliment. I've seen the pictures. Your mother was a beautiful woman."

Emmett gave her a heartbreaking smile. "So are you."

He walked her to the porch and stood with his hand raised until her footsteps were muffled in the woods. Samantha started singing softly to herself, "I go out walking, after midnight, out in the moonlight…" Her words trailed off and silence reigned. The horses were in the barn, the moon was a great ball of white light in the sky, and her husband was standing on the porch. Waiting. Smiling. Intensely focused on one thing. Her.

Samantha hurried up the steps to join him and he kissed her before looping his hands around her shoulders.

"Em all right?" She nodded. "You all right?" Another nod. "Well so am I. Guess I'd better shut up."

They stared out at the night sky and a burst of light streaked across the darkness, making her gasp. "What did you wish for?" Samantha asked.

"That our little one will grow up knowing his mama. That I'll sit here by your side when that beautiful hair of yours has gone silver, holding your hand in our rocking chairs until we're both old and feeble. Something Mama and Dad didn't get to do." For an instant, it was as if their ghosts were called up at his words.

Samantha turned to tip her head to Wyatt's, her heart full. "I wished that the baby will know you." She rose up and sealed her hopes and dreams with a kiss. Her stomach gave a grumble at that inconvenient time, setting her to giggling. "I guess that's it. Feeding time."

Wyatt took her hand and led her inside. There was apple pie and ice cream on the table with cups of cold milk, a lit candle, and a bunch of wild flowers in a vase. "What's this?" She asked incredulously.

"Dinner. Thought I'd spoil you, make your life easier." He pulled out her chair and sat down beside her once she was pushed in. The first bite and his eyes closed in ecstasy. "You should go into business, woman."

When the last crumb was gone, the spoons licked clean, and the dishes in the sink, Wyatt took hold of her chair and pulled it closer until they were knee to knee. "Honestly. I wasn't really hungry. I woke up and all I could think about was you." He picked her up and slid her onto his lap, his hand cupping the back of her head, his lips finding hers.

Samantha let loose a breath she'd been holding and threaded her fingers through his hair. "Are you sure about this, Wy? What if it happens to you again? I'm scared."

Wyatt bowed his head to hers and pinned her with his dark, steady gaze. "I'm scared too, but we can't live that way, Sammie, or we won't be living at all. All I know is it's been over two months since we made love. If it's safe for you, I'd like to try. I'll give it my best shot."

Samantha's smile trembled, but it held. "That's the only thing you know how to do. You're a Henry."

She stood and took his hand. They walked slowly up the stairs, Wyatt with one arm around her, one on the railing. When his leg didn't want to cooperate and his arm became heavy, Samantha was strong enough to help him. They took each other's clothing off, ever so gently, as if they could shatter at a touch. Both knew how fleeting this wonderful, terrible thing called life could be.

Wyatt laid down on the bed and brought her with him. He stroked her skin tenderly and Samantha returned the favor. So gentle. So easy. So soft. As if they might break.

When it was over, her head was in the crook of his arm and his hand massaged her belly round and round. Wyatt whispered. "This—this is all I could ever want or need, all I could hope for. I prayed every day in that hospital that the good Lord would give me one more chance to spend the rest of my life with you."

"Let's never waste another minute, Wyatt. I love you." Samantha buried her face in his chest and they both slipped off into sleep. Neither cared if they ever moved again.

CHAPTER 13

*D*ad! God, help me! Emmett, come quick!"
Wyatt ran like he'd never run before, not in a hundred baseball games or track meets, sprinting across the field, a field that seemed to stretch out longer the farther he ran. Emmett, out mending fences, somehow heard his shout. For a split second, his brother froze in horror at the sight of the behemoth tractor and their father pinned beneath it, then his feet kicked into motion.

Hell-bent and charging like an infuriated bull, the brothers arrived at the same time. In unison, they both squatted and took hold of the tractor, fighting a losing battle to lift something that weighed well over a ton. Wyatt pulled, pulled until his muscles stretched past the limit of endurance, until they started to tear, and still he pulled some more. Emmett, his face on fire and tears running down, bellowed in pain and frustration. All the while, Jackson Henry struggled to breathe, going whiter by the second.

"Boys—" The word came out in a tortured gasp, but they heard him, and dropped to the ground, each taking a hand, marveling at the strength of their father's grip. He was pinned at the waist and the John Deere was slowly crushing the life out of him. "Boys—enough—enough. You can't—can't—do—anything—more. God, I—love— the both—of you—Just—just stay—stay—with— me."

They stayed. Until he took his last breath. Until his fingers uncurled and went limp. Until the light was snuffed out of his eyes.

Emmett waited by their father's side because it was the only right thing to do while Wyatt made the longest journey of his life back to the house to call an ambulance and neighbors to lift the tractor. He returned with a shovel, digging their father out, joining his brother's vigil over Jackson Henry's body. The two remained as the paramedics loaded him into the back of the ambulance and drove away.

Only then did they move, holding on to each other, stumbling toward the house. Emmett's legs gave halfway there and a mournful howl rose up, the saddest sound a man could make. Wyatt hit his knees beside him and bowed his head. It was the first time in his life that he didn't know how to pray.

⌘⌘⌘

Wyatt came up quick with a gasp, his face wet and his head throbbing, but not nearly as much as his heart. The day his father left this earth was one of the darkest of his life. He wished it did not stay with him with such clarity. He kicked his feet over the side of the glider on the porch and threaded his fingers through his hair.

Slowly, the dream let go of him, making it possible to breathe again. Wyatt stood up slowly and his leg almost buckled. He bent at the waist and pressed his hands to his knees, waiting to find his balance. Samantha had gone to town while he finished up the morning chores with the herd. He'd been standing at the fence, enjoying the sight of the fine animals when a wave of exhaustion rolled in and nearly flattened him.

Strange how it could just hit him like that. One moment, he was teasing his wife, giving her a kiss, thinking about holding her in his arms, and the next it was near impossible to get to the house. His leg started to drag again, it was so heavy, a sure sign of overdoing it. Leaning on his cane for all he was worth, Wyatt managed to make it to the glider. His head was pounding and his left arm wasn't cooperating. Finally, he flung it over his eyes, terrified that something might be happening to him again. Waiting for his brain to erupt, he faded into sleep only to be trapped in his unbearable nightmare. Bad enough that tragedy happened, but to be forced to relive it?

Wyatt's leg finally held, and he grabbed his cane. His feet moved forward with a will of their own, propelling him off the porch. '*Now, don't you overdo it. You've got to…*' Samantha's admonishment echoed in his mind as he stumbled through the woods and nearly went flat on his face when his left foot caught on a root.

He stopped, breathing hard, focusing on his conversation with his wife to steady himself, find a slip of peace…

೧೯೧

"Listen to my body. I know. What if my body wants yours?"

Samantha turned so that he could get a good look at her profile. "There's definitely enough of me to go around. You really think I'm sexy?"

He took her in his arms, cursing when the left started to drop, but she set it back in place. "Sexiest woman I've ever seen, more beautiful now than ever before. You're ripe and glowing. Your eyes have got this sparkle about them and your hair…"His fingers trailed through the heavy strands. "It's like gold." She tipped her head back and revealed the pale, soft skin under her chin, the pulse at the base of her neck beating wildly. Wyatt set his mouth on that sweet spot and his head started to spin.

೧೯೧

What he wouldn't give to let her hold him, make this pain go away, but there was only one other person who could understand what Wyatt was going through right now, who had any chance of filling the hole in his heart that had just been ripped wide open. He pushed on, fighting his way through the woods, up the steps, to his brother's door. *My father's house.* No matter how much time passed, this would always be Jackson Henry's house.

Wyatt latched on to the doorknob and started pounding for all he was worth, falling in when Emmett opened the door. His brother caught him and helped him to the couch. "Wy, what's wrong? You're scaring me. How did you get here? I didn't hear the truck."

"Walked, dragged, and limped the whole, pitiful way." Wyatt's voice broke, and it spilled out. All of it. The nightmare, one they both bore witness to, a part of their shared history. No one knew this pain except Emmett. Others could imagine and sympathize. Only his little brother had lived it and walked in his shoes.

"He taught us to make mountains into molehills—but we couldn't move that mountain, Em, no matter how hard we tried. We couldn't do it!"

As the last of the words ran out, Wyatt started to cry uncontrollably and Emmett held on. *Just—stay—with—me, boys.* The Henry brothers had done so. For their father and for each other.

Emmett was still holding on when Samantha burst through the door, shouting, "Emmett, have you seen Wyatt?"

Rapid footsteps pounded through the house and she hit the living room, one hand on her baby belly, eyes wide with fright.

She came to a sudden stop at the sight of them and retreated to the kitchen. The scent of coffee drifted their way shortly after, along with soft music, something soothing.

Wyatt cleared his throat and sat up straight, scraping an arm across his face. "I'm sorry, Em. I know you've got enough on your plate. I didn't mean to unload on you."

Emmett grabbed his arm. "Don't you ever apologize because you need to talk, especially about Dad. I'm always here for you, Wy." His fierce expression fooled Wyatt for an instant. It was still hard to believe that his brother couldn't see out of those flaming eyes.

The two stood and traveled the short distance to the kitchen. Samantha slid out of her chair and went to Wyatt, resting her hand on his cheek. "You're all right?" She looked intently from one to the other.

Wyatt nodded and gathered her in his arms. "I just dreamt about Dad, what happened that day." His throat started to choke up and he pushed the anguish back. "A talk with Em helped."

She nodded and pulled away. "Okay. Why don't you two sit down and have some coffee? I'll whip up a snack or something."

As both sat before steaming cups, Wyatt snagged Samantha around the waist and settled her on his lap. "Forget about cooking. Why don't we all go to Sonny's?"

Emmett set down his cup of coffee and crossed his arms. "You two go ahead. I'm staying put."

Wyatt leaned forward and gripped his brother's arm. Ever since Emmett's sight had been taken from him, touching him was more important than ever. Human contact could deliver a message that the eyes could not. "We all need a night off from our worries, just a night off. Sammie, me, you. Come on, Em. You haven't gone out with us since this happened."

Emmett pulled away, kicking back his chair and backing into the stove, making it rattle. "No. Not gonna happen. You kids have fun."

Wyatt came after him and grabbed him by his shirt collar, giving it a little shake. "You listen, and you listen well. If I can go with this cane, then you can go with yours. It's time you started living again."

Emmett's head bowed and his hands settled on his hips. The clock ticked on the wall, the only sound, while all three waited in silence. Finally, Em lifted his chin. "All right." Resolved, he set off for the door. "I'll go, but that doesn't mean I have to like it."

"That's the attitude," Wyatt joked, offering Samantha his hand.

They joined Emmett and walked out to the truck, piling in, and taking a fifteen minute drive that seemed twice as long as their reluctant passenger remained rigid and tight-lipped the entire way. He didn't loosen up until they stepped inside Sonny's Side Up where they were surrounded by delicious smells, the noise of a busy diner, and shouts of greeting.

Townspeople stepped up left and right, offering all three hugs, giving the Henry brothers a pounding on the back, offering to buy them dinner. "Are my eyes fooling me or is that really the Henry boys and the lovely Samantha?" A large man with a gleaming, bald head stepped out from the kitchen, his face lit up with a smile, his deep brown eyes filled with warmth. He proceeded to give each a hug that nearly suffocated them. "Oh, this is a wonderful day! We have missed you terribly. Go sit and I'll take care of you myself." Sonny, the owner, had a big heart and a generous spirt that he willingly shared with his town. The Henrys could expect nothing else.

Wyatt gave a little bow and Samantha led the way, Emmett following the sound of her footsteps, Wy bringing up the rear. Thankfully, his nap and rest at his brother's house made it possible to get to the table without mishap. They all settled, Emmett letting out a long sigh. He looked like the firing squad might shoot at any instant.

"What can I get you, boys? Whatever it is, it's on the house. This is an occasion indeed when some of my most beloved customers are well enough to join me again. As for you, Miss Samantha—" Sonny beamed at her and kissed her hand. "—lovely, absolutely lovely. I cannot wait to meet the little one on the way. What can I get you? If you do not choose, I will simply bring you one of everything on the menu."

That had everyone laughing and, just like that, it was like old times. Ordering three of the house special, a meatball parmigiana sub that was out of this world, the three ate, talked, and laughed until their sides hurt. The owner sat with them for a while and caught up on the latest, sharing doings in town.

When they left with a huge sack of food and an entire chocolate cream pie to tide them over, Wyatt felt truly relaxed for the first time that day. As he settled into the front seat, Emmett went loose beside him. "That felt good. Nerve-wracking, but good."

"See? I'm your big brother, and I know what's best for you. Besides, you can't run from your troubles, Em. They'll always catch up to you."

They were quiet on the ride back to Emmett's, everyone in a contemplative mood.

Emmett said good night at the truck and made the trek to the house with his cane. He turned and raised a hand in a wave as they prepared to leave. "Thanks for getting me out of my comfort zone. Have a good night. Love you guys."

Samantha waited until he was in the house before turning the truck around and heading home. As they pulled in, she cut the engine and set her hand on Wyatt's knee. "Remember you can come to me for help any time, Wy."

He gave her a slip of a grin. "Okay. How about now? Want to help me get everyone in their stalls? I can do the rest."

With no arguments, she followed him out to the pasture, shaking a small bucket of oats. It was a signal the herd had learned well and most ambled to the barn for dinner. A few lingered but Wyatt patiently got them situated. He was in no hurry with his girl waiting on him and his nightmare held at bay.

Samantha was sitting on a hay bale when he closed the last stall. He turned and gave into the hold she had on him, deep down in his gut, drawing him closer, even as his leg started to fight him again. She stood and spared him any more steps. "Let's go, gimp. I think you need a hot bath, a massage, and a good night's sleep—in that order."

Wyatt leaned his forehead on hers and smiled. "Okay, wise woman. I'll do it if you will too."

Her laughter followed them all the way into the house.

He had to sit while she drew a bath. His body wouldn't let him do otherwise. The first week of taking care of the horses was wearing on him. Wyatt rested his hands on his knees and waited, enjoying the view as his wife sat on the side of the tub, a sight for sore eyes. When she turned his way, he stood slowly and his hands came up to undo her blouse.

She took hold of his wrists. "This is for you. You need it more than I do."

Wyatt shook his head and kissed her tenderly. "You're tired too. You work hard, too hard to keep this place together, to keep me together, especially since this happened." His hands became clumsy with his weariness. Samantha helped him to finish the job, shedding his clothes as well in a puddle at their feet. He insisted she step in and get settled first then eased himself into the warm suds. "Heaven. This is heaven."

She leaned against his chest and Wyatt let his head fall back. He closed his eyes and neither moved or made a sound, enjoying the simple pleasure of a warm bath and each other's touch.

Nothing was pressing on them, no obligations that had to be met. They were given the brief gift of a quiet evening together.

"Wy?" Samantha's voice drifted over him, snapping his head up before sleep won. He stroked her hair with one hand, his other resting on her belly. *Their child.* The realization never ceased to amaze him. "Wyatt, are you awake?"

"Barely." He couldn't help but smile as he watched her skin turn pink from the heat and her hair started to curl. Kissing the top of her head, he received a smile in return. Samantha set her hands on his as if she held a treasure. "What do you want to talk about?"

She hesitated a moment, thinking things through, only to plow ahead. "Tell me something good you remember about Dad."

He kissed her again and let out a long sigh. Sammie understood him so well. She always knew what he needed and right now Wyatt needed a distraction from his final memories of his father, those that overshadowed the hundreds of happy ones that were strung together over the years.

Samantha squeezed his hand, prompting him to speak. "Something good? Where do I begin? I knew from the start that I'd been blessed with the best for a father. I can still remember the first time he put me up on his horse, Ricky Ricardo, and I learned how to ride. Then there was the time a bad storm hit and he came in to build a blanket fort with us. We camped out in the living room, told ghost stories, and roasted hot dogs over the fire. Marshmallows too, I almost forgot the marshmallows." Wyatt started to chuckle, picturing that night. "That was one of the most favorite nights of my life." He grew quiet, immersed in the past, and his voice dropped down low. "I remember Mama cooking us breakfast while Em and I waited and Dad came in to steal her bacon. She gave him a swat with her spatula and the next thing you know, he had Mama bowed back all the way to the floor, kissing her senseless. She was worried that we were watching. Daddy said we lived on a horse farm. We'd have to learn some time."

His words ran out, a flood of emotions rising up and threatening to carry him away. Samantha picked up where he'd left off. "What about that time senior year when we were making out in the hay in the barn? Dad took us by surprise, coming out to the barn for something, and I'll never forget that grin or what he said. 'If you kids are going to carry on like rabbits, I hope you're ready for the consequences.'"

That had Wyatt choking with laughter, on a teeter totter that went from extreme sadness to overwhelming joy. "You skedaddled your way home pretty fast if I recall correctly. Would've given a jack rabbit competition. It's not like we would have done anything, not really."

Samantha sat up and turned to face him, taking his chin in her hand, meeting him with a level stare. "You bet your boots we would've done something, and knowing the way things work, we'd have learned our lesson the hard way. That was one of the things I loved most about your father. He steered us in the right direction but always left the decision up to us." Her mouth took a downward turn and her lip began to tremble. "I really miss him, Wy."

Wyatt nodded and somehow found the words that had to be said as he pressed her palm to his chest, right over the steady beating of his heart. "Me too, but he's here." Her hand shifted to rest on his temple. "And here." Finally, he cupped her bulging stomach with his hands and bowed his head as if in benediction. "And we both know that Jackson Henry's legacy will be carried on by the incredible person who is taking shape inside of you. God, but he'd be thrilled to pieces about his grandbaby, Sammie."

Samantha looked up and took his face in her hands so that she could graze his mouth with a kiss, one tear slipping down. "I'm sure he is thrilled, Wyatt, and he's watching over us every minute of every day until we are all together again."

He wrapped her in his arms and tucked his wife under his chin. In the dim light of their bathroom in the house that had been home to his grandparents and his father, a young mother and father looked to the future generation that would carry on the Henry tradition.

CHAPTER 14

Wyatt, I want to start on the nursery."

They were sprawled out on the couch, enjoying the cheerful crackle and warmth of the fireplace on an especially bitter day in early November. Wyatt had come in with his face wind-burnt, his leg arguing from the cold and that's when Samantha took charge, ordering him to the living room.

He played with a strand of her hair, wrapping it around his finger, a smile tugging at the corners of his mouth. "I can't believe how thick your hair has grown and how much it shines. You have never been more beautiful. How about I keep you pregnant all the time?"

She swatted his leg in answer. "You dare to ask me that when I feel like a beached whale—and two more months to go yet?" Samantha blew her bangs out of her face and rested her hands on her stomach. "I can't even see my toes anymore, but that's not what I wanted to talk about. Did you hear what I said about the nursery?"

Wyatt leaned over to kiss her on the side of her neck, setting her body to trembling and her heart to pounding. How did he still have such power over her? She was beginning to forget the question herself. "What was that…something about the nursery? If that's your definition of taking it easy, I had better get back out to the barn."

Inexplicably, her eyes started to sting. Her emotions were up and down like a yo-yo, running the gamut on a daily basis. "Wy, I didn't mean right now. I just want to start thinking about it. January isn't that far off, and if you think I'm going to put the baby in a dresser drawer until we pull something together—" She choked on her words, a sobbing rant on the way, and swallowed hard as the tears trickled down her cheeks.

Wyatt set his hands on her shoulders. "Hey, hey now. I was just teasing you, and you're right. Let's go upstairs and take a look at the room to get some ideas about what you want to do with it."

Samantha stood up on shaky feet and helped him up, relieved when she saw him steady himself without his cane. He slung an arm around her shoulders and they took the stairs together, down the hallway, to the room across from theirs. It had once belonged to Wyatt's father. Fitting that his grandchild would claim it next.

Wyatt hit the light switch and they gazed at a space that had been relatively untouched for years. Childhood mementos, trophies, and pictures still decorated the shelves and dresser. One caught Samantha's attention in particular. She crossed the room to pick up a photograph of Jackson Henry when he couldn't be much more than twenty, dressed in a plaid button down and jeans. Beside him was a beautiful, blonde girl who only had big blue eyes for him, dressed for a party in a dress covered in pink rosebuds. He looked at her like she hung the moon. Inhaling sharply with a catch, Samantha glanced over her shoulder at her husband, propped against the door jamb. She'd seen Wyatt look at her the same way many times. Loving so completely appeared to be a Henry trait.

"Your mother was so lovely, Wy." She ran her finger over the picture. Staring into the familiar face of her father-in-law, she felt a longing that was so strong it was physical. If only he was still with them.

"You remind me of her." Wyatt joined her and tucked her in his arms. They stood quietly for a moment before sitting side by side on the twin bed against the wall, holding hands as they so often did. "So, I'll clear all this out, pack up all of Dad's things, and then we can paint, put up wallpaper, whatever you want. As for furniture, you've got a few options. We can buy new or I can bring down the set in the attic, the one that my grandfather built that was used for my brother and me."

Samantha squeezed his hand tightly. "Oh, I want to

use yours, of course! How perfect! A piece of Henry history!"

Wyatt stood and motioned to different parts of the room. "We could put the crib there and the charging table over there. The dresser could go against that wall. There's a bassinet that can go by our bed in the beginning, and you can't forget the rocking chair! That can go in that corner. Let me show you, Sammie! You're going to love all of it!"

Caught up in his excitement, Samantha followed him up the attic steps. Wyatt hit the light switch, illuminating their path. It was hard to stay focused with so many great finds scattered along the way. She'd have to come back up here another day for a treasure hunt. Somehow, forays into the top floor hadn't happened in all the years they'd been married. Wyatt would store the Christmas decorations, insisting on doing all of the grunt work himself.

At the far end of the attic, there was an assorted collection covered under white sheets, looking like bulky ghosts had taken up residence. Wyatt whipped the bedding off with a flourish, revealing lovely pieces in black cherry, each an example of fine craftsmanship, furniture that would withstand the test of time for generations to come. Samantha ran her finger along the railing of the crib and the tears were back, this time as a sign of happiness too strong to hold inside her very full heart. "Oh, Wy! These are incredible! I'd no idea Grandpa Henry could do such works of art."

Wyatt joined her and his hands gripped the foot of the crib, his knuckles going white he was holding on so tight. He bowed his head as his jaw tightened. "I still remember how excited Mama was when she knew a new baby was on the way. She made Daddy drag everything down from our attic to set the room up early. Everything was…pretty, so pretty. Mama was sure it would be a girl."

His mouth clamped shut, unable or unwilling to say anything more. Samantha set her hand on his. "What are you talking about? I didn't know your mother was expecting. What happened?"

One look at the shadows forming dark clouds in his gaze, and she could have bit her tongue. An aneurysm. That's what happened.

Wyatt moved away from the crib and sat in the rocker, resting his palms on his knees. He spoke so quietly she had to strain to hear him. "We think she was about three months along, happy enough she could burst, and Daddy—Dad was just as excited. It rubbed off on Em and me. We helped every way we could—until the day our world ended. Dad was really upset. We stayed here for a few weeks after until he could face going home. When we did, the baby furniture was gone and the nursery was a spare room again. Grandpa and my uncles brought everything here. It was too much for Dad to bear."

Samantha knelt down beside Wyatt, a difficult feat, and rested her hands on his. "If it's too much for you, we don't have to use it. We can go shopping. I don't mind, really."

He scraped a hand across his face and pressed a kiss to her forehead. "No, I think it's time this baby furniture had a Henry baby in it again." Wyatt stood and drew her up with him. He gazed down at her and a tremulous smile began to grow. "I just can't stand the wait, Sammie. I want to meet him and hold him in my arms, teach him everything I know. Find out if he looks like you or has some of Dad and Mama in him."

Samantha stood on tiptoe and planted a kiss on his lips. "It could be a girl, Wy. What will you do then?" Her stomach gave a sharp twist. What if he had his heart set on a boy?

Wyatt sank down on his knees and laid both hands on her stomach. "Then I will cherish her as much as her mother and watch her grow into a beautiful blossom that will give me more happiness than any man could possibly deserve in a lifetime."

He leaned forward and kissed her bulging belly button.

Samantha slowly lowered herself down so that she could look in his eyes. "You deserve to be happy, Wy. You've had enough sad."

A flood of tears was on the way. He cradled her in his arms and joined her.

e∕ɔe∕ɔ

"That looks perfect. Right there. Don't change a thing," Emmett said.

He stood in the center of the room with a great big grin, full of mischief. He'd been recruited to help with the heavy work, bringing the old furniture up to the attic, carrying the baby furniture down. With guidance and patience, plus a dash of pure stubbornness, he could manage.

Wyatt, his hands on his knees to catch his breath, managed to nudge his brother with his shoulder. "All right, that's enough, wise guy. We've got to wait for Sam. She'll tell us where to put everything."

"Right. She's the boss when it comes to baby stuff. I'm really glad you're turning this mausoleum into the little tyke's room. Where is Sammie anyway?" Emmett reached out and found the rocking chair. He sat down and set it in motion.

Wyatt had to laugh. His brother looked like a kid! "She's staying out of our way until we're ready for her."

As if on cue, Samantha walked in at that moment, huffing and puffing. She waddled more by the hour. Her cheeks were flushed and she waved a towel at her face. "Lord, is it hot in here? I feel like I'm having a hot flash. Between that and taking my hundredth trip to the bathroom, I've about had enough of this." She rubbed at her side. "Oof. Junior has been sitting on my bladder all morning, kicking me in the kidneys."

Emmett stood up and bowed with a flourish. "My lady, your chariot awaits." He offered his hand and she accepted. "Really, Sammie. Sit down and take a load off." His palm brushed over her stomach and his eyebrows sprang up. "Whoah! It feels like you've got a basketball in there."

Samantha leaned back and closed her eyes. "I *feel* like there's a basketball in here. Do me a favor, boys. Get it out."

"Sorry. No can do. The little tyke needs to cook a while longer yet." Wyatt stepped up beside her and began to knead at her neck, shoulders, and back. Carrying that extra weight all the time was making her sore everywhere and tired. Lord, she'd never been so tired in all her life. Samantha could sleep for a week. "Tell us where you want things and then you can go lie down for a nap."

Samantha found his hand and entwined her fingers with his. "Oh, you don't know how good that sounds. I think I'll take you up on the offer. The past few days of painting has really got me whooped." A sigh rose up and almost carried her off to sleep.

With a little shake, Samantha stood up and glanced around the room. It was a cheerful yellow that brought in a touch of the sun. Wyatt had done the hardest part when it came to painting, down on his hands and knees to do the molding around the floor, up and down with great strokes for the two coats it took to cover the old white, climbing up on the ladder to do the trim work at the top. Samantha had used her creative abilities to paint murals that included Pooh Bear, Piglet, Tigger, and Eeyore. It was a very cheerful place. One where a child would grow and bloom. Happiness lived here.

"How about the crib over there? You can set the changing table and dresser over there. Don't forget your grandmother's cedar chest. That would look really nice under the window and could be another place to sit once I put a cushion on it." Samantha glanced from brother to brother and saw them roll their eyes.

"Another trip up those stairs? What are you trying to do to us, Sam?" Emmett propped himself against the wall and crossed his arms, positively glowering.

"Fine! I'll do it myself!" She heaved herself out of the chair and took a step toward the door.

Emmett was faster, blocking her way and setting his hands on her arms after a few fumbles. "Don't be crazy! I'm just kidding. Go lie down, and you can come back to see it when it's done. Doc's orders." Emmett leaned forward and dropped a kiss on the top of her head. Taking a step behind her, he pressed Samantha gently in the small of her back. "Let's go. Into bed, now. The baby needs rest. All the books say so."

She didn't have it in her to argue. Her pillow was calling her name. She slid under delightfully cool sheets, laid down her head, and was out almost the second her eyes closed.

"Sammie? Hey Sammie! Wake up, sweetie." Wyatt was shaking her gently, sitting on the edge of the bed.

Samantha peeked one eye open a slit and saw that it was dark outside. She sat up in a rush. "Oh my goodness! I slept the whole day away! I'm so sorry, Wy. You and Emmett must be starving."

Wyatt gave her the grin she loved so well and dropped a kiss on her nose. "We're not cavemen, Sam. We managed to get something to keep us squared away. Come see the nursery!" His excitement was contagious.

Samantha nodded and stood up next to him, groaning as she did. "Hold on. Bathroom first. I don't know how I could possibly have to go again."

She went as quickly as possible, trying to ignore the fact that her stomach was the size of an ample watermelon. No cute, little baby belly for this girl, no sirree. Wyatt was waiting when she walked out. He took her hand and led her down the hall, stopping outside the door to whip a bandanna out of his pocket. "Hold up. Close your eyes."

He tied the strip of cloth around her head and wrapped an arm around her shoulders.

"Okay?" she asked.

His answer was to take a few steps forward. "All right. What do you think?" Wyatt slipped the bandanna down and stepped back, wearing the biggest smile she'd seen in quite a while. Emmett waited beside the crib, pointing to it like a salesman.

Samantha's jaw dropped as she slowly turned in a circle. Not only was everything in place, Wyatt had hung the mobile of clouds, sun, and airplanes over the crib.

The bedding was in the crib with a large, dark brown teddy bear wearing a big, red bow sitting on top. He wore a tag in Emmett's untidy scrawl, that read, *"To My Nephew or Niece, Baby Henry—Love, Your Uncle Em."* A lamp with Winnie the Pooh sat on the dresser and basic baby supplies were lined up on the changing table. A colorful, braided rug that matched the room's fresh paint, sat on the floor. The rocker even had new cushions while another transformed the cedar chest into an inviting seat. Cheerful, checkered curtains hung at the windows, adding to the bright atmosphere.

"Oh—oh my. You boys have been busy. Thank you, fellas. Thank you so much." She gave both a hug and a kiss, her heart light. The baby's room was ready. Taking their hands, she gave a gentle tug. "Let's go downstairs, and I'll make you dinner."

There were no protests there. They journeyed to the first floor together, into the kitchen, and Samantha almost started to cry. The table was set and the dishes were already filled with steaming stew. Emmett gave her a clumsy kiss on the side of the head. "We figured it was the cook's night off. I made the stew and Wyatt made the bread. I didn't know he could make bread."

Wyatt shrugged and pulled out a chair for Samantha. "I don't like to let on about my culinary skills, you know. I don't want Sammie to feel like I'm taking over her territory."

The brothers sat down and everyone linked hands.

Samantha was grateful. She needed to give thanks while it was fresh in her mind. "Dear Lord, thank you for the food at this table, for the amazing men in my life, our beautiful nursery, and this life blooming inside of me. My cup runneth over."

Wyatt poured drinks, and they all clinked glasses. "I'd say it's overflowing for all of us."

They shared a meal and talked well into the night about baby names, if it would be a boy or a girl, and when the tot would arrive. When Emmett started to fall asleep at the table, Wyatt steered him to the spare room where they used to sleep as kids.

Samantha was waiting up for her husband, propped against the pillows, when he came into bed. She took her fill of watching him as he unbuttoned his flannel and set in on a chair, slipped out of his jeans, and pulled on pajama bottoms, not even bothering to change his white undershirt.

He was too tired for that.

"Hey," she called out softly.

He turned the lights off and crossed the room, sliding into bed next to her. The moonlight cast him in a silver glow, his eyes a glistening gray that drew her into his arms. Wyatt kissed her, his rough palm grazing her cheek. "Hey, yourself."

They snuggled under the covers, Samantha tucked against his side, as close as the baby belly would allow her to be, while Wyatt stroked her hair, making the knots in her body come undone. When he wasn't turning her on, her husband had such a soothing effect on her.

"Thanks for all you did today."

"No thanks are needed. It's my baby too, right? I'm glad Em decided to stay. I'd feel better if he'd stay all the time." Wyatt's hand stilled and he let out a long, slow breath, as if he'd been holding it.

Samantha rested her palm on his heart and felt the steady rhythm of its beating. She used it to center herself. "You can't keep him in a bubble, and you can't watch him all the time."

"I know. I just wish I could keep an eye out, you know, just in case he ran into trouble. Winter's coming. I don't know how he'll make out then."

She heard the fear and uncertainty in his voice. It was her turn to give comfort. Samantha rolled over and began to run her fingers through Wyatt's hair. "We'll check in on him all the time and make regular pests of ourselves, okay? If it's really bad, I'll insist he stays. Emmett can never tell me no."

Wyatt smiled and gently kissed her. "I can never tell you no. Love you."

"Love you more."

The words seemed to float out and hung on the air for an instant as Samantha closed her eyes. When she opened them, the sunlight was peeking in and a mum from her garden was on her bed stand. She couldn't help but smile even as annoyance poked at her. The blasted man had let her sleep in again. He'd managed to leave her tea and toast too. It was still hot.

∼∻∼

"Well, Samantha, my girl, you're coming along just fine." Doc Smith patted her knee and turned around while she got off the table and slipped into her clothes.

It was a glorious day in November, the sun casting the room in a warm glow as the last of the fall leaves floated down outside the examining room window. Samantha stared out at the fields and rolling hills in the distance and had the sudden impulse to go for a walk, taking in all that nature held for her, to keep going until she reached the horizon. The baby gave her a hearty jab that snatched her breath away and she held on to her stomach with two hands. She wouldn't be getting far in this state. "Are you sure, Doc? I feel like an elephant—or a Volkswagen bus. I'm not sure which."

He turned to face her, his green eyes sparkling and his lively grin giving a boost to her spirits. "Now, now. You're not even close to the size of a Beetle, much less a bus." The doctor took her by the arm and led her to the door. "Why don't you send that brother-in-law in here next? Hopefully, he's not scaring off any patients with that scowl of his. I don't blame him for glowering, but it could ruin my reputation." He gave her a wink and sent her into the waiting room.

Emmett sat with his arms crossed, eyes trained on the wall straight ahead. The sun was shining full on his face, making his eyes gleam brightly, turning them to a golden honey. Samantha couldn't breathe staring at them, seeing how beautiful they were, and stood with her hand gripping a chair.

Sensing something, he stood slowly and turned toward the direction of her first footsteps. "Everything okay, Sam?" A crease formed between his eyes, prompting her to move.

She crossed the room and took his hand. "Fine. Everything's more than fine. Doc Smith wants to see you."

A groan rose up, but Emmett allowed her to lead him to the examining room. Fortunately, no other patients were around on a day that was quiet for a change. Samantha stepped back as Em shut the door to leave him some privacy. A half hour later, it opened again, Doc Smith guiding her brother-in-law to her side.

The kindly, elderly man met Samantha's questioning gaze and gave a shake of his head. He ran a hand through the wispy strands of his snowy hair, making it stand on end. "I'm sorry, Em. Every time you come in or I drop by to check in on you, I hope to give you some good news— and every time it's no change."

Emmett caught the doctor's arm and gave it a good squeeze, pulling out a smile. Samantha often wondered how he found the strength. She would've run out of smiles when the lights went out. "I'd rather no change than for it to get worse. At least there's no sign of an aneurysm, right? Should I go in for X-rays just to be safe?"

Doc Smith shook his head. "Not unless you have symptoms. I think you've had enough poking and prodding for one lifetime. I still can't believe it happened to Wyatt. You're sure he's all right?" At their reassurances, he closed his eyes in gratitude. "Thank the Lord I never will get over what happened to your mother." The doctor gave Samantha a pat on the back. "I can't wait to deliver your baby. It's high time we bring another Henry into this world."

The doctor insisted on walking them onto the front porch. As he approached the steps, his breathing became labored, and he grimaced in pain. His hand caught the railing while Samantha took his arm.

"Doc Smith, what's wrong?" she asked.

Emmett held him on his other side, concern for the elderly man pushing aside all other thoughts. The doctor took a few breaths and steadied himself. He waved them off. "Just a little twinge in my chest is all. I had some spicy food for lunch today. I've got to remember I'm not a kid with a cast iron stomach anymore. Thank you, kids. I really am fine."

He gave them both a hug and a reassuring smile. Samantha kept a close eye on him all the way to the car. His smile and his wave followed her in the rearview mirror until they drove out of sight.

They drove for several minutes, each lost in thought.

Samantha couldn't stop worrying about Doc Smith. Hopefully, he wasn't lying to them. Catching Emmett's brooding expression out of the corner of her eye, she took his hand. "He's fine, right? He's a doctor. Doc Smith would tell us if something was wrong. Now, what do you say to a stop at Mom and Dad's? Mom will probably have apple pie."

His favorite dessert, baked by the expert hands of her mother, was enough to have him sold. Emmett's eyes lit up and he licked his lips. "Sounds good to me. I'll never turn down your mother's cooking, Sam."

Her parents responded in a typical way, falling over themselves to give Samantha and Emmett the royal carpet treatment. While David took care of guiding Emmett to the living room and getting him settled with a beer, Angela ushered Samantha into the kitchen and took her hands. "Let me look at you. You have never been more lovely." She set her hands on Samantha's belly and her blue eyes simply glowed. "I'd say you're just about ripe. Any day now. How was your appointment?"

"Fine, just fine, and Emmett checked out okay too. Doc Smith always checks up on him too, you know. Wyatt isn't using his cane as much. He's getting much stronger. I'm sure he'll get rid of it soon. I'd say things are on track." Samantha accepted her mother's hug and the heat rose up in her face. "Um, Mom, I don't mean to impose, but is there any chance you've got some of your prize winning apple pie around?"

Her mother patted her cheek. "I can do even better." She turned and grabbed an oven mitt as the timer on the stove began to chime. Efficient as always, the older woman whipped the door open and nimbly set *two* pies on the counter. "We'll have some now and the other is going home with you. Your father and I were going to drive out later on."

Samantha started to laugh and wrapped her arms around her mother. "Oh, Mama, you're too good to me!"

The women worked side by side to slice the pie, dish out scoops of ice cream, and set them on a tray. As they walked to the living room, Angela nudged Samantha's hip. "I wasn't only thinking about you, sweetheart. Those handsome Henry boys have got to eat. Isn't that right, Emmett?"

Em straightened up on the couch and lifted his nose to the air. His eyes drifted closed as a smile grew. "You've got that right, Mrs. O'Dell. I'll be your slave for that pie of yours. I fight all the others off at the fair to be the first to taste your pie, and I always vote for you. I might bump into a few things around here, but you put me to work and pay me with pies. I'll consider that more than fair."

Laughter rose up for everyone, and it took them all a moment to settle down before they gave Samantha's mother's pie all due respect. When Sam and Emmett pulled in the driveway, Wyatt was waiting on the porch.

"What's this about a pie? Your mother just called. You didn't eat it all on the way home, did you?"

Samantha and Emmett had their second helping of the day. As for Wyatt, he made up for missing the first go around with two, large helpings and a large glass of ice cold milk. Generous soul that her husband was, he insisted on sending the leftovers with Emmett. A fresh pie was waiting for him when he came in from the barn the next morning. The trip to the bedroom was well worth it for Samantha.

As Wyatt massaged her feet and legs until she turned to jelly, Sam groaned in pleasure. "Apple pie is all you need to give me this kind of treatment?"

He nodded and kissed the pad of her foot, making her wriggle and want more than a massage.

She reached for his hand, a promise of what was ahead in her eyes. "You'll have one every morning."

CHAPTER 15

He couldn't stop shaking. Three times, Wyatt had to pull over to try and get control of his body. His leg was fighting him, his arm was fighting him, his hand was slipping off the wheel. As he stared out at the snow whipping by, the storm's bitter chill took up residence in his bones. The sound of his gasping filled the cab of the truck while the tears ran down his face and he couldn't stop shaking.

Wyatt took a deep breath, swiped his sleeve across his eyes, and put the truck in gear again. *Five minutes. Just five more minutes, and you'll be home.* The truck rolled back on to the highway into a white wall. making him slow to a snail's pace. The squall came up out of nowhere, following him all the way from town. Nerve-wracking at any time, the weather was more than he could take today. Wyatt's hand dropped down to his leg again and he cursed in frustration. Any time he was over-tired or under a strain, it acted up again. *Not now, damn it! Not now!* He just wanted to get home.

Finally, the light at the end of the driveway glowed like a beacon. Wyatt plowed through six inches of fresh snow and stopped by the front door. He turned the truck off and rested his head on the steering wheel. He'd made it. Straightening up, his gaze swept the house. The front porch and several lights glowed on the first floor while the nursery was lit as well. Samantha was rocking by the window, waiting for him. Anxious. What was meant to be a short trip had turned into hours.

Wyatt swallowed hard and steeled himself for the walk to the front door. He hadn't brought his cane, hadn't needed it when he left earlier that day. The return trip was a different story. He opened the door and took great care to set his feet firmly on the ground. *Don't you dare give out on me now!* His mind barked orders at his leg, and he was granted a small miracle. It held. It was shaky and dragged, but carried him up the walkway, three steps, and to the door where his wife stood with open arms.

"Wy, what happened?" Samantha asked the moment she saw his face.

She ducked under his left arm and offered him badly needed support, guiding him to the living room where he sank down on the sofa. Struggling to get down on her knees with her growing belly, Sammie managed anyway and slipped off his shoes. All the while, he was still shaking. "Wyatt Henry, you talk to me! I've been pacing the floor up and down for two hours. I thought you had an accident!"

Her voice rose in pitch, her fear washing over him as she pulled herself to her feet and grabbed a blanket off the back of the couch. Samantha sat beside him and wrapped her arm around him. At his side. His rock. His comfort, but he still couldn't stop shaking.

Wyatt leaned forward and propped his elbows on his knees, covering his face with his hands. "I'm—I'm sorry, Sam. I should've called—but it all happened so fast—and then I couldn't even think straight."

"*What* happened? I sent you to the grocery store for ice cream and a couple of things for dinner. That was three hours ago, Wyatt! One hour I could see because you know the whole town, but three? And then the snow storm hit. I've been going out of my mind with worry. I was ready to walk to town to find out what happened to you. Please talk to me!"

He nodded and took her hand in his with his right while the left dropped. Seeing him struggle, Samantha began to massage his weak hand and arm to improve the circulation, the pins and needles sensation making him wince. Wyatt took a deep breath. He couldn't put her off any longer. "I was finishing up at the checkout, headed for the door, when Doc Smith walked in. He—he—gave me a pat on the back—said I looked mighty fine—asked about you—as always—" The words broke off. Too hard. What he had to say was too hard.

"Wyatt, you're scaring me." Samantha was holding on tight to both of his hands, her knuckles white with the strength of her grip. Wyatt needed that strength right now.

"I invited him for Thanksgiving, and Doc said he wouldn't miss your cooking and company for the world when his face twisted up in pain. He grabbed at his arm—and then Doc just dropped. I—I caught him and lowered him down, called for help, did CPR—" The tears were coming again, and Wyatt couldn't stop them. He turned to Samantha and buried his face in her shoulder. "There was nothing anyone could do, Sam. Doc Smith had a heart attack—and he's gone." The shaking took over, and he gave in, didn't fight any more. Let it have him.

"Oh—oh, no, Wyatt. No!"

Her wail rose up, and it was his turn to comfort her. He stroked her hair and massaged her back, his hand running in soothing circles. His wife trembled in his arms, and the baby stirred, as if responding to a mother's strong emotions.

There was nothing Wyatt could do, that any of them could do, but hold on.

The clock ticked over the fireplace and the fire crackled cheerfully on the hearth, but the ice wouldn't melt inside of him. Samantha wiped at her cheeks, her eyes puffy and face red from her crying as she took his face in her hands. "You're freezing, Wy. Let me get you something hot to drink."

He shook his head. "No, you don't need to. Just sit with me, Sam. Sit a bit."

She took a shuddering breath. "I can't believe it. Doc Smith, gone. He was my doctor all of my life—and yours. He was supposed to be there to welcome the next Henry." Her hands rested on her belly and the baby stilled as her tears splattered down.

Wyatt laid his hands on hers. "I know—he's been there for all of us forever. For Mama and Dad too. The world won't seem right without him."

They sat side by side, stunned into silence, holding hands, trying to keep it together as they stared into the flames. Samantha gave his hand a squeeze. "I'd best make us a little something for dinner." For some reason, food was a balm to the spirit.

Wyatt stood and crossed the room with faltering steps to grab his cane. He returned to Samantha's side and bent down to kiss the crown of her head. "I've got something I have to do first. I have to tell Emmett and it has to be in person. Some things can't be told over the phone."

e/ɔe/ɔ

His brother took it hard, harder than anyone else. Doc Smith had been Emmett's champion, every day in the hospital, sitting with him sometimes for hours, just holding his hand, not saying a word. Making a point to see him every week since his injury. More than that, Doctor Edmond Smith was one more tie to their parents that had been broken. Except for their Henry uncles, their namesakes that had farms nearby, the brothers were all that was left of their legacy. When Wyatt told his little brother about Doc's passing, Emmett hit his knees and sobbed like he never had for himself. The only thing left to do? Help him to his feet, something the brothers had done for each other many times before, and it wouldn't be the last.

☙❧

Edmond Smith was buried the Sunday before Thanksgiving, on a clear day without a cloud in the sky, the last few straggling geese flying overhead, the sun so bright it hurt Wyatt's eyes. He had volunteered to be a pall bearer along with other members of their community who banded together as the family Doc Smith had never had of his own.

Wyatt stood at the front, Emmett behind him. His brother didn't need to see to do his part and carry a weight that was light compared to the burden on all of their hearts. It was the least that the Henry brothers could do as a final duty to a man who was more like a grandfather to them than a doctor.

As they approached the grave, Wyatt held his head high and did not look at the mourners waiting nearby, somber in their dark winter coats and hats. He could not meet Samantha's eye. Her pain was more than he could bear. Heaped on top of his, it would break him. He could hear the sound of Emmett's boots thudding on the barely frozen ground behind him, his breathing labored. Em was still having a hard time of it. Everyone was grieving hard for a man who was beloved by all.

After what seemed to take forever and yet happened much too soon, they set the casket down on the lowering device over the grave. Gazing down in the hole, Wyatt was badly shaken, brought back to another burial that had hit home not too long ago. As before, such a small pit in the ground was not nearly large enough to swallow Doc Smith. Like Jackson Henry, he was too big of a man for the earth to contain. Wyatt bowed his head and tried to pray. It didn't come easily.

A hand gripped him by the shoulder. "Come on, Wy. They're waiting," Emmett told him gruffly. Scraping at his cheeks, Wyatt took his brother by the crook of his arm and led him to an empty seat beside Samantha.

Samantha's eyes were red from crying and she was pale. Sleep had eluded her the night before, the baby restless, her spirits low. Neither of them had eaten that morning, too heartsick for food. The last thing she needed was to be sitting in the cold in a cemetery. Pushing his own sorrow aside, Wyatt wrapped an arm around her shoulders and let her rest her head on his shoulder. "It will be over soon," he murmured with a confidence that did not exist.

He lied. When someone you loved died, the pain was never over. In the beginning, it was an open wound. Gaping. Bleeding. Stabbing at you and stealing your breath away. Over time, the gap would close, but never fully heal. A bad day, a memory, a sudden longing and it would fester again.

A hand hovered on the edge of his vision, Emmett feeling a pain that was for more than Doc Smith. Today's funeral ripped off the scabs for the loss of Jackson Henry—and far off in the distant past, Beth Henry, leaving them wide open.

The pastor finished his prayer and blessing. Wyatt didn't even hear the words. Did they really matter when they were all the same in essence? And all of them left him feeling empty, inadequate to give him any peace. The cemetery staff began to shovel in the dirt and Samantha broke down, crying in earnest. Wyatt held her, Emmett held his hand, and they created a final circle, unbroken, as the rest of the visitors drifted away.

When his wife began to shiver from the cold, enough was enough. "Come on, Sammie. Let's get you home." She nodded and let Wyatt lead her to the truck, Emmett by his side.

છ৩છ৩

"How's Sam?"

Emmett sat on the sofa, shoulders hunched as he leaned toward the fireplace. Periodically, a spasm ran through his body with a chill neither brother could shake. Wyatt suspected it was more emotional than physical.

"She's lying down. She's had a rough time these past few days. Except for Dad, a loss like that hasn't hit her." He sat down with a sigh and handed his brother a cup of coffee.

Emmett murmured his thanks and took a long draw on the steaming brew. He let out a long, pent-up breath, shuddering once more. They'd both changed into flannel shirts and jeans as soon as they got home. While they might be more comfortable, clothing did little to ease their spirits. "You never get used to it."

Wyatt slung an arm over his brother's shoulders. "That you don't. I wish I could've spared it happening to you so young, Em."

Emmett's mouth turned up in a poor attempt at a grin. "I could say the same for you, Wy."

They drained their cups, and Wyatt's body went loose for the first time that day. He dropped back against the couch and pressed an arm to his eyes. Maybe sleep would come to him, just for a little while. Beside him, Emmett was fading fast, both of them exhausted. Consciousness was slowly slipping away when a shriek ran right through Wyatt and had him taking the steps two at a time, cursing when his leg caved at the top. Emmett was at his side and hooked an arm around his waist, helping him to regain his footing. Another shriek and the brothers sprinted. Somehow, Emmett didn't crash into anything.

Wyatt threw the bedroom door open and found Samantha sitting up in bed, trembling, the tears streaming down her cheeks. She was holding her belly and looked terrified.

"Sammie, what's wrong? Is it the baby?"

She accepted Wyatt's hand and Emmett's as her brother-in-law sat by her side. Struggling to get a hold of herself, her words came out in a stammer. "I dreamt—I dreamt that I went into labor, here, in our bed—and there was blood, so much blood. It was everywhere. Doc Smith wasn't here to help, and you were gone. I had to do it all by myself and when the baby came—it was too soon. He didn't make it, and the blood kept coming. I was going to go with him—and Wyatt?"

He kissed her fingers and rubbed her hand. "What, honey? What is it?"

Her blue eyes stared at him and her fear reached out to him, sending a chill down his spine, making his stomach clench. "Wy—I wanted to go with the baby." He could barely hear her whisper, but knew his heart stopped for an instant.

Wyatt pulled her in against the wall of his chest, reassured that she was solid and warm, the baby giving him a jab in the stomach that made him weak. If anything happened to Samantha or this baby, that would be more than one man could take. "It was only a dream. No one is going to leave you alone when it's time for this baby to get here, and you aren't going anywhere, Sam. It would kill me. Might as well dig another grave for me."

"Hell, forget that. I'll deliver the next Henry." Emmett made them all laugh, although a sheen of tears made his eyes glisten.

Unwilling to dwell on the nightmare or the sadness that hung over them all like a dark cloud, they all went downstairs and sat together. Emmett made hot chocolate, Wyatt made popcorn, and they watched an old comedy to help carry them over the hump. Only together could they get through life's storms.

∽∾∽

"Mom! Dad! Happy Thanksgiving. Let me hang up your coats." Wyatt accepted hugs and kisses as he gathered his in-laws' winter wear and shut the door. "Brr! It's a cold one out there. Feels more like Christmas!"

David waited while his wife bustled off to the kitchen, dusting snow off of his hair. "You've got that right. Nearly a foot fell last night. I think we're in for a tough one. So, what's my girl up to?"

Wyatt gripped him by the shoulder and gave his father-in-law a helpful push. "Take a look. She's been at it since I went out to take care of the horses this morning. I don't know how she manages, but Sammie outdoes her-self every year."

"That's my daughter. Always raising the bar, like a Henry." Samantha's father stepped into the kitchen and wrapped his daughter in a hug. Standing in the doorway, watching them, the need for Jackson Henry was strong. Holidays were one of those times when Wyatt missed his father the most.

Shaking it off, he gloried in the sight of his wife, her cheeks flushed from the heat of cooking, her sunny hair falling in soft waves around her face and down her back. With every day of her pregnancy, she only became more beautiful. *She's a sight to see, Dad. Wish you could be here for the baby.*

Unwilling to let a gloomy mood ruin a day of grati-tude, Wyatt stepped into the living room to find Angela hugging his brother. "Let me look at you, Emmett. My, but you are looking well."

Self-conscious, he ducked his head and smiled at her compliment. "Thank you, Mrs. O'Dell. I'm feeling well for the first time in a long time."

She pressed a hand to his cheek. "It's Angela or Mom, remember. You're getting enough rest and no more headaches?"

A fleeting shadow passed over his face, but his brother spoke lightly. "Rest is no problem. I've got all the time in the world. The headaches hit from time to time, but that's to be expected. At least the seizures haven't come back."

She patted him softly on the back. "That's true. Sit down, Emmett, and I'll bring you something to drink."

"Just a beer, Mrs—Mom. Thanks."

Angela beamed when he remembered to use the term of endearment and turned to go, pulling up short when she saw Wyatt.

"I'll get one for you too, young man. Sit with your brother and put on the game." She tilted her head sideways, inspecting him with a keen eye. Apparently, her mother's instincts made her unhappy with what she saw. Angela cupped his face in her palms and her expression softened. "You've been working too hard, Wyatt. You've been through a terrible strain, first a physical one, now an emotional one. I need you to stick around for my daughter and grandchild. Promise me you'll take better care of yourself."

"I promise, Mom." Wyatt pulled the small woman in for a hug, imagining holding his own mother would feel this way. The memory was faded, but not completely forgotten, a feeling like coming home.

Angela shook her head, her eyes suspiciously bright. "You're humoring me of course. You Henrys are stubborn as they come." She pulled away to pat her hair and straighten her skirt, collecting herself, and gestured to the couch. "Like I said, join your brother. Your father-in-law will be with your shortly. I've got to chase him out of the kitchen. You know what they say about too many cooks."

Emmett wore a knowing grin when Wyatt sank down beside him with a sigh and they settled in with David to watch the Patriots take on the Giants. Two beers later, the men joined the women at the dining room table. As head of the Henry household, carving and grace were left up to Wyatt. After the serving platters were passed around, he stood and Samantha joined him, taking his hand, his gaze resting on every face at his table. In his mind, he also saw those who were missing. His gratitude knew no bounds that his in-laws were still here for his wife and for their unborn child.

"Dear God, I'm thankful, more thankful than I can say that I stand here with all of you today, that my brother is still with us after all he's gone through, and my beautiful wife continues to be a blessing from above. Thank you for everyone at this table, for the little one who will join us next Thanksgiving, and for the delicious food my wife and Mom have worked so hard to prepare. My cup runneth over. Amen."

"Amen," echoed around the room as Samantha looped her arms around his neck and gave him a kiss. Wyatt knelt down to kiss her baby bump next, creating a blend of smiles and tears before they shared their meal on a day of giving thanks. The Henry House and his heart was full.

CHAPTER 16

Samantha rolled over and simply stared at her husband. She didn't get the opportunity often. If he didn't slip out quietly to the barn before her eyes cracked open for the day, the sound of the shower would pull her reluctantly from sleep. Her hand massaged her belly as she watched the even rise and fall of Wyatt's chest, a sight that gave her a reason to smile. So close. She'd come so close to losing him. What she wouldn't give to linger in bed by his side. These days, she was tired all the time.

So was her husband. Resisting the urge to close her eyes and let sleep take her back under, she carefully heaved herself out of bed and waddled to the bathroom. Lowering herself down to a seated position wasn't getting any easier. Finished with her morning business, Samantha washed up, brushed her teeth, and pulled her hair away from her face in a hasty braid. She didn't have patience to do anything else with it.

A sigh of pleasure rose up from her toes as she slipped her swollen feet—*Balloons! They're blasted balloons!*—into cushy slippers Wyatt was considerate enough to buy for her when shoes were no longer possible. Her robe was last. Samantha groaned inwardly in her poor attempt to tie the belt. The ends hardly met. Tucking end over end, she blew her bangs out of her eyes in exasperation and did her daily penguin act down to the kitchen.

The scent of fresh coffee called to her like the Pied Piper. A smile took root and sprouted the instant she stepped into the kitchen. Emmett was already at the table, cupping his mug in two hands and sipping the brew like it was the elixir of life.

Samantha scuffed her way across the kitchen, poured her own cup, heavy on the cream and sugar, light on the coffee. Too much caffeine and the baby did power gymnastics all day long as she'd found out the hard way. Trial and error, that's what pregnancy was. *Pregnancy? How about raising babies? What about life?* She pressed Emmett's shoulder and grazed his cheek with a kiss before sinking into a chair next to him. "What are you doing up so early?"

He shrugged. "I know Wy will be down soon and I felt like being here for him like he has been for me since everything went to crap." Emmett's face darkened as he appeared to stare down at his cup. "I wish I wasn't so useless."

Samantha set her coffee cup down and gripped his wrist. "You're a Henry and that means that you are a gift beyond measure. Your eyes are not the only thing that defines you. You have an incredible strength of character. You helped your brother to get through his worst crisis the same way that Wyatt helped you through yours. That means more to him than helping in the barn. Because of you, your brother is sane and whole."

"Thanks, Sam. You've always been so good to me. You used to let me tag along when Wy said no when we were kids. You're still letting me tag along, always looking out for me." Emmett leaned in to give her a hug and went back to his coffee.

Wyatt came down the stairs at that moment, whistling cheerfully, lighting a fire inside of Samantha. Since Doc's death, her husband's mood had taken a nosedive. Last night at Thanksgiving had been a turning point. "What's the big doins' today?" He filled his mug and messed his brother's hair, followed by giving Sam a kiss that could make her melt. Wyatt chuckled as he tapped Emmett's arm. "Sorry, I'm not kissing you good morning too."

While Wy took a swig of his coffee, eyes warm with appreciation, Em sat back and crossed his arms. "I've been sitting here wishing I could be of some use out in the barn. I feel guilty as hell that you have to do it all and I miss my horses, damn it!"

Wyatt drained his cup and stood up, hauling Emmett up with him. "Come out to the barn with me then. I'll put you to work. Besides," he winked at Samantha and patted his little brother's stomach. "I think you're getting a little soft in the middle."

He got a punch in the arm for that one. Nothing could be farther from the truth. Em was leaner than before if possible what with all of his walks out in the field, something Samantha had managed to keep a secret. Laughing, the brothers pulled on winter boots, coats, hats, and gloves.

Wyatt and Emmett walked out together as snow fluttered down and the sun made its first appearance for the day. Samantha stood at the window, coffee cup in her hand, and watched them. As the sky went from purple to pink and finally was painted a heavy gray, their silhouettes were swallowed up by the barn.

Her emotions went haywire, making her eyes sting at the sight of the Henrys headed out to their horses again. Biting her lip and chalking it up to pregnancy, she took up her chores for the day. Nothing was accomplished quickly anymore. Dishes, laundry, dusting, sweeping, mopping, vacuuming, and cooking left her exhausted. Pacing herself was key and an afternoon nap was a must because if she didn't get off her feet, Samantha would cry.

She decided to check in on her men before surrendering to her pillow and quilt on the couch, the journey up the stairs more of a bother than it was worth. Samantha fought to swing the heavy door open, panting with exertion, and stepped into the welcome warmth of the barn to find Emmett carrying buckets of oats to each stall while his brother sent the herd out.

Wyatt caught sight of her and ate up the space between them, concern turning his eyes to a dark slate. "What's wrong? You're really flushed and you look tired. Do you need me?"

Emmett stopped what he was doing to take a few steps their way. Samantha smiled wearily and kissed Wyatt's cheek. "I'm fine, fine," she answered breathlessly. The baby pressed on her diaphragm, making it hard to inhale deeply. "I'm just winding down like a clock these days, Wy. Only a few more weeks to go, you know? I left you two lunch on the table. I'm going to go lie down now, okay?"

"I'll walk her in, make sure she's all right," Emmett offered, extending his hand. Considering the snow was getting deep and she'd slipped a few times on the way, Samantha willingly accepted.

The two made their way slowly back to the house, her heart fluttering madly when an icy patch threw her off balance. Emmett caught her and wrapped an arm around her waist. "You've got to be more careful, Sam. You *shouldn't* be coming out here by yourself. It's too dangerous for you and the baby."

She swallowed to wet a mouth gone dry from a shot of panic. "You're right. I won't again, promise." Samantha held his arm as they stood in the hallway once the door closed, leaving the bitter fingers of icy air outside. "You need to take your own advice," she told him reproachfully. "If you ever fell or got hurt out walking that field…" She couldn't say anymore, shuddering at the thought.

"I promise I'll be careful, but I've got to get out, Sammie. If I stay in that house, in my head, all the time, I'll go crazy." Emmett knelt down and eased her boots off first, wincing at the size of her feet. His fingers fumbled by the wall until they rested on her slippers. He set one on each foot, making her giggle. He grinned at the sound. "I feel like the prince from Cinderella." He took his own boots off next, then hung up their coats. Finally, his arm rested on her shoulders and he steered her toward the living room.

When Emmett's knee nudged the couch, he reached out and found her blanket. He folded it back and gave a little bow. "All right, princess. Time for your beauty rest." His hand gently patted her hard, full belly. "You too, little one." He drew the quilt to her chin and bent over to kiss her forehead. "Rest, Sam. Thanks for letting me stay last night. It felt like old times."

She caught his sleeve and gave it a tug. "You don't

need to thank me, Em. We love having you here, any time, as much as you want." As he turned to go, she blurted out, "Your brother wants you to move back in with us, just until the winter is over. He worries about you, all alone over there, you know?"

Emmett froze, his hands resting on his hips as he bowed his head. He took a deep breath and turned around to face her, his face strained. "I can't do that, Sam. You don't know what a temptation it is, to let you guys take care of me, to have your company all the time, but this isn't going away and I've got to deal with it, every day, all year. I've fought too hard to come this far. I can't take a step back like that."

Samantha pulled on his hand until he took a step closer. "I know and I understand. I had to try."

He kissed the top of her head and gave her a bittersweet smile. "Just like I have to say no, but thanks, Sammie. You know how much I love you guys. Enough talking. You need your rest. I'll be out in the kitchen. You call if you need me, okay?"

"Okay. Love you too, Em." She listened to the reassuring sound of his footsteps and his movements in the kitchen. Her eyes became heavy, drooping shut as the door opened and shut, Wyatt stomping his boots off on the entryway rug. The low rumble of his voice met with Emmett's, their soft laughter traveling her way and her whole body relaxed at the soothing sound. Everything was going loose, her joints and her bones preparing for that miracle when her body would open up wide enough to let the future out.

Samantha fell asleep dreaming of their slumber party the night before, all of them sprawled out on the rug, a movie sending them teetering off the edge of wakefulness as the fire snapped and popped into the wee hours of the morning. Sometime in the darkness, Wyatt had covered her and drawn her in close, keeping her warm while Emmett snored softly only a few feet away. Her whole word in one room. What more could a woman ask for?

∾∽∾

"Come on, Sammie. Please come for just a little while. Em's planned dinner for us all day." Wyatt stood by the rocking chair and set his hand on her neck, kneading at muscles gone tight as her head drooped. She'd been taking refuge in the nursery more and more. Perhaps this was the nesting instinct her mother had told her about. "Please, Samantha, for Emmett."

Her head snapped up and she glared at him, her words coming out in a hiss. "I have two weeks to go, Wy! Two weeks and I can barely waddle my way through that door. You'll have to roll me down the stairs soon. I can't even get my boots on my feet are so huge. I just want to stay here." *Wonderful. I'm starting to whine.*

He moved around in front of her and knelt down, cupping her cheek with his palm, forcing her to meet his gaze. "I know you're tired and you've had enough, but I think it would do you good to get out for a bit. We won't stay long, I promise. Em said something about decorating for Christmas. Let's go see how he made out."

Wyatt's eyes were dark with longing, his expression so pleading that she couldn't deny him, nor Emmett. *Licked before you started, and you know it.* "Oh, all right! But only for a little while, you understand?"

With a whoop, he came up fast and snatched a kiss. His strong arms scooped her up and her crazy husband carried her down the stairs.

"What do you think you're doing, Wy? I'm an awful strain on that leg."

He stopped at the bottom and set her down gently, his face grim. "If I can't carry my wife, you can decommission me. Come on now. Let's get a move on. I'm getting hungry."

Samantha giggled as she patted her stomach with a rueful grin. "Maybe that's why I've been eating everything in sight. Junior has an appetite like yours and I have to keep up with him." Before she could say anything more, Wyatt slipped her swollen feet into a pair of his winter boots. He wrapped his coat around her and grabbed Jackson Henry's flannel off of the hooks.

When she started to sputter, he'd hear none of it. "The truck is right here and I've got it warming up. I'll be fine. You have precious cargo on board and your coat is not going to fit right now so don't argue with me." He walked closely by her side, his arm supporting her, ensuring she would not fall.

As he gave her a boost into the truck, Samantha rested her hands on his shoulders. "Thank you for being so good to me and putting up with my miserable moods, Wyatt."

He tossed her a playful wink. "You're entitled. That's my baby in there making you so moody." Wyatt walked around to the driver's side, climbed in, and pulled the door shut. Kicking the truck into four wheel drive, he turned on the headlights as the daylight started to fade. Snow sprinkled down along the way as the sky bled with the closing of the day.

Samantha grabbed his hand and sucked in hard. "Oh, Wy! Look how lovely!"

He glanced at her. "Yes, you are." At her jab in his side, he laughed. "Oh, you mean the sky, it is pretty special. Good thing I pried you out of that nursery or you would have missed it. You'll have plenty of time to spend in that room soon, Sam. Be patient."

"Easy for you to say. You're not about to give birth to a wooly mammoth." That had him laughing so hard that Samantha couldn't help but join him. They turned down Emmett's lane and she covered her mouth when they pulled up by the house. "How? How did he do it?" She asked faintly.

A large wreath hung on the door with a bright, red bow. White lights were strung across the shrubbery and a

Christmas tree twinkled in the window where their father had always placed the holiday evergreen each year.

Wyatt sat frozen beside her, his eyes beginning to water. He cleared his throat and took her hand. "I don't know. The only thing I did was lug a few boxes of decorations down from the attic. Em did the rest."

He shook himself and stepped out of the truck to come around to her side. His strong hands rested on her waist and carefully lowered her to the ground. Samantha could only marvel at such strength.

She leaned against him for a moment and patted his chest when a voice called out, "Well, are you going to keep me waiting all night? Dinner's ready."

Emmett sat in a chair on the porch, the lights from the shrubbery casting a glow on his face and making his golden eyes shimmer.

Samantha could see tiny sparkles reflected in his pupils, like fairy fire.

She nodded to Wyatt and they traveled the walkway that had been thoroughly cleared. More of her brother-in-law's handiwork. Strength, indeed.

As Samantha's foot clomped up the steps, their host stood and met them halfway to the door. "How's the house look from the outside?" Uncertainty was etched into his face.

She threw her arms around him and gave him a hug. "Beautiful, just beautiful. You did this all by yourself, chopped a tree down and everything?"

He shrugged modestly. "It wasn't that big of a deal. Finding the tree, that was the hardest part."

Wyatt clapped him on the back. "I'm impressed brother and I'm starving. I hope you cooked for an army."

"No problem there. Dad taught me that. You never know who will show up." With that, Emmett opened the door and voices shouted out from every direction, "Surprise!"

Samantha's jaw dropped and her feet wouldn't move. Her family, friends, neighbors, and townspeople were all gathered around, streamers and balloons dressing the place for a baby shower. When she finally regained her power of speech, she shook an accusing finger at Wyatt. "So this is why you made me get out of the house, to ambush me? And as for you, Em," Samantha snagged his sweater and wouldn't let go. "You did *all* of this without any help?"

He kissed her hot cheek, a blush creeping up in his own. "Well, I did the Christmas stuff on my own. Everyone else got in on the act for your shower." His face softened and he engulfed her in a hug. "It's a big deal, Sammie. It's not every day we get the chance to welcome another Henry into this world."

She couldn't speak. Her heart was too full. Samantha let Wyatt escort her to the seat of honor, another rocking chair, "Because you could always use a spare," her father called out. This was no ordinary shower. Men, women, and children of all ages filled the house to the brim. The gifts rained down, stunning her with the generosity of everyone around her.

The food and drinks never stopped, many of the dishes supplied by Emmett. It hadn't all been a lie. "Just stretched the truth a bit," her husband whispered in her ear. They stayed late into the night, until well past her bedtime, singing Christmas carols, eating cake, enjoying a moment too precious to be ignored.

As Wyatt carried her up to bed at the end of the night, staggering a bit with weariness, they didn't even bother getting undressed. He slid under the covers and tucked her into his side. Samantha turned to face him and pressed her nose to his. "Thank you for making me go. That was the best surprise ever."

He grinned sleepily and patted her stomach. "No, the mystery guest in here, that will be the best surprise—and our greatest gift. I can't wait to unwrap it. Good night, Sam. Love you."

"Love you too," she murmured as the stars winked at her window and the man in the moon smiled down on them in benediction.

CHAPTER 17

What do you mean you're not coming? It's Christmas Eve, for God's sake!" Wyatt stood by the hearth with his arms crossed, glowering at his brother, even though it didn't do a lick of good. "Sam's waiting in the truck for you and believe me, the fact that she is out there is quite a feat. She doesn't want to go anywhere these days and I can't blame her. Get your butt in gear and let's go."

Emmett shifted in his seat, his jaw set and shoulders tight. His gaze was turned toward the crackling hearth as if he was losing himself in the flames. "Me and the Man Upstairs are having a difference of opinion right now. If I go with you, I'm afraid I'm going to have words with Him. I may not be particularly nice. Now please, Wy." He leaned forward and propped his forehead on one hand, rubbing at his temple. Warding off another migraine? "Just go."

Fighting every fiber of his being that told him to bodily pick up his brother and wrestle him out into the chilly, star-filled night, Wyatt stomped his way out, slamming the door for good measure.

"I take it he's not coming," Samantha murmured quietly, her hand resting on his, calming the burning in the pit of his stomach.

He waited one more minute, hoping against hope, then peeled out. "No, no he's not. Stubborn. God, but he's stubborn!" His jaw clenched and he slammed his hand against the wheel.

Samantha's voice wore a smile. "You mean like you?"

He glanced at her and gave her a half-hearted grin. "Exactly like me—and my father—and my grandfather before me. Stubborn runs strong in Henry blood."

They were quiet the rest of the drive to the small country church. Wyatt's gaze traveled to the small cemetery where his parents slept. *Merry Christmas, Mama and Dad.* He pulled up as close to the door as possible and stepped out of the truck, moving swiftly to Samantha's side lest she get any ideas about setting out on her own. One slip could mean disaster.

She took his hand and eased herself to the ground, her breath coming out in a rush. It was getting harder and harder for her to get about. Like the animals on the farm, he could see all the signs and could see her body was preparing. Soon. Their baby would be here soon.

Wyatt wrapped his arm around her waist and paced himself, shortening the length of his steps, taking as much time as she needed. He took her coat and draped it over the pew, lending her his strength as she pressed one hand into the small of her back and eased herself down. Samantha rolled her eyes as he joined her. "You'll need a tractor to haul me out of here at the end of mass. Heaven help us all if I have to go to the bathroom. I feel like the Hindenburg!"

He kissed her cheek and tickled her side, getting a giggle in response. "Not even close. You're adorable."

They sat back and listened to the organ music, nodding and calling to friends as they streamed into church. Handshakes, hugs, and kisses were passed around, many coming to ooh and ahh over Samantha. "Now, now, little mother. Don't you get up! Just look at you, blooming like a Christmas blossom," was the main gist of most every conversation.

The music became louder, signaling the pastor was about to make his entrance when footsteps approached, accompanied by the clicking of a cane on the wooden floor. Emmett, in jeans and a dark brown sweater, stood at the end of the pew. Emily Hasting gave them a little wave and moved to her family pew across the way. That's how it was here. They kept traditions, just like the Henrys had sat in this scuffed pew for generations. Wyatt and Emmett's names were carved underneath, mischief committed when they were young.

Wyatt could barely speak as his brother worked his way in beside him. He gripped Emmett at the nape of his neck and gave it a hard squeeze. "It means a lot to me, your coming tonight."

Emmett cleared his throat. "The Man Upstairs and I hashed it out at home. He told me to get my butt in gear and get going. Sounded just like you." He slid him a grin. "Besides, Emily showed up and wouldn't take no for an answer."

Wyatt's eyes burned and he had to blink hard to avoid embarrassing himself. His little brother reached past him, his hand skimming over Samantha's belly. She laughed and grabbed hold. "We're so glad you're here, Em. It wouldn't be right without you."

He stepped in front of Wyatt and gave her a kiss on the cheek. "I figured that out. Merry Christmas Eve, Sam."

The pastor made his entrance then and Midnight Mass was underway with songs, prayers, and the Christmas story retold as it had been for hundreds of years. When the service was concluded, the Henry family shook hands with their church leader and stepped out into a gentle snowfall.

Emmett tipped his face back and called out quietly, "Thanks for sharing, Mama and Daddy. You always did love the snow."

As the rest of the congregation trailed out to their vehicles, Wyatt turned toward the cemetery, a bouquet of roses in his hand; they'd rested on an empty space on the pew until it was time to leave. Samantha held Emmett's hand as they followed close behind. A few feet in, under an old oak tree, a simple stone waited with his parents' names and dates. *Beloved mother and father* put it well. Straightforward and simple, the Henry way.

Wyatt knelt in the snow and laid the flowers down, bowing his head. Samantha rested a hand on his shoulder while Emmett found his way to a spot beside him, his hand reaching out to hold on to the cold, solid stone. His brother was trembling and tears streamed down his face. "Miss you, Mama, Dad. Christmas just isn't right without you."

Wyatt wrapped an arm around his brother's shoulder and let him lean his way. That's what big brothers were for, to shoulder the load when it was too heavy to bear. Emmett took a shaky breath and stood up. Samantha took one hand, Wyatt the other, and they slowly wended their way to the truck. Everyone weary at such a late hour, they all turned in as soon as they arrived home. Wyatt slept easy with his brother under the same roof.

ഗ~ഗ~ഗ

Up early to meet the sun on Christmas morning as was his way, Wyatt bundled up with so many layers he could barely move. The air was so cold his breath practically turned to ice on the way to the barn. He'd keep the herd in, muck out their stalls later. Making sure all were fed and watered with some fresh hay, his boots eagerly carried him back into the welcome warmth of his cozy home.

The house was quiet, everyone else enjoying the respite from the regular routine, sleeping in a bit. Wyatt plugged in the Christmas tree, made coffee, and sat down at the kitchen table. If he turned his chair at the right angle, he could see the bright lights twinkling on the great white pine harvested from the edge of his own property. Samantha's pick of course, a granddaddy of a tree that was a real bear coming in and worth every bit of the strain to see her beaming with pleasure, flitting around all that day, adding this decoration and that. Creating magic with her touch.

Thinking of his greatest blessing, the woman upstairs, in his bed, in his heart, Wyatt bowed his head and prayed. Every night, every morning, and every minute in between, he said the same prayer. *Make my brother whole. Give him back his sight.* On Christmas morning, this most holy of days, he had high hopes. After all, it was the season of miracles. His heart fell when his prayer was not answered. Emmett felt his way in, gave him a hug, and scraped a hand through his hair, making it stand on end until he resembled a porcupine. His little brother accepted a cup of coffee for himself.

A half hour later, Wyatt had a change of heart sitting on the couch with his wife leaning against him, his fingers playing with her hair while her hands circled around the baby she was carrying. Perhaps a man could only be given so many miracles in his life. An amazing wife. A baby on the way. The return of his strength. His brother, against all odds, still alive.

Feeling lazy, no one wanted to move. A knock sounded at the door, footsteps receded, and a car pulled away. Wyatt wandered out and looked outside to discover a basket with a big red bow on the porch. He stepped out to see a pair of the sweetest brown eyes staring up at him. His heart melting, he picked up the gift and carried it in to the living room. "Sam, we've got a Christmas visitor."

A German shepherd puppy sprang onto the rug and scampered to Samantha, jumping up on her legs, wriggling fit to come right out of his wrinkled skin. Wyatt lifted the shepherd up and the pup started licking her face all over. "Oh my! Where did this critter come from?"

Seeing a tag poking out from the dog's collar, Wyatt snatched it. All the while, Emmett wore a secretive smile. "It says 'Merry Christmas! My name is Chucky, and I'll give you a practice run before the baby comes. For all you've done for me and continue to do every day, love, Emmett.'"

Samantha was crying in earnest, laughing at the same time as the puppy crawled all over her. Wyatt hauled his brother in for a hug and settled him on the couch to get an introduction to the newest addition to the family. Christmas dinner and all of the other gifts could wait. They were all in love.

∽∾∽

"Ready, Em?"

Wyatt sat at the front of the toboggan that had been passed down for generations. Another Henry tradition the brothers were bound to keep.

Emmett held on tight on the back. "It's Christmas night. Let's do this!" A nudge and the sled shot down the hill, gliding through the fresh powder, rocketing toward the pastures below. Their father had taken this ride many a winter's day with his brothers and now it was their turn, their time. Samantha stood on the porch, hand raised in a wave as they sailed by. Too far along in her pregnancy to take such a bumpy ride, she'd have to sit this one out.

Wyatt let out a great whoop as the sled picked up speed and he felt his brother's death grip, followed by a shout of exhilaration. "My God, Wy! It feels like we're flying!" Inspired by his little brother's words, Wyatt closed his eyes as well and had to agree. Any moment, they'd have lift off and touch the sky.

They took the long climb back up the hill until their feet were too tired to carry them and the cold had seeped into their bones, making them shiver uncontrollably. Samantha had blankets, slippers, and hot chocolate waiting.

The brothers stripped down to their long underwear, settled in a nest of quilts on the living room floor with the new puppy, and topped off the day with one more time-honored tradition, "It's a Wonderful Life."

As the movie wound down to the closing scene and the bell rang to celebrate Clarence's wings, Samantha wiped the tears from her face. "His name should be George Henry," she told Wyatt, sniffling even though she smiled.

Wyatt hooked an arm around her neck and planted a kiss on her golden head. "You remind me of Mary, always there for me, building me up, believing in me, making this house a home. Making sure I feel loved."

She settled against him with a sigh and closed her eyes. "You Henrys are easy to love."

Only a few feet away, Emmett was sound asleep, Chucky curled up on his chest, snuggling with him. Gazing at his brother, holding on to his wife, Wyatt knew her words to be true. As the old year neared its end, his heart was full with love for Henrys—Em, Sam, and the Henry on the way, more love than many would ever know.

ဗာဗာ

On the dawn of the new year, everything was eerily still, as if the world was holding its breath. A bank of gray clouds pressed down on his shoulders, heavy enough to drive Wyatt into the ground as he let the horses out of the barn—and cold, Lord but it was cold. It hurt to breathe, made his bones ache, had his leg and arm arguing a bit with him. He needed to go in and take a hot soak. The snow started on his way in, bringing a sense of foreboding that he couldn't shake.

He shucked his jacket, a shiver running through him, and rubbed at his arms on his way through the kitchen. Samantha stood at the sink, her hand gripping the edge as a wince of pain flashed across her face. A wrinkle and it was gone.

"What's wrong?" Wyatt stood behind her, putting his hands to work as he rubbed her shoulders, her back, and kneaded the spot where it bowed in with the weight of their baby.

Her body gave and she waved him off. "Just cramps." She turned to face him and breathed in deep. "You smell like winter."

"I brought it in with me." Wyatt shook the snow out of his hair and made her laugh until concern made her study him more closely, the way he favored his leg.

"Go get off your feet. The cold is getting to you, isn't it?" Samantha took his left hand in hers. It was colder than his other hand and had that annoying pins and needles feeling that could really bother him. She started to rub at it to get the circulation going and he squeezed his eyes shut.

"I'm going to soak in the tub a while. You should take it easy too." Reassured by her promise to do exactly that, Wyatt headed up to the bathroom and sank into the glory of a steaming bath. He nearly dozed off for a good hour. When he finally got out, his skin wrinkled like a prune, he found Samantha lying on their bed, sound asleep. Gazing at her, he couldn't help but smile. *When in Rome…*

Wyatt stretched out beside her, spoon style, and held their baby while Chucky curled up at their feet.

The day wore on, the snow continued, and his wife became restless. She got out of bed, went to the bathroom, began to wander from room to room. Her unease reflected Wyatt's as he gazed out at the wall of white that continued to fall.

Sometime after lunch, he tried Emmett to check in. No one answered, setting him on edge.

Samantha joined him at the window and set her hand on the small of his back. "It's really coming down, isn't it?" Wyatt didn't answer, his forehead furrowed with worry. She rose up on tiptoe to kiss his cheek. "Go see him will you? You're driving me up a wall." Her face softened. "I'm worried too. You go or I will."

Wyatt turned to face her and looked at her hard, his hands on her shoulders. "Are you sure you're all right? I know you haven't felt like yourself today, even though you've been trying to hide it."

She set her hands on his cheeks. "Look in my eyes. I am fine, Wyatt Henry. Go now and make sure that other stubborn Henry is all right."

❧❦❧

Aggravated, he wanted to punch his little brother. Wyatt stomped his way through the woods, shivering, wishing he had a shovel to cut through the foot of snow that had fallen that day. He packed a few snowballs and launched them at the towering pines, finding little satisfaction when they exploded in a burst of white upon impact.

Emmett made him so angry he could scream. Nearly a year had passed since his brother was blinded, and he'd become so damned independent. All well and good, but Wyatt wanted to keep him close until this storm passed—till the winter was over—*Admit it. Until he can see again.* A few more snowballs and Wyatt stopped and put his hands on his hips, debating on whether he should go back to physically drag his brother with him.

His jaw clenched and his heart hammered in his chest. Fat chance. Em told him he could go ahead and try, but it wouldn't be pretty. That sent Wyatt walking in circles, torn. A full-fledged blizzard was underway. Who knew how long it would last? That was what sent him to his brother's in the first place when no one answered the phone. To have everyone under one roof. Was that so wrong? He knew Emmett could handle himself, but what if something went wrong? The migraines still hit, taking him down for a couple days and each time, Wyatt expected an atomic bomb of an aneurysm to hit another Henry.

He hesitated another second and plowed toward home. Sammie was on his mind, pulling him in the opposite direction. The first of the new year was here, making her two weeks overdue. She was miserable. She'd been feeling cramps that morning. What if it was more than cramps? That had him pushing on even as the snow came down harder and he knew there would be no getting out if that baby decided to come. Wyatt started to pray like never before and continued on.

Darkness had fallen when he hit their door. Wyatt was met by Samantha's wail, so loud it shook him to the core. His feet took the stairs two at a time to find her in the tub—in labor—and his heart thudded so hard in his chest he thought it would shatter.

CHAPTER 18

The cramps started first thing in the morning, snatching her breath away while she cooked breakfast. Samantha recognized them for what they were. Mild and sporadic at first, she didn't see any reason to bring them to Wyatt's attention. After all, they'd seen labor stretch on for days with the horses and hadn't her mother pointed out time and again how Samantha put *her* through the wringer for three days?

Prepared to settle in for the long haul, Samantha carried on with her routine while anticipation bloomed inside of her. *Soon! I'm going to meet you soon!* She thought with a small smile of satisfaction, standing at the window as her hand circled round and round throughout the next set of tremors that shook her body. The snow started coming down in a pure sheet of white, sending the first trickle of fear skittering through her. She pushed it to the back of her mind. *You'll have plenty of time to wait out the storm and get to the hospital.*

Wyatt was fretful. Done with the horses early on, his body struggling with the cold, he tried to relax. First in the tub, then by her side as she lay down in a pretense of sleep, trying to give her body the rest Samantha knew would be necessary for the long stretch of hours ahead. Giving up all efforts, he paced, picked up the phone to dial his brother's place, cursed when Emmett failed to answer, and went to the window for the umpteenth time, a study in tension.

Samantha stood behind him and rested her hands on the small of his back. His spine was rigid, each knob standing out. She might as well have grabbed hold of a live wire. "Go on now and see him. I'm worried too. If you don't go, I will."

It took some bending the truth to reassure him that she was fine, but Wyatt finally set off to his brother's a couple of hours before dark. Samantha stood at the window and watched his retreating figure as he was swallowed up by the storm and a sense of foreboding poked at her. She swatted at it mentally as if shooing away a pesky fly. *Plenty of time. You've got plenty of time.*

The next pain hit, bending her over at the waist. She gripped the windowsill and breathed through her nose. In and out. In and out, glancing at the clock on the living room wall to keep track of how long. Thirty seconds or so. Not a worry. Not yet. The pain let go and she sighed in relief. Her feet carried her aimlessly from room to room, Chucky following her like a shadow, hunkering down by her feet each time a contraction made her go still. Unable to reach down and pet the pup, she rubbed him with her toe and smiled weakly. "It's all right, sweet-ie. Your mama went through this too, Lord knows how many times. We'll get through this."

Somehow, she found herself in the nursery again and eased herself down on the rocker. Samantha pushed off, setting the chair to swaying, and the repetitive motion eased her fears some until the pains started hitting more often. Her eyes kept being drawn to the small clock on the baby's dresser each time a contraction set in. Thirty minutes apart. Twenty minutes apart. Ten minutes apart and panic was creeping up, starting to strangle her, mak-ing her gasp as she clamped her mouth shut and gritted her teeth through the next round. What if her dream came true, and she had to go solo?

When a horrible groan pried its way out between her teeth, Chucky got up on his hind legs, his paws in her lap, and whimpered pitifully, burying his face in her belly. Samantha swiped her sleeve over her forehead and gave him a smile, her hand resting on his head. "It's all right, little guy. It's all right."

Unable to sit any longer, Samantha heaved herself out of her chair and filled the tub, hoping the warm water would give her some relief, easing the intense cramping of her uterus for any kind of respite. The next contraction was the worst yet, making her feel like her insides were being ripped apart.

"Wyatt—Wyatt, please come home soon!" Samantha said the words out loud, her urgent prayer, willing her husband to find his way home. Another half hour went by, and she hit it. The magic number five. Five minutes apart. *Dear God. Please don't make me do this by myself in a bathtub.*

Her head tipped back when the next contraction rolled over her in a wave, grabbing hold, nearly crushing her with its weight—and she screamed bloody murder.

"Sammie?!" Footsteps pounded her way, Wyatt taking the stairs two at a time, racing into the bathroom to kneel by her. "Sam—are you all right?"

The pain let up, and she exhaled hard. "Sorry. Figured I was alone, might as well scream as loud as I wanted."

He stroked her hair from her face and cupped her cheek, his thumb stroking away a tear she couldn't hold back. "Go ahead. Scream all you want. Why didn't you call me?'

Samantha laughed softly, although she was ready to sob from exhaustion. "You know what they say. First babies are supposed to take forever. I figured I had time."

"How far apart are you?" His hand moved to her neck and began to massage the knots out of muscles gone tight. Her head dropped on her chest and she slowly breathed out through her nose. *This. All I need is this. Just give me a few minutes. Please.*

"I was at ten for a good while—I'm down to five." She sucked in hard, her teeth sinking into her bottom lip as another contraction took hold. Samantha grabbed Wyatt's arm.

He cursed quietly. "I don't think you're going to take forever and there's no way we're getting out, Sam. No one is coming in either. It's a blizzard out there."

She forced a smile as soon as her body gave her a badly needed break. "Well," she said lightly, "I guess you'll have to use those capable Henry hands to do it yourself."

Wyatt pressed his forehead against hers. "Would've preferred to let a doctor do it—but it's a family tradition. Em and I were born at home. We'll get through this together."

Samantha snorted with a grimace. "What's this we stuff? I don't see a baby coming out of you." At his hurt expression, she reached out to stroke his cheek. "I'll need you every minute, and you do not know how grateful I am that you're here. I thought I would have to do it alone." Another pain set in, snatching her breath away, putting everything on hold. "Mmm. That felt like forever."

"They're about a minute long now, three minutes apart. You're getting really close, Sam. Will you be all right while I get the bedroom ready?" At her nod, he left in a rush. Samantha held her thighs and pressed her back into the tub when the next one hit, nearly biting through her lip.

What seemed only seconds later, Wyatt was back. One look at her face as she wilted forward, and he climbed in, sinking into the water behind her, his legs sliding alongside of hers. One powerful, callused hand kneaded at the base of her spine, making her groan so hard he started trembling, his other hand cupping her abdomen, massaging as the muscles tightened yet again. Wyatt rubbed hard, murmuring to her softly, putting her at ease, just like he gentled the horses. She'd seen him do the same time and again delivering foals.

"So, what did you do in the delivery room?" Her eyes drooped shut. Tired. She was so tired. If only the pain could let go for a little while, fifteen minutes even, but the next one set in and her whole body went tight, Wyatt right along with her.

"Easy. Easy now. You're doing just fine, Sam." He began to stroke her hair again while his other hand continued to massage her tender, swollen belly. When her body went loose and she sagged against him, he told her hoarsely, "I stripped the bed, put down a plastic table cloth and old sheets. Set out towels, hot water, twine, scissors, alcohol for my hands—I think I've got it covered."

"Wyatt." The word drifted on the air so softly he had to lean in closer, straining to hear her.

"Hmm," he whispered, his mouth brushing her ear, sending a ripple through her from her head to her toes.

"You're still wearing your jeans." She hoped Wyatt could hear the smile in her voice since he couldn't see it from his angle.

A deep chuckle rumbled down deep in his chest, vibrating against her back. "So I am. I guess I was a little preoccupied." His fingers trailed through her sweat-dampened hair, his quiet humming soothing on a spirit worn raw over the past few hours. Another pain hit and his heart pounded like thunder against her back. "Two minutes apart now, Sam."

"I want to lie down, Wy." She pushed the words through clenched teeth, her jaw so tight it hurt. Wyatt gave her hand a squeeze, stood to step out of the tub, and fought his way out of his wet clothes. He hooked an arm around her waist and practically lifted her out, gently drying her, slipping a cotton nightgown over her head. Once she was lying in bed, propped up by a mountain of pillows, he found dry clothes for himself.

Another pain wracked her body, and Wyatt took hold of both of her hands. "Go on, Sammie. Scream as much as you want." She shook her head, determined to ride it out. After an eternity, it finally let go of her.

The phone started to ring and Wyatt snatched a kiss. "I'll be right back." He sprinted downstairs. Chucky put his front paws on the bed, stretching as far as he could to lick her face.

Samantha rested her hand on his furry, head and rubbed behind his ears. "Sorry, little guy. I know this has to be scary for you." The pain slammed into her, making her body begin to shake, yanking out a scream that even scared her, making her throat go raw. Chucky ducked out of sight and took cover. She couldn't blame the poor thing. Samantha wanted to hide too.

Wyatt rushed back into the room and kneeled down beside her to touch her face. Against all odds, he wore a shaky smile. No matter how terrified her husband might be, he didn't show it. "You won't believe it, baby. Doc Smith's replacement broke down and ended up at Emmett's. They're on the way now. Just hang in there a few more minutes."

She gave a little nod. "We'll have to see—what the little tyke has to say about that." The pain began to stir. "How—" Her tongue flicked over her lips. "How are they getting here?" Her words came out on a gasp as every muscle in her body tensed and she leaned forward, an ungodly sound rising up out of her and bouncing off the walls.

Wyatt didn't back down, remaining at her side, allowing her to dig her nails into his arm without even flinching. "Em's guiding her here on the path."

Samantha sagged back against the pillows, closing her eyes, her mind filled with terrifying pictures of her brother-in-law and the doctor floundering in the snow, getting lost, freezing to death. Her body didn't let her fret about it too long, the next contraction pushing aside all other thoughts and bending her nearly in half.

Wyatt gave her both hands and she clamped down. This one was the worst yet, over a minute long, with only a minute to spare since the last and Samantha screamed herself hoarse. Tears flowed unchecked. It was so bad, she was on the verge of being sick.

Wyatt bowed his head. "You're killing me, Sam."

Her body went loose after being through the wringer all day long, each contraction building in intensity. There was no doubt in her mind. Their baby was coming before this night was through. "Now you know why I didn't call. I didn't want to put you through any more than I had to. This is how I felt—when you were in the hospital—and I watched you—suffer. So helpless."

Wyatt kissed her swiftly, framing her face in his palms. "But that's why I'm here, Sam, to be by your side, through thick and thin, the good and the bad, in sickness and in health. Don't shut me out again." Her rock. Always and forever, never backing down. She nodded, the tears coming again, only to gasp. No one honestly understood what a woman went through in labor. You had to live it for yourself.

"Oh God, oh God! Wyatt, I can't take much more. Make it stop!" The scream tore through her with the agony, and she thought dying would be better.

The door slammed below, footsteps bounded their way, and a young woman burst through the door, followed by Emmett, solidly reassuring in jeans and flannel. Wyatt met the doctor's deep green gaze that made him think of still waters, a fishing hole, or his favorite pond. A dark curtain of hair fell past her shoulders, giving her an exotic appearance. Any more first impressions would have to wait.

He gave Samantha's neck a squeeze and met the stranger part way across the room, offering his hand in greeting. Wyatt eased up when he saw her wince with the strength of his grip and pulled out a smile. "Thank God, you're here. I'm Wyatt. I knew I should've brought her to the hospital earlier today, taken a precaution, what with the weather. Sammie was fractious all morning, testy to no end, fighting cramps. Stubborn woman, didn't want to pester me with the fact that she'd been in labor all along. She figured there was no sense bothering me until they got close." With an insistent tug, he urged the young doctor to his wife's side. "They got close in no time. A little over a minute apart now. No going slow for this one. She's always been a full speed ahead kind of girl. Sam," Wyatt's voice softened and his hand cupped her cheek. "The doctor's here, honey. You're going to be all right."

"I'm Casey Mitchell. Don't you worry. Babies tend to take care of coming on their own. We just help as the cheering and clean-up committee."

Samantha willingly borrowed the doctor's strength when she offered her hands in support. At the same time, she tried not to grind Casey's bones into dust.

Another shriek rose up, followed by a strong gust of air pushed out of her lungs and Sam managed a weak smile. Only a blink or two passed, hardly enough time to catch her breath, and unbearable pressure jabbed at her between the legs. "Oh, Lord—I feel like I need to push. I've got to push!" Her voice was rising again to ear-splitting decimals, a terrifying sound.

The doctor stepped away to wash her hands in the basin of water on the dresser. She moved swiftly to the foot of the bed and threw back the sheet. "All right, Sammie. You're looking good down here. On the next one, go ahead, give it that push!"

Wyatt grabbed a stool and slid it behind Casey, getting a wink for his troubles. The doctor took up her position, waiting patiently to act as welcoming committee for the new arrival. *Finally, it's time! Please, God! Please get this over with now!*

A chair scraped across the floor, snagging Samantha's attention in the space between pains. Emmett, covered with sweat, peeled out of his flannel shirt. He felt his way up the bed.

ཀྵ

Hanging back, feeling a need to step up, Emmett peeled off his flannel shirt, sweating to no end in the plunge from frigid to heat wave. His hand fumbled its way along her body, gently grazing her belly before skimming upward before flitting over her cheek. She latched on to his hand, marveling at his strength.

Emmett brushed the dampened hair out of her face on the tail end of the lull and pressed a kiss to her hot cheek, his forehead touching hers. "Well, little sister, this is it. Showtime. Ready for the grand finale?"

Sam snorted loudly, followed by a grunt as her whole body tensed, shaking the bed. Emmett leaned forward and braced himself, intent on giving her everything he had. There was a disruption and some jostling.

Wyatt had climbed up behind his wife and was taking on the role of coach, shouting, "Come on, Baby Doll! You can do this! You're the toughest woman I know. Let's bring this baby home!"

The doctor urged her on as well, her concentration intense as she devoted all of her attention to Samantha's uterus. All the while, Wyatt dug his fist into Casey's back, easing her pain some as he continued to talk her through it.

Being a Henry, Emmett was doing his part as well. His forehead pressed against the mattress as Samantha made his arm bleed with the bite of her fingernails. Regardless, Emmett would not shirk his duties or leave her high and dry, no matter how uncomfortable he was. As the contraction let up, Samantha gazed through a fog of pain to see him smiling at her.

Casey brushed hair out of her eyes with her forearm and cleared her throat. "Okay, okay Samantha. You're doing fine. Rest now while you can because the baby's about to crown." She sprinted to the dresser to grab a few towels just as Sam grimaced and her whole body became rigid once more.

The doctor helped her, pushing her legs back to ease her position and shouted, "Now, Sam! Push with everything you've got!"

Unbidden and uncontrollable, Samantha's scream ripped through the night, Chucky began howling mournfully, and a thin wailing joined the chorus. It was impossible not to cry.

"He's here, Mama! You have yourself a boy, Daddy!" The young doctor was efficient, cleaning the little man, swaddling him in a towel, and laying him down long enough to snip the umbilical cord. Casey set him in Wyatt's arms and pressed gently on the new mother's stomach. Sam wanted to cry and push her away, the pain awful after the rigors of labor, but the afterbirth was expelled on a towel, and more towels were packed between her legs. Finally, it was over.

Crying freely and not caring one lick about it, Wyatt set their son in Samantha's arms. Her tears joined his as they both gazed at the wonder that was their son. Glancing at the others in the room who would forever be remembered for sharing in this moment, Samantha couldn't help but be caught up in Casey Mitchell's smile until she saw Emmett and wanted to comfort him.

His forehead was pressed to the bed, his jaw

clenched, both hands fisted in the covers. A shudder ran through him, and then he shook it off, sitting up and putting on his game face. Emmett didn't fool Samantha for an instant. She reached for him—but he couldn't see. Still, perhaps by gut instinct, his hand caught hers. Casey and Wyatt whisked the baby off for an instant to clean him up and dress him, swiftly returning to settle him in his mother's arms. The last thing Samantha wanted to do was let go, but his uncle *needed* to hold his nephew.

"Em, do you want to hold him?" Her voice wasn't her own, gone hoarse after all of the screaming. Shredded. That's what having a baby did to a woman. One look at the expression on Emmett's face when her little one was placed in his arms, and she had to correct that assumption because the man looked shattered. The tears were streaming down as he grazed his lips over the baby's cheek, easing up his grip when the little bundle sent up a tiny mewling sound.

Wyatt stepped up from behind and wrapped his brother in a bear hug. "Uncle Emmett, meet Jackson Emmett Henry."

Emmett laughed softly as he scraped at his cheek with the back of his hand, dashing his tears away. His other hand held their precious bundle securely against his chest. "That first name is perfect, Dad would be proud, but Emmett? You trying to torture the poor Little Man? I mean, *we* had to suffer the penalty of bearing Dad's brothers' names, but why pass on the burden?"

Wyatt's face softened, and his hand game up to grasp his little brother by the nape of his neck. "We needed a name for someone who would be strong like the mountains, someone who would not crumble no matter what life threw at them. We chose the names of the best men I have ever known."

Watching the Henry men standing together. Samantha held her breath. Graced by the first name of a man who was as big as they come, her son was in good company.

CHAPTER 19

Long before the sun was up, Wyatt was awake and out of bed. Staring out the window, nearly sagging with relief that the snow finally stopped. Something about the idea of being penned in when Samantha and Jackson might need medical attention sent a rush of adrenalin coursing through his body, making it impossible to lie still another second.

He turned and gazed at his wife, illuminated by moonlight, her mouth curved in a small smile. Finally at peace, the work of birth was done and she could rest—for now. Wyatt couldn't resist tiptoeing to the bassinet at Samantha's side to peek in at their boy. *My son!* The rush of love and pride was too much to be contained, pulling him to his knees as he watched the slight rise and fall of the light blanket covering the tiny infant. Casey had guessed Jackson weighed about ten pounds. *Ten pounds of some kind of wonderful!*

Wyatt studied his sleeping child for a few minutes more. Reluctant to leave, he blew a silent kiss to mother and baby before gathering some clothes from the dresser. He padded down the hall in bare feet, shrugging into his typical winter wear of jeans, a T-shirt, flannel, and wool socks. Filled with energy born from the eagerness to do what had to be done, the coffee pot was bubbling away in no time. Wyatt popped some bread in the toaster, hastily ate it over the sink, and snatched his coffee mug off the counter. A few, scalding sips had him nursing a burnt tongue before putting himself through another dose of abuse. It had to be done. Coffee was a must to kick start his day.

A close look at the thermometer through the porch window had him cursing. Below freezing! That meant overalls, a heavy coat, warm boots, hat, and gloves. Dressed from head to toe in the works, Wyatt ventured out into a blast of cold air that should've taken his breath and dropped it in a massive ice cube at his feet. He took on the horses first, feeding and watering, pulling out the truck with a plow to clear the field. That accomplished, the driveway was the next priority. If anything happened, his wife and baby would get out. *Please God, don't let anything happen.*

He whistled to himself as the pick-up ran up and down the driveway, moving snow out of the way with each sweep, making it easier for him to breathe. Wyatt knew his fears were unreasonable. Samantha and Jackson were fine, with no signs of trouble. That and having a doctor in the house should have reassured him, but things happened. Unexpected things with dire consequences. The Henry brothers knew that through personal experience.

The sun broke the horizon, casting a splash of brilliant color across the fresh snow, as he took the final pass on their driveway. Mission accomplished and more at ease, Wyatt stomped his way to the house and took up a shovel, quickly sending the snow flying to clear a path to his front door.

A white trail of smoke drifting up over the pines made him take pause and reminded him of Emily Hastings. Ever since she was widowed some five years ago, Wyatt had taken his elderly neighbor under his wing, making a point of personally taking care of her plowing, mowing, and any odds and ends around the house. The thought of heading over to her house made the warm glow of contentment inside of him blaze up into a bonfire. He would have the great pleasure of being the first to tell that sweet, old lady the news.

A few more shovels full of snow and Wyatt reached the porch. He kicked his boots clean and stepped inside, peeling out of his outer wear. Inside, the house was quiet, everyone still in bed. He set a new pot on the stove to perk and hopped from foot to foot, waiting for the circulation to come back and send the numbness away. His hands actually hurt from the bitterness and he cupped them to his mouth, blowing on them to bring back some warmth. Cradling a fresh cup of coffee helped nicely.

A few sips and Wyatt couldn't stand waiting any longer. He quietly prepared a tray. Toast, orange juice, and coffee would curb Samantha's appetite until his plowing was done when a full breakfast would be in order. She'd have to be ravenous after all their son put her through the day before. That thought made him snort. *Try nine months before.* How the human race was not extinct, he did not know.

His first step into their bedroom and he couldn't move, couldn't breathe, couldn't do anything but fill his eyes with the sight waiting in his bed. Samantha had the pillows propped up behind her and Jackson was in her arms, wrapped in a powder blue blanket, his mouth attached to her breast as he nursed hungrily, the noise of his suckling loud enough to reach across the room. She looked up, a beautiful blush rising up in her cheeks, her blue eyes sparkling bright enough to outshine the signs of exhaustion that clung to her. Her smile grabbed his heart and drew him to her side.

Carefully setting the tray on the dresser, Wyatt eased himself down on the mattress beside his wife and son to drop a feather kiss on her lips. "Good morning, little mama."

Samantha's hand drifted up and threaded through his

hair, bringing him back for another kiss, one that was sweet with love and longing. "Good morning, Daddy. Where have you been? You've brought the cold with you and your cheeks are wind-burnt. Brr!"

She shivered dramatically and Jackson wriggled in her arms.

Wyatt bowed his head to press a kiss to the fine cap of his son's hair and stroked it gently. He spoke softly in a low rumble, unwilling to disturb the infant's meal. "Oh, I took care of the horses, plowed their field, and cleared our driveway. If you and Jackson have an emergency, you'll get out all right."

She shook a finger at him reproachfully. "Wy, the emergency already happened! We're fine. Come rest with us and snuggle. You're getting tired. You know you're going to pay if you push it."

Wyatt gave her a goofy grin, just couldn't seem to wipe it off his face. He buried his face in the sunshine of her hair and inhaled deeply, smelling the scent that belonged to her, mingled with the sweetness of baby powder. "I'm all right. I want to take care of Miss Emily and see to it that everyone else is squared away and then I'll be back in an hour or two. Save me a spot and keep it warm, all right?" One more kiss and he brought the tray to her, setting it up on a table she could reach. "Make sure you eat. Love you."

Samantha snagged him by the collar of his flannel shirt and reeled him in for one more kiss, rubbing noses and scraping her cheek against his five-o'clock shadow. "Love you more. Hurry back."

One hour turned into several, what with a long visit at Emily's and about five other aging neighbors who had no one else to do for them. It was well past lunch time when his truck bumped its way back down their driveway and rolled to a stop in front of the Henry House. Footprints and other tire tracks suggested someone had come and gone, probably getting Emmett back to his place and Casey Mitchell on her way. With fatigue creeping up and making his body heavy, Wyatt had to admit he was relieved. Alone time with his little family sounded really good about now.

He stepped onto the ground and everything caught up with him, his leg nearly folding. A wild grab at the door kept him from falling. Wyatt sucked in hard and pushed his breath out between clenched teeth, watching the white cloud drift away. *All right now. Get this done.* Steeling himself, he walked from the old pick-up to the house, his leg dragging all the way, forcing him to stop every few feet. Wyatt cursed the steps, the railing the only thing that kept him moving forward. His wife would *not* find a frozen hunk of a man on their front porch. He finally reached the door and hung on the knob, breathing in gasps, waiting to get his strength back.

The chills set in next as Wyatt went to war with his gloves, coat, and boots, leaving everything in an untidy, soaked pile in the hallway. It would be waiting for him later when he was up to the task. Too cold to bear it, he warmed the coffee on the stove, his hand shaking and sloshing the hot brew over the side of the mug as he poured. The tremors didn't stop when he brought it to his mouth. When his left hand kept slipping off and dropping to the counter, Wyatt had no choice but to listen to his body and lie down. His wife and son were waiting for him and there was no place he'd rather be.

The staircase was one more obstacle that made him want to sit on the bottom step and wait until morning. '*Make that mountain into a molehill!*' Jackson's voice rang out, reminding Wyatt that the steps might be a struggle but nothing could keep him from reaching his family. He grabbed the railing and counted his way up. His leg gave a few times, quivering harder the farther he went, but Wyatt went the distance.

When he finally took hold of the bedroom door, hanging on to steady himself and wipe away the sweat on his forehead, a small prayer of gratitude rose up to the heavens above. *Thanks, Dad. You too, God.*

Samantha was sound asleep, Jackson lying next to her, off to dream whatever baby's dreamed about. Wyatt closed the gap, overcoming the final hurdle, and managed to tug his flannel shirt over his head before his body finally gave out. The bed caught him, giving him the respite he so badly needed.

He stretched out and rested his right arm against his son's warm, tiny body. Samantha opened one eye lazily and her hand came out to find a home on his hip. Wyatt felt himself slipping under fast. No doubt he could sleep for a week.

"Did you see how Casey looked at Em?" Samantha's quiet whisper pulled him back from the edge.

He murmured, "Hmm hmm." Somehow, his body slid a little closer, and Wyatt nuzzled her neck.

She giggled and returned the favor. "I think he likes her too. Did you see how he acted around her?"

"Hmm…hmm…Maybe…I had my mind on other things last night." His mouth quirked up at the corner and he kissed her.

"Don't you want to talk about Em's future?" Samantha laid a hand on his cheek. He opened his eyes to find her staring at him intently, her blue eyes sparking with excitement.

"He'll be all right. Em's turning his mountains into molehills. I'm sure the doc can help. Now if you don't mind, I'd really like to study the inside of my eyelids right now. I'm not complaining, but I'm a little tired, Sam." Wyatt's thumb went round and round on the soft, smooth skin of her cheek. Beautiful. No woman was more beautiful than his wife.

"Go to sleep, Wy. Jackson's really good at it. He'll teach us both how it's done." Samantha's words trailed off, sleep taking her once more and Wyatt went with her.

Some hours later, close to sunset judging by the angle of the sunlight streaming through the window, Wyatt slowly awakened. He watched the sun touching on Samantha's hair first, making it glow, grazing their son's cheek next. *Dear God, I must be the most blessed man alive.*

Jackson didn't stir but Samantha opened one eye of brilliant blue and met Wyatt's stare. "Give me a moment and I'll go down, make some dinner."

He shook his head and ran a hand through her hair. "No. Stay put. I don't want you to move. I'm not going anywhere either. The horses can wait. The rest of the world can wait. Just lay still and let me look at you. The both of you."

Her face softened and she set her hand on his hip. Wyatt continued to hold her gaze as the sun illuminated the room, changing it from pink, to purple, before a curtain of darkness marked the close of another day. The color rose up in her cheeks. "Wy—I love you—love you so much. You were incredible last night."

"I love you more." He leaned in and set his mouth on hers. A low humming started at his toes, traveled up his body, all the way to his head, making him dizzy. Wyatt held on tight. Sam wouldn't let him go.

Her hands rested on his chest and his heart thumped steadily under her palms. Wyatt set his thumb on the beating pulse at the base of her neck. Music, she was his music, a song that could never grow old. Samantha's face lit up. "You're humming, do you know that?"

His hand traveled to her cheek and began to circle

round and round. "I can't help it. You put a song in my heart and you have ever since the first time I laid eyes on you—even as we fought over that teeter totter. From elementary school and through all these years in between, I've never been able to get enough of you, Sammie. I never will."

The baby stirred at that moment and began to fuss. Wyatt sat up, thankful that he could again, especially now that he was a father. He scooped his son into his arms and laid Jackson on Samantha's chest. Her arms encircled their son and the little tyke started to nurse again. As Wyatt watched, his eyes filled with tears and he hastily brushed them away.

"Wyatt, what's wrong?" Samantha asked him quietly.

"Nothing, nothing at all. Sometimes, a man is so overwhelmingly happy he has to cry. I'm just going to lie here all night and cry over the wonder that is you." He propped his chin on his hand and gave her his undivided attention.

Samantha laughed softly and gazed at their son. It was her turn for her eyes to fill. "Oh, little Jackson, my little man. I've been waiting so long to meet you."

"And now you'll have a lifetime to get to know us, little guy." Wyatt rested his palm on his son's head and marveled at how tiny the newest member of the Henry family was. His hand practically swallowed up his baby boy. "It still won't be enough time."

Samantha reached out to take his hand. "But we'll make every minute count, won't we?"

"And we'll be sure to teach him how to make mountains into molehills, the same way his grandpa did. God, but I wish Dad was here for this." Wyatt bit off any more words, afraid he'd break. Now was not a time for sadness.

"He's here. I know that Jackson Henry is with us every day." Samantha gave him a smile that made up for the lone tear making its way down her cheek.

Wyatt wiped it away and moved in closer to prop himself up against the headboard, drawing his wife snug against his chest, his arm coming around to cradle Sammie and little Jackson at the same time. Through the days, months, and years ahead, he had one goal in life. To be their shield and love them well.

The Henry way.

About the Author

Heidi Sprouse lives in upstate NY in historic Johnstown. She attended college at St. Rose in Albany, knowing all along her two loves were teaching and English. It took four years before she landed the teaching job of her dreams, but over twenty years later she is still nurturing little ones in pre-K. She loves the privilege of watching brand-new little humans as they discover and begin to shape their own worlds.

Knowing what she wants and going after it in relentless pursuit is Sprouse's gift. Deciding to become an author can be downright unnerving, but Sprouse bit into the challenge, took off, and never looked back. Her perseverance proves success is not a matter of luck. It's a matter of finding what speaks to your heart and committing to do that thing until it makes a difference.

When she isn't busy teaching or with her husband Jim, her son Patrick, and her canine kids Chuck and Dale, she's cooking up her next novel. She dabbles in sweet romances, historical fiction, and suspense thrillers, depending on what pleases her reader's eye at any given moment. Sprouse is always in search of the extraordinary in the ordinary, writing about strong men with old-fashioned values and the women who pick them up when they fall. She'll tell anyone it's never too late to chase after your dreams, no dream is too small or insignificant, and any mountain can be moved with a proposal and a good plan.

Her past works include: *All the Little Things*, *Lightning Can Strike Twice*, *Aging Gracefully*, *Sunny Side Up*, *Against the Grain*, *Hope's Rise From Ashes*, *Adirondack Sundown*, *The Edge of Forgiveness on Blue Mountain*, *Sunrise Over Indian Lake*, *Deserted on Lake Desolation*, *One Last Adirondack Summer*, *Whispers of Liberty*, *Liberty's Promise*, *Liberty's Legacy*, *and Rosie and Her Ragamuffin Sam*. Stay tuned for more to come!